Sam Spallucci:
Ghosts From The Past

A.S.Chambers

First published in Great Britain 2014 by A.S.Chambers.
Copyright © 2014 A.S.Chambers.

"It begins with a blessing but it ends with a curse" by Kevin Cawley Ayers, Blackhill Music ltd (prs). All rights administered by Warner/Chappell Music ltd.
"The Confessions Of Doctor Dream" by Kevin Cawley Ayers, Blackhill Music ltd (prs). All rights administered by Warner/Chappell Music ltd.

Cover art by Kate Evan © 2014 Red Maiden Art

ISBN-10: 1497402050
ISBN-13: 978-1497402058

DEDICATION

For my muse and the fact that she is always there
through thick and thin.

Also by A.S.Chambers:

Sam Spallucci books:
The Casebook of Sam Spallucci
Sam Spallucci: Shadows of Lancaster (due out 2015)

Short story collections:
Oh Taste And See
All Things Dark And Dangerous (due out Christmas 2014)

ACKNOWLEDGMENTS

Many thanks to Theresa Main for being a fantastic proof-reader and continuing to make me look like a grammatical wonder.
My absolute admiration to Kate Evans of Red Maiden Art for her fantastic dragon artwork.
My utmost gratitude to Edith Lobo from Warner/Chappell for guiding me gently through the process of song lyric licensing.
Also, my thanks go out to all those fans who come and see me at conventions or chat with me over Twitter and Facebook. Your encouragement has kept me going through a very hard year.

PROLOGUE

Anything is possible.

That's what they say. We've heard it all before: the gurus, the salesmen, the politicians.

Anything is possible.

It roughly translates as, "Give us your money, sucker. You're so unhappy with your miserable life that we will sell you a barrel-load of hokum and hogwash which you will drink up with such a beatific smile on your face as you think you're getting a wonderful life-changing deal. Just you wait until we're out of town and you realise that you've been had once again. Just you wait while we're laughing all the way to the bank with your hard-earned cash."

Anything is possible.

It never is, not normally. Not for normal schmoes like thee and me. We have to make do and mend with our little lot in life: the ups and downs, the to-ing and fro-ing. No, nothing is possible for us unless someone gives us a break and helps us better ourselves. But even then there is always a catch. Always a bitter pill to swallow when you realise you've sold your soul to the devil.

Anything is possible.

Imagine, just imagine if that were the truth. Imagine if you could obtain your wildest dreams. What would that actually do to your life? Would you be happy? Would you be satisfied? Or would you want more? Would you crave that little morsel that was just out of sight? What would that craving make you do? What would you become in order to satisfy your hunger?

Anything is possible.

I once met a man who told me about this tribe in India. They were a simple but happy people. Living in a small forest, they hunted pig to feed themselves. They had all that they needed to survive. Then corporations came and told them that they could have so much more. They were shown glossy photographs and hi-res Powerpoint presentations. The world was their proverbial oyster. But there was a catch, as there always is. The forest had to go. It was needed for resources and building space, but the sacrifice that the people made would be worthwhile and their lives would be improved. So the trees were cut down and the factories were thrown up; spewed out of the gut of multi-national corporations. It was only a few months later that the villagers realised that there were no more pigs - the animals' habitat had been ruined. This meant they had lost their staple food and had to depend on the corporation to feed them and sustain them. Within a year the village was no more and the tribe had become just another workforce under the rule of a cruel, capitalist overlord.

Anything is possible.

Tell me, what did you do yesterday? Did you wake up, eat breakfast, wander round the house scratching your butt before going to work? Did you idle the day away wondering what your life *might* have been? Did you watch that guy with the green hair shamble past your office at five to two just like he always does? Did you come home, have tea, watch a bit of telly then go to bed?

Anything is possible.

Or did you even *exist* yesterday? How can you be sure of that?

"But I remember it!" I hear you say. Says who? Says your memory? How can you trust that old thing? What if yesterday you were someone completely different? What if you had a different job? What if you were, in fact, someone of importance in society? What if you had been wealthy, rich beyond your wildest dreams? What if you were the sort of person that you actually loathed?

How would you know?

Anything is possible.

What if someone changed everything?

Because, you know what? Someone did.

CHAPTER 1

I stood and gawped out of the door to my office.

The previous week had been somewhat stressful, to say the least. Satanists, Vampires, Fairies...

And one big, bad-ass werewolf.

I had just finished typing it all up. My eyes were sore and every muscle in my sleep-deprived body ached.

Now I had to deal with this.

Caroline. The love of my life from those final days at Luneside University when my face was a mask of glee whilst my stomach was a pit of agony at the knowledge that my father, two hundred miles away, was dying a slow, painful death.

Caroline had been, to put it not too biblically, my succour and my refuge. When the terrors had come, she had been the one to hold me while I shook. When the tears had threatened to drown me in their deluge, she had been the one to dab my eyes with a convenient tissue.

She had given me so much.

But there was that one thing that she had never been able to hand to me on a plate and that was why I had walked away.

She had never given me her love.

So what do you say to someone who you haven't seen for sixteen years and whose heart you crushed? How do you express all the angst and regret that has been bottled up inside your stomach like a dormant volcano ready to erupt at any moment in an outpouring of tears and self-loathing? How do you start to make amends for an unforgivable act so heinous that you cannot begin to imagine the sleepless nights of torment and anger that your former lover has endured? What words can even begin to break down all that anguish?

"Hi," I said.

"Hello," she replied.

It seemed a bit of an anti-climax.

"Can I come in?"

I nodded, stood back and Caroline crossed the threshold. As she passed me, I caught the scent of her perfume - patchouli, jasmine, summer fruit - and I was transported back to that summer of my final year. A warm evening at the bottom of a vicarage garden. The neatly mown grass beneath us. The warmth of her body close to mine. The soft touch of her lips on my mouth. The delicate shades of blonde framing her face.

I blinked.

"Your hair's brown."

She stood in the middle of my office, "Some things change," she said wafting her gloved hand through the fug of cigarette smoke; "unlike others." Her eye caught the numerous dog ends in the overflowing ashtray. "Haven't you quit yet?"

"It's been one of those weeks."

"Nothing new there then." Acid. I flinched inwardly.

Silence descended.

The clocks ticked. She eyed them but said nothing.

Apart from the hair she really hadn't changed that much. Slim, youthful, pretty, immaculately dressed with dark brown eyes. I'd missed those eyes.

Why was she here?

"Why are you here?"

"I need your help."

"I should have guessed it wasn't a social call."

"And why on Earth would you expect one of those?"

"You could have kept in touch."

"Kept in touch? Sam, we split up."

"I know, but..."

"Oh, for Christ's sake!"

"You know Daddy hates it when you blaspheme."

"Don't bring my father into this."

"Why not? He runs your life."

"He just wants what's best for me."

"Like choosing adequate boyfriends?"

"At least my father cared for me."

The clocks ticked.

I clenched my hands.

"And what does *that* mean?"

Caroline closed her eyes. "Sorry. I didn't mean that. Sam, can we just talk about work?"

"Screw work. Let's talk about Dad. What did you mean?"

"Sam, I said I was sorry..." She opened those dark, brown eyes again and she did look truly sorry, but she had waved the red rag to the bull and, after the week I had just endured, there was no stopping me now.

"That was always your problem, you know? So bloody superior. You had the better life. You had the better school. You had the better house. You had the better father. The sweet little vicar's daughter. 'Yes, Daddy. No, Daddy. Butter wouldn't melt, Daddy.' But he never knew the half of it, did he? His little sweetness and light was a minx, a tramp. Out all night and climbing back in her window before dawn. And not once did he suspect. Not once did he have to worry. No, because the next day you were back to miss prim and proper. Miss studious and meticulous at school. You were... you were..."

Caroline was crying.

I stumbled to a stop, breathing heavily.

"Caroline..."

She held up a hand. "No, Sam. It's okay. You're right. You're totally right," she sniffed, drawing a tissue out of her purse and dabbing her eyes, "and one day he found out. So we don't exactly talk anymore."

"Ah..." My words had dried up in the heat of my anger. I tapped my teeth as I wracked my brains for what to do next. Here she was after all these years, just walking back into my life and I was *so* not coping with it.

The emotions inside were complex to say the least. They ranged from the hatred that had made me rant to the desire to just scoop her up and kiss her.

I guessed the middle ground would be best.

"Why don't you sit down while I put the kettle on?" I suggested.

She agreed.

I darted into the kitchen and started to clatter about the place. My hands were trembling as I snapped the lid off the tea caddy. "Get a grip, Sam," I mumbled to myself and the bags of dark brown leaves. "No psychotic Satanists, no vamps, no werewolves - just Caroline." I sighed deeply as I filled the kettle and flicked it on. My face felt hot, my cheeks were flushed. I was exhausted from the frenetic energy of writing with no sleep and I desperately wanted to crash in my bed, on the sofa, on the floor - *anywhere* - but now *this* had happened and I was suddenly locking down the harness on the roller-coaster for a second spin and I knew my stomach was going to churn up something unpleasant.

As the kettle started to hiss and crackle, I dumped two teabags into the pot and breathed in deep the soothing, aromatic fragrance.

I closed my eyes and it was just shy of sixteen years ago.

A balmy summer's afternoon. My head was still a touch hazy from the events of the previous night with the phantom Gerald, Malcolm Wallace and Wallace's mysterious high-heeled benefactor. I had consequently chewed so many mints that my stomach could have been dished up as a dessert haggis. Saint Cuthbert's vicarage was very much old school - an ironstone edifice nestled in rambling ivy and climbing roses surrounded by ornate and lengthy gardens which were suitable for tea and cucumber sandwiches in the summer, or stalls selling mulled wine at the Christmas fair in the winter. It was a parish which had obviously been extremely wealthy when it had been founded. The church was an immense size for what I estimated to be a small rural congregation and it dominated the village. The priest's home overlooked the green to the side of the church. A gravel path wound its way through immaculate borders; flowers of all shapes, colour and perfume decorated my way up to the large, oak door.

I looked for a bell, saw none and knocked as loudly as my knuckles would allow on the wood that had been hewn from a tree long before my grandfather had been born. I fidgeted as I waited and ran my hands through my curls in a vain attempt to tame my unruly hair. Sleeping half the night with your head on a kitchen table does wonders for the shabby chic look.

There was a rattling behind the door and it creaked open. A blonde teenage girl stood in the crack between the door and the frame. "Can I help you?"

For a moment I struggled to find any suitable words. My brain had forgotten it possessed the ability to communicate with other beings, it was far too busy taking in what it could see and pumping necessary hormones around my weary body.

She was slight of build, standing just short of my nose. Bobbed hair framed a pretty face with a slightly upturned nose which sat precisely between two deep, dark brown eyes.

And she was smiling. It wasn't one of those, "Wow, I'm really happy!" smiles. No, it was one of those, "Oh, *hello*. I think you look cute," smiles.

I tried to work my mouth into intelligible consonants and syllables but nothing ventured out past my lips.

She raised a light coloured eyebrow and half-turned her head to shout back into the house, "Dad! The guy's here about the placement." Then she stood back to open the door and gestured with her hand, "I think you'd better come in."

So I did.

The kettle clicked off, snapping me out of my reverie. I snatched it up and drowned my daydream along with the teabags. The past was the past. It belonged to a time that was gone and finished. What was important was the here and now. I placed the pot, two mismatched mugs, some teaspoons and a bowl of sugar on a tray and ventured back into my office. Caroline was seated nervously on the edge of the sofa. I wasn't sure if she was nervous about being here in general or about the possibility that the accumulated debris of the room would leap up like a garbage golem and grab her by the throat. I chided myself for letting the room slip towards Spliffness and lay the tray on the table.

"Do you want sugar? I'm afraid I don't have any milk."

She shook her head. "Just black will be fine."

I spooned two big heaps into my mug and splashed tea onto the white granules. It was still rather weak, so I prodded the bags with my teaspoon to encourage them in their work. On the second attempt the tea poured somewhat darker. I decided it would do.

Caroline took her mug and blew over the hot liquid causing a small puff of steam to blow up over her face. I sat in my office chair cradling my drink and waited. Even now, after all these years, I was still at a loss as to what I should say around her so, for a while, we just sat and sipped tea, the rumbling of past memories bouncing between us in a noisy silence.

Inevitably it was Caroline who spoke first. "I have a son. He's my life, my all. I never made the big time. Still stuck here in this provincial hole working for a tin pot little rag owned by a self-inflated moron who believes the most effective way to get something decent out his workforce is to berate and bully them until they submit to his will."

She had always wanted to be a reporter and the description of her boss sounded incredibly familiar. "You work on the Lancaster Chronicle? For Hector Swarbrick?"

Caroline nodded.

"I met him last week."

That old smile caressed her lips and hormones stroked my palpitating heart along with a slightly baser organ. "I know. I hear you had some *fun*."

I shrugged. Then I frowned. "Wait. Has *he* sent you?"

Caroline quickly shook her head. "No! God no. If he knew I was here he would fire me instantly. I'm here because my son's in trouble."

"Your *son*?"

"Yes." Those big, brown eyes kept a firm hold on me. My heart sighed and I desperately tried to ignore it; stay professional, Sam. "He's in trouble, I'm sure of it."

I concentrated on letting my mind pore over the facts. It was hurriedly trying to make a connection here. There was Hector Swarbrick, owner of the Lancaster Chronicle and bullying father of Billy Swarbrick. Billy was a pupil at Saint Edmund Campion. I had been at Saint Edmund's last week. My heart waved an image in front of my brain - a glass figurine being smashed in anger - and at once I knew who Caroline's son was.

"John," I said.

"John," his mother confirmed.

It had been there, right in front of me, last week - John's blonde hair, the glass animal, the over-protective mother - but I just hadn't made the full connection. The whole business with Billy had sort of edged it out of the limelight. I thought about the bright-eyed youth and his bubbly demeanour. He had seemed just like any other teenage lad, possibly even more well-adjusted than most. He certainly hadn't come across as the sort to get himself into trouble. Sex and drugs or fast cars had not seemed to be on his agenda. "So what's the problem?"

Caroline fidgeted with her fingernails. They were highly polished and lacquered in a clear varnish - professional, not tarty. "Here's the deal. A few weeks ago John and a few of his mates picked up a leaflet in town about a youth group that meets locally and provides what it calls a "safe environment" for teenagers to go and hang out. There's no drink, no drugs, no hanky-panky - all very clean and above board. I thought to myself, 'Okay, no bad. It'll give him something to do,' and for the first week or so, everything seemed fine, but then he started spending more and more time with the group and I guess the *worried mum* gene kicked in. I challenged him about it and he said that everything was cool. He and his friends were having a great time and learning stuff about how to succeed in life."

"No real harm in that," I shrugged. "A bit driven perhaps, but apart from that...?"

Caroline shook her head emphatically. "No. Something was wrong; I knew it. They all started wearing these wrist band things."

"Lilac-coloured ones?"

She nodded.

"I saw them last week. Lots of kids were wearing them."

"It's not just the kids. I rang school and voiced my concerns. I spoke to some young girl who sounded fresh out of college and she brushed me off saying that the society was perfectly safe and even members of staff there belonged to it."

"She may have a point. It could be nothing," I volunteered. So John had described his little group as *life-changing*, but then, to a teenage lad, every latest, greatest thing was life-changing: the X-Box Kinect, Facebook, banana-flavoured ice-cream.

Caroline stood up and made to leave. I leapt up after her. "Where are you going?"

"This was a mistake," she snapped back at me. "You obviously think I'm neurotic and don't want to help."

For a split-second I hesitated. This woman was one of the greatest failures of my past. Could I really turn my back on her right now? Whether she was over-reacting or not, surely I had to try and make things right?

"Of course I'll help you."

She turned back to face me. "Really?"

"Really."

A smile tugged at her mouth and my heart melted. "Really, really?"

I nodded, remembering the last time we had exchanged those words. It had been the other way round. We had been cosied up together in her dad's garden and my heart had been pounding louder than an atomic blast. "Really," I said again. "John gave me a leaflet last week. I'll start with that."

"Thanks, Sam," Caroline smiled and all the pain of the previous week melted away. I searched my head frantically for a reason, any reason to delay her departure. It had been so long and my heart had missed her so much.

"I'd better take your number," I finally said, "so I can contact you."

"Sure. You have some paper?"

I grabbed a pad off my desk and passed it over with a pen. As she neatly wrote the number down I darted over to the windows and opened them as wide as I could to remove the stale cigarette smoke. She had always hated my habit. "Cancer sticks," she had called them on numerous occasions. Her father was very high church but also curiously puritanical and certain things had rubbed off on her. I remember her stealing my packet of fags and sitting on them until I promised not to smoke another for the rest of the day. When I had finally extricated them from underneath her, it became all too apparent that those particular Luckies would not be being smoked that day or any other; they had been squashed flatter than a child's innocence when it sees its parents filling stockings over the fireplace on Christmas Eve.

"Here you go." She handed the pad back to me, still smiling that sweet little lop-sided smile.

"Thank you." I took my phone out and entered the number into my contacts. "Listen you want to stay for a bit? There must be all sorts of things we need to catch up on."

She waggled back and forth uncertainly as if weighing up the pros and cons of my suggestions until finally she said, "Sorry, Sam. I can't. I need to get back to work. Another time, perhaps?"

My heart slouched down and rested its head morosely on its hand. "Sure, okay."

"But how about you ring me tomorrow and we can meet up to discuss your findings?"

My heart bounced out of its doldrums and started cartwheeling around my chest. "Okay. That sounds good." I waved the pad in front of me. "I have your number."

She chuckled then something dawned on me. Something which, as yet, had gone unmentioned. "Erm... what does John's father think about all of this?"

The lop-sided grin fixed me in its grip as her brown eyes twinkled. "I never married him. It's just me and John."

I smiled back at her. "Cool... I mean..." I coughed, "Okay. I'll ring you tomorrow then."

"Tomorrow," she grinned as she turned and left me standing like a young boy excited at the prospect that soon he will be holding hands with the prettiest girl in the class. But that was tomorrow. First I had to knuckle down to some work.

After Caroline left, the first thing I did was just sit and stare blankly into space. Life, I decided, was a funny old thing. It was rather like a trusted, old car. It ran and ran for years with no problems whatsoever, then you decided to upgrade something in the engine to make it supposedly better. After the upgrade, things started to happen. You might use more fuel or you might start to hear an annoying rumble every time it went above forty miles per hour. The car that you once loved was just not the same any more. Yes, it was running faster and smoother, but those little things just seemed to bug away at you.

Was this my life now? Had my self-imposed upgrade thrust me into some sort of spotlight that would make me a target for all things weird?

Well at least it would not be boring.

I lit a Lucky and glanced at the mantle clock on

the window. It was just past ten. I yawned loudly as my body reminded me that I was still lacking that vital component of rest and rejuvenation: a good night's sleep. I glanced over at the welcoming upholstery of the sofa but shook my head. I had matters to attend to.

John, John, John. What to do about John? I reached over to my jacket which was draped on a chair and rummaged around for the leaflet he had given me. I scrutinised the front cover of the three-fold A4 leaflet.

Emblazoned across the middle was the lilac-coloured emblem that resembled an upper-case T enwrapped with two spiralling lines and there, underneath, was the eponymous call to action: "Anything Is Possible."

Anything? Get that killer promotion? Run the London Marathon? Pass your degree with no student loan? Con your way onto the International Space Station? Or how about something *really* hard – get to the post office on a Monday morning before the grey-haired attack force of old age pensioners make you stand in the queue out the door for five hours?

Okay, so perhaps I exaggerate just a touch but the organisation, which appeared to call itself *Credete,* might as well have suggested them as it seemed to promise just about anything. There was healthy living, job satisfaction and international harmony to name but a few. I sighed. I had seen all this sort of stuff before. Before I was a student, I had taken a year out (that's what you youngsters call a *gap year* these days, just in case you were wondering) and explored the various facets of the rough-hewn diamond called the Church.

Many people see it as one coherent body and get all confused when they see it squabbling over such things as gay marriage or women bishops. Well let me tell you this, the Church of England is somewhat like a swan. It has all the grace and decorum on the surface, but underneath there is a chaos of legs paddling maniacally trying to keep it afloat. The difference between the swan and the good old C of E is that the legs of the swan succeed, whereas the legs of the Church are in constant chance of tripping over each other and splitting it apart. You have the ecumenicals, the catholics, the evangelicals, the conservatives, the liberals and the list goes on and on.

So, during my academic sabbatical, I decided to try my hand at as many of these groups as possible, just to verify where I was most comfortable. Looking back, I'm amazed that I came through it still wanting to wear my shirt back to front, but I did and that led on to Caroline, which in turn led me to this train of thought.

A weird kind of synchronicity, don't you think?

The ones that I guess freaked me out the most were the evangelicals. It all seemed far too *happy*. I'm the cynical sort, by nature, and I kept waiting for the drop. You know what I mean: they're all aliens, they're all sadomasochists, they're all bank managers. Something bizarre or evil like that.

Anyway, the evangelical meetings I went to always followed the same pattern, there would be lots of singing, clapping, affirmation, praising the Lord and then utter condemnation of anyone who didn't see the world through their vindictive little spectacles.

I once went to this rally... (Oops! Sorry. That should be *conference...*) which was being held by a society that called itself *Jesus Loves Us*. It was full of young people bathed in the healthy glow of self-righteousness who continually proclaimed just how much good *The Lord* (yes they *did* speak in emphasised italics) had imparted on them since they had turned away from darkness to Jesus Christ.

That deep, dark cynical part of me knew it was a farce from the moment that I walked in the door. It was like *Songs of Praise* meets *The Stepford Wives*. There was no individualism whatsoever. They all dressed the same (clean t-shirt with blue jeans). They all sang the same hymns (*Shine Jesus Shine* was normally the one that tended to be the favourite. Whatever you do, *don't* google it; you'll be humming it *ad nauseam*). They all had that beatific cleanly scrubbed glow to their faces that comes with far too much soap and sanctity.

I was subjected to hour upon hour of pious indoctrination. Time after time I was pounded over the head with the undoubtable fact that Jesus was born from a virgin and that he *had* to be the Son of God. To think anything else was totally incredible when one looked at the wonderful deeds he performed in the lives of the society's members. Any divergent opinion was the work of *The Devil*. To believe that there was any vestige of truth in any other religions was the work of *The Devil*. To over-indulge in any practice that could be vaguely construed as *fun* was the work of *The Devil*. To pass wind on a Sunday was the work of *The Devil*.

You get my drift?

Mind you, being the open-minded sort of bloke that I am (and the fact that I had a specific return train booked to save me a bundle of cash), I was willing to give them the benefit of the doubt.

Perhaps all these fundamentalist tenets were just the face of an over-bloated managerial hierarchy?

Perhaps the grass roots members were just good, honest youths who were there to nod and smile sagely during the day but would let their hair down and boogie like there's no tomorrow once the lights were out?

Perhaps penguins fly north for the summer?

"Hi... er... *Sam*." It was a clean-shaven boy in his late teens who was performing a remarkable job of reading the three letters (one of them in upper-case) on my name badge. As he smiled that Stepford smile, the mountain-fresh aroma of middle class Marks and Spencers drifted up to my nose causing my face to grimace. Unfortunately he took this to be a welcoming smile and he continued his introduction. "Peace be with you. My name is Luke."

Fortunately, at that point, my common sense gene kicked in and, realising that the name was biblical, stopped my numpty gene from blurting out something along the lines of, "Great to meet you. Killed any Sith recently?" Instead, I just mumbled a vaguely audible, "Hi."

Unperturbed by my non-committal grunt, Luke carried on in his irritatingly friendly manner, "So what brought you to *Jesus Loves Us*."

Again, I swerved past the obvious answer, which would have been, "A train." The answer I gave was far more sensible (or so I thought at the time). I explained that I was just kicking my heels for a year before university and was looking for something suitable to stick on my CV.

"Ah!" he sighed as if being lifted up in the Rapture. "God does move in *mysterious ways.*" Whatever that had to do with a CV, I had no idea. "What university are you going to?"

I informed him that it would be Luneside University, where I would read Religious Studies.

This was the point where I had to undertake a little introduction: knife meet atmosphere; atmosphere meet knife.

"*Religious* studies?" The mask of happiness slipped and a look of perturbed confusion assumed its place. "Does that include *other* religions?"

I explained that yes, it encompassed many other varied faiths.

Luke shook his head. "No, Sam. There is only *one true faith.*" His demeanour became that of one futilely trying to explain to a serial killer why he should stop listening to that little voice in his head. "All the others are *false religions.* The only true faith is the way of *The Cross.*"

I begged to differ with him. I especially thought that there were aspects of Buddhism which were very *green*...

"The Green movement is *New Age,* Sam. It is the work of *Satan himself.*"

Words left me as I was stunned into silence.

"Brothers! Brothers!" Luke called out to

surrounding members. "We must lay our healing hands on this poor wretch..."

Wretch?

"... and pray that the evil demon..."

Demon?

"... that is dwelling within him will leave, so that he will return to Christ."

Christ!

I rose sharply from my chair and bolted to the door in order to make a hasty exit. As my hand grasped the door-knob, a wicked smile touched my lips and an idea bubbled up in my mind. I turned a raised hand as if in a pseudo-blessing and said, "Don't worry, my friends. I am sure that Crom Cruach will forgive you."

There were screams of horror as I shot out of the building and ran for the nearest main road to hitch a lift home. Apparently none of them had ever read up on ancient Irish religions. Philistines.

So yes, I have very little time for any group which promises a divine thunderbolt that will bring peace, love and fluffy bunnies into your mundane existence. I'm more of a "stop the whinging and get on with it" kind of guy. If your life is crap then it is up to you to sort it out, not constantly wait for a supernatural intervention.

I am also the kind of guy that needs his sleep, and as I sat there, finishing off my cigarette I felt the abuse of the last few days catching up with me and my eyebrows drooped. Stretching, I curled up on the sofa.

I would just close my eyes for a bit. A little doze would sort me out.

Within seconds I was snoring like an asthmatic

camel.

It actually started out like any normal dream. I was wandering through my mum's house: all her toby jugs were smiling down at me, the thick carpet felt warm under my bare feet and sunshine was streaming in through the French windows.

I smiled. For once a dream I could enjoy.

It didn't last, of course.

I turned the handles on the French windows and the tall glass doors swung outwards into the sweet-smelling summer garden. There, in the middle of the immaculate lawn, a young boy of about seven played with his Action Man dolls. He was dressed like a soldier himself: green jumper and purple beret. As he positioned the dolls in various poses around about him he made squawking noises that sounded like military radios whilst making the characters in his stories interact with each other.

There were light footsteps to my side and I was aware of someone stood next to me. "You remember this day?" A clipped, educated, female voice.

I nodded as I turned to face the stranger. She was about my height, immaculately dressed in a light-green two-piece skirt and jacket suit. Her dark hair was tied up in a severe bun and dark-rimmed glasses were perched on her aquiline nose.

She looked, for all intent and purpose like a librarian.

I shuddered involuntarily.

"Of course I remember this day. It was the first

day that I heard things that weren't there."

She continued to gaze at my younger self. "What was it you heard?"

"Voices."

"Where did you hear them coming from?"

"Well, from..." I paused and looked back at my younger self. He was staring up at me with a frown on his face and the memory of that day clarified in my head. I had been playing in the garden on a hot, summer's day when suddenly I had been aware of voices. They had been coming from my house, but I could not see anyone there. I had not been able to make out any words, but it had felt like there had been two people talking there.

I spun towards the neatly-dressed woman, my mouth open in disbelief.

"Don't forget the child you were, Samuel," she said, her fiery eyes locked on me through her glasses before she faded into nothingness and I was left alone.

Then there was a pelican wearing a purple scarf and Buddy Holly spectacles hovering overhead squawking in an extremely irritating tone.

"That'll be my phone, then," I sighed. "Time to wake up."

So I did.

CHAPTER 2

Half an hour later I had splashed some cold water on my face in a vain attempt to awaken my senses, roughly run my fingers through my hair to try and make myself look vaguely presentable and legged it up the road to the police station hoping not to keep a certain punctual DCI waiting.

I think I just about managed the last of this trio, as for the others.... ah well.

The first time I had ever been in a police station had been when I was about eight. Our dog, a black and white border collie named Shep (every collie in the seventies was called Shep – such was the popularity of John Noakes and his four-legged friend) had done a runner. Again. My parents had bought him for my seventh birthday. For some bizarre reason, they had presumed that the joy that overflowed from a young lad at snuggling up to his newly acquired furry bundle of fun would form itself into that self-same boy exercising said dog twice a day.

Fat chance.

I was far more involved in curling up in my room with my latest super-hero comic whilst my dad grumbled loudly and slammed the door with extreme volume as he stomped out into the rain with "the sodding dog." A few weeks of this saw Shep exercising himself in the back garden rather than in the fields at the end of our street. This, in turn, led to young Samuel refusing to play out in the fresh air as treading in something warm and brown lying in the grass was not his idea of fun. End result: dog got bored in garden, I withdrew into my science fiction, one very pissed-off father.

I'm sure there are parents everywhere nodding their head in recognition of this scenario.

Anyway, back to the matter at hand. One frequent consequence of Shep being imprisoned in our luscious, green, rear-of-the-house dog toilet was that he tended to get bored and longed for the company of other canines, especially female ones. This inevitably led to an already angry father getting even more annoyed as he wandered the local streets searching in vain for a randy escapee.

On the occasion that I mentioned earlier, Shep had been picked up by a local bobby and driven to the town nick where they kept cells for canines as well as humans. My mum was out when the phone call came in and, as a result, my dad dragged me out of my pit and forced me to accompany him in bailing out the four-legged fugitive.

So, as I sat in the corridor outside of Jitendra's office and my watch ticked its way round to one in the afternoon, my mind was cast back to that little vignette from my childhood and I started to dwell on the various freudian baggage that went with it. I had the overwhelming feeling that I was in trouble again and that my father was scowling down at me from Heaven whilst muttering profanities quietly enough that I could not pick them up and repeat them but with enough volume to know that I had incurred his wrath.

The look on Jitendra's face when he opened his office door did nothing to allay my anxiety. "Hello, Sam," he said. "You'd better come in."

His office was more or less as I had expected it to be. It was totally pristine: clean and fresh with a delicate hint of an essential oil that I could not quite place. Sandalwood perhaps? I had the feeling that Jitendra was the sort that had to go over a room and titivate it to his exacting wishes after the cleaner has supposedly already done the job. There was a wide, open window looking out over Thurnam Street and the side of the town hall. Next to that was a lusciously green swiss cheese plant with immaculately polished leaves and trimmed roots. Down the wall to my right were bookcases lined with meticulously filed and labelled folders next to three imposing filing cabinets. The third wall of the room was dominated by Jitendra's mammoth desk and this was the sole exception to his rule of precision. It was littered with hastily scribbled notes on sheets of A4 paper which were piled up on top of a number of books that were in the process of being read, annotated and dissected. My eyes were drawn to a reproduction of a woodcut of a werewolf standing in all its slavering glory.

Jitendra noticed the direction of my gaze and quietly closed the book shut, sliding it under the notes which he shuffled together on top of it.

Not a word did he say; not a comment did I make.

For a moment we stood in the ominously awkward silence that occupies the space between two individuals who know that sooner or later they will have to confront the elephant in the room but figure that perhaps now is not the appropriate time to crack out the peanuts.

He gestured to the chair in front of his desk.

I coughed and gladly took it.

"It's regarding your abductors from John O'Gaunt Media." Direct, no-nonsense, to the point.

"Ah. I guess I'd almost forgotten about them." I leaned back in the chair and stretched my arms, stifling the desperate urge to yawn. I really did need a decent night's sleep. "How's it coming along? Have they," I formed quotation marks with my fingers, "*confessed*?"

Jitendra shook his head. "Not exactly. In fact three of them were found dead in their cells this morning."

Jitendra did not keep the same sort of liquid refreshment that I did. His filing cabinets may have been purely following the manufacturer's recommendation but someone in the station sure made a decent cup of coffee. I've been told many times that I should avoid caffeine as it affects the ringing in my ears, but right then I didn't give a damn. I was already dropping on my feet from lack of sleep and it now felt like the rug had been viciously yanked out from under the self-same appendages.

Haversham, Baines and Sothwell had been found dead that morning in their holding cells. All three of them had chewed at their wrists until they had ruptured a vein (Or is it an artery? I can never remember.) before bleeding to death. Apparently it had not been a pretty sight.

I could have murdered for a Lucky, but I didn't dare to mess with the precisely positioned molecules of the air in Jitendra's office.

"What about the other two?" I finally managed.

"Brande tried the same trick but must have hesitated for some reason. As a result she didn't bleed out as vigorously as the others and we got to her in time. Philips..." the policeman let out a short puff of breath, leaned back in his chair and tossed a pen onto his desk. "Philips is exactly the same as when we arrested him."

I raised a questioning eyebrow.

"Lights on; nobody home," he rumbled as he reached over for a buff-coloured file similar in style to the one he had loaned me regarding a certain lycanthrope. "He flicked through a few sheets of paper, chewing his bottom lip. "There's loads of medical jargon in here, but the long and the short of it is he's switched off. He eats, he sleeps, he performs the usual bodily functions but he will not, cannot communicate with anyone."

I drummed my fingernails against my teeth as little bells rang fiercely in my head. "This is all very well and good, but why did you need to see me. Surely you could have told me this over the phone?"

"True," Jitendra grunted, reaching for another file. "There is, however, something else. Before he died, Baines left us a message in his blood. It's not exactly *The Da Vinci Code* but I need to know if it means anything to you." He slid an A4 colour photo across the desk. There, scrawled in a dying man's blood was the phrase:

"*The Divergence is coming.*"

I looked Jitendra straight in the eye. "I need to see Brande right now."

"Oh, and why would that be?"

"You have to trust me on this one."

The asian policeman threw back his head and barked one sharp, resonant laugh then glowered at me. "Like I had to trust you to take a walk in the park? Is this to do with the werewolf?"

I fidgeted in my chair. "No."

He continued to fix me in his scalpel-sharp stare.

I remained silent and fidgety.

"Well?"

"Honest, it's nothing to do with the werewolf... I think."

"You *think*?" Jitendra's voice was dripping with the most potent sarcasm that I think I had ever heard. "Well *there's* a novel idea."

"It's not to do with werewolves and it's nothing to do with the suicides."

"Really?" His fingers were steepled and he peered over the top of them. "So Baines just decided to compose a little bit of random abstract poetry whilst his blood oozed out of his lacerated wrist? Is that it? That's what you're telling me? Bullshit, Sam. Tell me what it means!"

I winced as his voice raised. "I've heard the phrase once before, last week."

He nodded. "Go on."

"From a client."

"And..."

"They were a vampire."

That good, old familiar awkward silence walked back into the room and sat itself down neatly between us atop Jitendra's desk. It crossed and uncrossed its legs expectantly before carefully examining its nails and eventually buggering off when Jitendra quietly and calmly said, "I think you need to tell me all about last week, and any other little tales of ghosties and goblins, right now."

So I did. It was all still fresh in my mind from having cathartically typed it all out. I began with Satanists, moved onto vampires, nipped back some years to phantoms before coming back to poltergeists which were really fairies and then finished with one big, bad-ass werewolf.

You know what, I think he actually believed it. I was impressed.

"So you have no idea what this Divergence is?" he finally asked.

I shook my head. "No. But I got the impression that it's bad enough to share the shit out of Bram Stoker's favourite friends."

"Then I agree," he said as he rearranged his desk and stood, straightening his tie, "that you need to speak to Miss Brande."

The young woman who was led into the grey, oppressive interrogation room was not the same young woman who I had met just the week previous. This creature was a wreck, a shell of a person. Her insides had been scooped out and she had been left hollow: a mere simulacrum. I watched through the ubiquitous one way mirror as two uniformed constables guided her somewhat unwillingly in. Her hair was unbrushed, her skin missing its multilayered coats of slap and her feet shod in tattered trainers rather than some fancy brand of expensive high heels. Having said that, the vicious little spark was still there. I know that I would have struggled to take the verbal abuse that she doled out without snapping back at her. Some of the things that she suggested they do to one another were quite anatomically impossible but they just carried out their duties and waited patiently until Jitendra led me inside; an inquisition party of two. He silently nodded to the constables and they left us alone with her.

Brande sat scowling at us in silence for a minute or so while Jitendra, apparently unconcerned with her being there, quietly flicked through his file and made notes with his fountain pen.

I thought it best to follow his lead, this not being my field of expertise. Was he trying to rile her; get her to blurt out something without thinking? Was he playing Good Cop, Bad Cop? If he was, what did that make me? Was I supposed to go and lean in the corner chewing on a tooth pick bottling up all my misogynistic anxiety, ready to snap and start berating the woman for the piece of crap that I saw her as? I hoped not. I was sure I'd make a much better Good Cop.

Eventually, my worries were proved pointless (not

to mention rather foolish and fanciful). Jitendra fished the same photo out of the file that he had shown me and slid it across the table. Brande's reaction said it all. Her eyes widened and her face visibly paled. "Oh, God," she moaned. "Where was this taken?"

Jitendra answered with his most matter-of-fact voice, "In Baines' cell shortly after he chewed himself to death. Care to enlighten us?"

The actress mumbled something inaudible.

"Sorry, Miss Brande," Jitendra's authoritative voice was cold, hard, "I didn't quite catch that."

She lifted up her head and tears were welling in her eyes. "None of us really believed him when he said it was going to happen."

"The Divergence?"

She nodded.

"What is it?"

"We... I... don't really know," she stammered. "He said it was going to be a wonderful thing. The world would change and all would be peaceful."

Something here did not make sense. I thought back to the cold, hard floor of John O'Gaunt Studios, a pentagram and a very sharp knife. "Forgive me if I don't quite believe you to be the butterflies, bunnies and unicorns type," I snapped. I ignored Jitendra's warning glance and carried on. "I'm still having nightmares about your little *peaceful* games."

"Oh, my heart just *bleeds* for you," she sneered, her lip curled up in derision.

"I didn't know ice had a pulse," I shot back.

She was silent for a moment then continued, "Do

you know what it's like to be used?"

The question burned into me as her dark-rimmed eyes scoured my face trying to rip an answer from my flesh.

"Yes I do." I thought about another woman. One who had waltzed into my life last week, fluttered her eyelids in my direction, fed me a sob story and tried to feed me to her crazed brother as a human-sized packet of *Winalot*.

"It cheapens you, doesn't it?" She closed her eyes, tears forcing their way out of the screwed up eyelids, trickling down her pale cheeks. She raised her arm and wiped them away with the fresh bandage that now swaddled her wrist. Brande opened her eyes and studied the damp dressing as if it was the first time that she had lain eyes upon it. Her eyes darted up and down its folds, examining the pattern of the tightly bound material. The tears started in earnest.

"The bastard!" she cried, "The fucking bastard. He promised us everything!"

I glanced at Jitendra. He gave an almost imperceptible shrug. He had no idea who the actress was talking about.

"Who used you Melanie?" I asked, my voice low and calm. I knew that I needed to win her over, to be a friend in her hour of need. Even if it was a total fabrication, it could win us some answers.

Then, in an instant, the little bitch of the previous week was back and I was looking at a middle finger standing upright. So much for the friendship approach. "You really think I'm gonna help an old perv like you?

Get kicks off damsels in distress do you?" She flicked her red hair that was tied back in a rough ponytail and leant back on her chair. "Yeah, that's it isn't it? You swank in and go all 'Hey, babe, you can trust me,' with those big dark eyes of yours and that tousled, wavy hair, but you know what? I see right through you. You're a knob who likes to play with himself when no-one's looking. You really get off on..."

"That's enough," Jitendra's deep baritone was calm and unobtrusive, but cut her off mid-rant.

She turned, looked at him as if he was a piece of unidentifiable slime that she had scraped off her shoe and spat out, "Screw you, *paki*."

Jitendra rose smoothly from his chair, walked over next to Brande, looked down into the smug little 'you can't lay a finger on me,' face, sighed and slammed said face down onto the table. His hand gripped the back of her head tight as he hissed into her ear. "Now you listen to me, you cheap little piece of trash. With all the crap you've given me and my people, I couldn't really care less whether you live or die. If you had bled yourself out last night, I actually think the world would have been a better place this morning, but to have three prisoners in my charge simultaneously kill themselves... Well that's just far too much paperwork. Letting another add herself onto that list would make it totally intolerable. So I'm going to let go now and you're going to be a nice helpful, little puppy. Do you understand? Roll over and play nicely."

Brande made a strained nodding motion against the hard surface and Jitendra yanked her upright before resuming his seat.

At that moment I have to say I actually felt sorry for her. She looked terrified, truly terrified.

Jitendra nonchalantly crossed his legs. "I believe Mister Spallucci asked you a question and you were about to answer him in a nice, polite manner that is pertaining to a young lady of your profession. Am I right?"

Brande looked from the chief inspector to me then back again. She opened her mouth to speak, her bottom lip trembled and more tears flooded out from her eyes. "I can't!" she screamed. "Believe me, I can't! He'll know and he'll come for me." She thrust the bandaged wrist forward. "You've seen what he made us do. Well this is nothing compared to what he's capable of. Please don't make me tell you. Please!" She sprang from her chair and darted towards me. Jitendra was up like a shot and lunged over the desk to grab at her shoulder but she dodged his outstretched arm and threw herself at my feet, her hands grabbing onto my trouser legs. "Please," she begged, "please, just go away and leave me alone. I can't take it anymore. He promised us so much. We didn't understand the price. The things he said to us. The things he said. It was too much.

"He came to me in my dreams. It was as if he was there in the cell with me. He kept telling me how worthless I was, how there was no way out of this and that I was a failure."

She drifted off to somewhere unpleasant. When she returned her voice sounded as fragile as a new-born baby's skull. One hard squeeze and she would be totally crushed. "His eyes. His eyes. They refused to release me. He stood there punishing me for my uselessness.

"I just wanted to die. It was all I could do to escape!"

She buried her head against my trouser leg and sobbed and sobbed and sobbed.

I looked up at Jitendra. The interview was over.

The roasted, smokey flavour tasted divine. I leaned my head against the brick wall and blew a rather impressive smoke ring.

"Neat trick. Feeling a bit better?"

I nodded and ran my free hand through my hair. "That was somewhat intense, wasn't it?"

Jitendra nodded, his arms crossed and one immaculately polished shoe resting under him against the wall. "I think it's safe to say that Miss Brande is somewhat messed up."

"Indeed." I drew in heavily and finished off the Lucky. It was only mid-afternoon but I was in desperate need of my bed but I wasn't finished here yet. "You don't think she's faking it, then?"

The DCI shook his head. "No. I've seen a lot try to claim the insanity thing, but that..." He let out a sharp breath. "That was pure fear." Jitendra pulled himself away from the wall, straightening his suit as he did. "Whoever played her has terrified her to the core. What do you make of that dream business?"

"She genuinely thinks that this guy made her try to kill herself." I drummed my fingers against my teeth. "Obviously there's part of me that is thinking *psychic powers* here, but perhaps we could do with looking at the more mundane too?"

He shook his head. "If you're thinking it might have been an inside job, I've already been there, examined it. Not one officer had contact with all five of them last night." He fished a notepad out of his jacket and ran a finger down a list. "Baines and Sothwell were checked on by one PC, Brande and Haversham by second, Philips by another. There was no link."

"Hmmm..." I pondered. "All the same, it might be worth just doing a bit of checking up in case the three officers have any connections outside of the force. Perhaps they were being used?"

"I'll look into it." He paused, looked me up and down then asked, "So, you up for another interview? Want to question Philips?"

"Sure, I shrugged. It can't get any worse can it?"

Little did I realise just how wrong I was.

The meeting with Philips began quite well. Okay, as well as a meeting with a man as responsive as a boiled cauliflower *can* go. We waited for him in the same oppressive interview room as before. He shuffled in, a PC on either arm, guiding him to his seat where they lowered him down and he sat, just staring off into middle distance.

The man seemed to have aged ten years in a week. The grey in his hair was far more pronounced and his face was weathered, wrinkled. His mole-man spectacles had been removed (I guessed these had been considered a possible tool for harming himself) and his eyes looked so much smaller, giving him a more rodent-like appearance. This was not helped by the manner in which he sat. His hands were drawn up in front of him like a pair of grasping paws and he twitched involuntarily every now and then. He was a small mammal waiting for a bird of prey to swoop down, snatch him up and rip him limb from limb.

My heart could not help but go out to him. He had, quite obviously, lost his mind.

"How long has he been like this?" I asked, my voice barely a whisper.

"Since we brought him in. He eats, sleeps drinks and performs normal bodily functions, but apart from that..." Jitendra waved a brown hand hopelessly towards the television producer. "What you see is what you get."

"Lights on, nobody home," I murmured. Cautiously, I rose from my chair and approached the hapless little man. "Mister Philips," I spoke gently as if trying to wake a slumbering baby, "can you hear me." He continued to stare off into space, oblivious of my presence. I waved my fedora up and down in from of his blank stare. He didn't even blink.

I drummed my fingers against my teeth and glanced over to Jitendra, who shrugged. "He's not responded to anything?"

"Nothing."

I crouched down, my knees creaking as I did so, until my head was level with my abductor's. Even with me this close, my breath on his skin, he did not move. In his world, wherever that was, I just did not exist. "We're not going to get anything from him," I finally conceded.

"We're not going to learn anything about the Divergence."

Philips' head slowly turned and his eyes fixed on mine. His black pupils widened and as he spoke, the frail, gravelly voice that crept from his lips caused the bells in my ears to shriek.

"The Divergence is coming," he rasped. His stale breath smothered my senses and spittle flecked my skin. "When dragons walk the Earth, then all creation shall tremble.

"Dragons walk among us."

Dragons.

My mind shot back to the dream I had suffered the previous week – two dragons, one red one black, viciously fighting each other, their gouged flesh ravaging the land where it landed. I tried to stand, but my tinnitus rose in volume and the room began to spin. I was vaguely aware of someone calling out my name over and over, a chair falling backwards, but then there was just the grey. Everything blurred and there was an almighty crash followed by men shouting.

I gave in and let it all wash over me.

When I came to, I was lying on the floor in the recovery position with a nicely tailored jacket under my head. My head was still spinning but it was bearable, just. I made to rise and felt a firm hand press down on my shoulder.

"Easy," came Jitendra's deep voice. "You went down heavy."

As I rose, I felt the muscles in my right shoulder

groan in protest, a testament to just *how* heavy I had gone down. Then I saw Philips. He was flat on his back on the floor.

Totally still and lifeless.

"What..?" I managed.

"Dead. And so is Brande."

I grabbed a chair and slumped down into it. "How?" I was content to go with sentences of just one word. It was all I could manage for the moment.

The DCI sighed deeply. "As of yet, we have no idea. One minute he was rambling on to you about dragons, the next he collapsed face first onto the table, blood trickling from his nose. We tried CPR but..." He ran a hand over his face. "Then an officer came in and said the same had happened to Brande."

I sat and stared at the body. Philips and Brande both together? She had been terrified of some anonymous threat and he had started to spill the beans about Divergences and Dragons.

This was not a coincidence.

CHAPTER 3

I staggered home from the police station. It must have taken me about five minutes but it felt more like five hours. My ears weren't just ringing, they were screeching. Someone had taken a blackboard, wedged it in my cochlea and was dragging a screwdriver down its surface. Bile rose in my throat and nausea swept over me with every staggered step. Passersby stared in disgust at me, convinced I was some sort of awful drunk as I lurched from one steadying lamp post to the next. It was obvious to them that I had just been kicked out of some dive bar. I'm sure that one woman actually turned her child's head away from me.

Or perhaps that was just paranoia. My condition tends to do that to me. I get convinced that people are watching, staring, plotting. If someone tries to help me, I convince myself that they have some ulterior motive and plough on past them regardless. Later on, when the spin has waned, I run my hand over my face groaning and praying to the god of lost causes that I was not *too* abusive to some Good Samaritan.

Eventually I reached the door to my stairwell. I pushed it open and it slammed violently against the wall. I tumbled through, crashing to my knees. I swore, kicked the door back into its frame and gripped the wall with my fingertips to heave myself vaguely upright.

The stairwell was swaying from side to side. I leant my back against the wall and closed my eyes. *Almost there. Almost there,* I told myself over and over again.

When my breathing had steadied, I tentatively prised my eyes open and approached the bottom of the mountain. So many step-shaped cliff faces rose up in front of me. I decided to use the old tried-and-tested technique; all fours.

I knelt down on the first step and slowly, so slowly, began my ascent. Hand over hand, knee over knee I climbed my personal Everest, eyes once again tightly shut, until I finally reached the door to my office. I fumbled into my pocket, fished out the key and, slouching in a heap on the floor, reached up to unlock the door.

As it swung in, I crawled after it then turned onto my back and closed it in the same manner as I had the one downstairs. I gave one of my clocks (cannot remember which one) a quick glance. It was about two thirty.

Now came the hard part.

Now came the reason why I surrounded myself with so many time pieces. Lying there on the floor, my trench coat splayed out making me look like a bird that has hit a window, I breathed deeply and *listened*.

There they were, my constantly ticking workmates. Slow ticks, fast ticks, low pitches, high pitches. All of them surrounding me in their beautiful, caressing embrace. I let the noise wash over me like I had been forced to do so many times before and their individual songs sang into my beleaguered ears. There was the napoleon hat mantle clock, there was the mechanical carriage, there was the station clock. Those and many more surrounded me and administered to me like angels in the desert. They brought me succour and relief; they fed me life-sustaining manna.

And eventually the ringing and screeching subsided.

It did not disappear completely, it never does, but it became tolerable, ignorable.

I rose to a sitting position and, when I was sure that I was not going to keel over, rose and went to my desk. I flipped my laptop open and there, staring at me, was the end of the work that I had been writing just that morning. Once again tiredness tried to claim my limbs. I looked up at the station clock. It was now three o'clock. I finished off what I had been typing when Caroline had arrived that morning, clicked save and sat back in my chair.

I reached into my desk drawer and rummaged around for a pack of Luckies. After a couple of pat downs and jabbing of sharp objects I found an unopened pack. Smiling, I made to unwrap it.

Then the shaking started. I tried to grasp the plastic tab but my fingers just would not cooperate, they juddered and jinked like a caffeine-addicted spider.

"Come on..." I grumbled. "Open, damn it!"

Then I felt it again.

The spinning.

This was not good. I knew instantly what was going on. I had overdone it. Stress, lack of sleep, crazy guys rambling on about dragons: all these things are known causes of Meniere's attacks.

I closed my eyes and tried to listen to my clocks.

They were nowhere to be heard. Not a tick. Not a tock. Instead the ringing was increasing in volume. The old serpent was rising from its shallow slumber and it was right royally pissed off at being disturbed.

I rose from my desk and lurched into the centre of my office as reality spun and swayed around me. I knelt down and curled up in as tight a ball as I could manage, clasping my hands tightly over my ears. It was a futile gesture, rather like King Cnut trying to stop the tide from coming in, but I had to do something. I had to try something.

Still the serpent slithered towards me, its mouth dripping with ravenous intent.

Still the bells rang.

Still the tintinnabulation chimed incessantly in my own personal hell.

I rocked backwards and forwards moaning quietly to myself, desperate to cover up the continual noise.

No good.

I hummed.

I hummed louder.

I hummed louder still.

No good. No good. No good.

The scaly beast was upon me now. It had wrapped its muscular coils around my chest and was squeezing every least breath from my lungs.

Tears were forming behind my eyelids and started to trickle down my cheeks and my nose. Angrily I brushed them off with the back of my hand before shoving my fingertips in my mouth and biting down hard.

No good. Even the pain could not deaden the infernal noise.

The serpent chuckled its infernal laugh. There was no escape for me now.

I rolled back up into a seated position and immediately regretted it. My head swayed and the room span, nausea rose from the pit of my stomach to the back of my throat. I lurched forward and grabbed the plastic bin by my desk, strewing its contents on the floor. I crouched there, sweat seeping from every pore of my body, a flush followed by a chill as I fought back the inevitable.

And still the merciless bells continued to peal.

Still the serpent laughed at my hopelessness.

I closed my eyes and pulled my face down into the bin. The vomit was somewhere waiting to erupt, lava from my fiery pit. I rocked back and forth dreading the sensation, knowing it would arrive any second. I tried to take my mind elsewhere, I truly did. I tried to think of open fields and fresh country air. I tried to imagine calm walks along a sandy beach with fresh sea water lapping my bare feet.

The only water I felt was mixed with bile and last night's tea.

I'll spare you the details. Let's just say it was unpleasant.

Afterwards, my body's muscles started to unknot and loosen as the serpent, finally satisfied, slithered back down into its rank, foul-smelling pool of stagnant hatred. I was cold, so cold, from the sheen of sweat under my shirt. I cleared one nostril then the other. Spat out whatever was left in my mouth and dragged myself and my bucket to the bathroom.

My head was still spinning but not quite as much now. I was able swill the bin out and flush the contents of my stomach down the toilet.

Carefully, I pulled myself up to the wash basin. The room began to spin again, but I knew the worst was over now. I ran the cold tap and splashed refreshing liquid onto my warm, clammy face before sluicing my mouth out with handfuls of heaven.

When I felt vaguely abluted I slumped down against the wall and rested my head not too far away from the toilet pan. Hormones were now racing around my body at an exponential rate. There was relief that I had *finally* been sick. There was revulsion that I had *actually* been sick and there was deep depression that I knew it would happen again at some indeterminate point in the future.

Time and time again it would happen over and over with no cessation. This was my life. This was my existence, staggering from one spin attack to the next, the life in between them was only a mild distraction.

The serpent would rise and I would plunge headlong into its crushing embrace.

It had to stop. Dear God, I would give anything for it to stop.

When I felt that my stomach was no longer in danger of belching out any more of its contents, I drew myself up to my feet, lurched sluggishly into the office and grabbed a bottle of Jack before stumbling upstairs to my flat and my merciful bedroom where, after a few long drinks of over the counter anaesthetic, I eventually passed out.

CHAPTER 4

The next morning I felt somewhat better. Well, by better I mean I felt as if all the fluid had been wrung out of my muscles and my brain had been walloped with an overstuffed trout, but at least my ears had calmed down.

After half an hour of my body working out which way was up, I levered myself out from under the snuggly safehold that was my duvet and shambled towards the bathroom. I took a slight detour via the kitchen to fill the kettle and flick its switch before stumbling into what they refer to in Star Wars as the *refresher*. Whilst I sat *refreshing* myself I took my mind off my current state of bleariness by pondering the matter of toilets in films. I'm all for keeping things clean and artistic but surely there has to be a certain amount of realism or people disconnect from what they are watching? Or perhaps it's just me. Perhaps I'm just far too pedantic and can't help remembering that super-heroes and space captains have bodily functions. Is it just me who, when Picard calls up an away team, wonders why none of them say, "Actually Captain, I just need to nip to the Enterprise's loo." Surely it would be practical to make sure the crew were refreshed before they teleported down to an alien planet? Who would know what might happen if Commander Riker took a leak behind some purple-coloured rock. For all he knows it might contain some extra-terrestrial element that reacted with urine, explode violently thus detaching his genitals and scuppering his romantic notions for Deanna Troi.

Hmmm. Yes, I think it's just me.

I obviously over-think these little matters.

Anyway, suitably refreshed, I washed my face, brushed my teeth and shaved my chin to within an inch of its life, the result of which left me awake and cleansed, ready for the day. I brewed a pot of tea, lit a Lucky and was fully equipped for whatever would be thrown at me.

As I sipped my brew I kept thinking over the previous day and the sudden re-insertion of Caroline into my life. Just what were my feelings to her? More to the point, what were her feelings to me? Was there a tiny spark of romance there that needed a slightest breath just to rekindle it? "Don't go there, Sammy," I grumbled to myself, stubbing out my cigarette, "Old wounds can easily re-open especially if they never really healed." That was the problem, of course. I had never really recovered from Caroline.

It had been brief.

It had been passionate.

It had been devastating.

I closed my eyes and thought back to that hot summer, the year of my graduation. I was standing in the cold verging on frosty atmosphere that encapsulated the study of my mentor-to-be.

"So, you're the boy they've sent to replace the Wallace lad, then?" Caroline's father was sat behind his desk, his eyes peering at me over the tops of his steel-framed, half-moon spectacles. They were the intense brown of his young daughter's, but whereas hers were overflowing with youthful mischief, the craggy lines that criss-crossed his face gave his windows on the world the aspect of a pair of black holes dragging in all that surrounded them, crushing them to oblivion.

Not a very pastoral look at all.

"I am, sir."

The black holes crinkled up under their eyelids and he snorted out a husking disparagement. "That's Father Adamson, sonny, or did you not notice this wrapped around my neck?" He tapped angrily at his dog collar.

"Sorry, Father Adamson," I quickly apologised, desperate to make a good first impression. "I didn't mean to cause offence."

"Oh, stop grovelling and take a seat."

So much for first impressions.

I was informed about the basics of parish life. The main services were on Sunday: said mass at eight, sung mass at ten and evensong at six in the evening. There were other services during the week; I was to look up what time they were on the notice board outside the church. I was to attend every single service without fail and I was to follow Father Adamson during his duties around the parish. He did not suffer fools and, in his opinion, fools were those who blabbed on about nothing at all whilst not paying attention to the world around them so I was to keep my mouth shut and my ears open.

"And one last thing," he said, his eyes fixing me firmly in their gravitation pull, "I am sure that you will have noticed that I have a beautiful, young daughter. Her name is Caroline and she is a sweet little thing as pure as the whitest rose. I am well aware of the licentiousness and crude goings-on that happen within the walls of our educational establishments. If I so much as catch a whiff of it here, you'll be out. Do I make myself clear?"

Back in the present I opened my eyes. "Very clear," I whispered hoarsely, shaking my head. If only the old fool had really known what his precious little daughter had really been like...

I chuckled to myself, drained the rest of the tea and glanced out of the window. It was turning into the sort of day that really appealed to me; cold and crisp. I stretched my arms and stood as my joints creaked. I decided that a brisk walk over to Luneside University was in order.

As I made my way through the sprawling campus I watched the students passing me by. Most ignored me; some gave the almost middle-aged guy in the mac and fedora a curious stare. How old did I look to them? I recalled that, when I was their age, anyone over the age of thirty was practically friends with Tutankhamen. They still had their whole lives in front of them: loves, losses, achievements, failures. I had been through many of these already and right now it was seeming that the negative ones were stalking me somewhat. I sighed and resolved to myself that this was going to be a *good* day. The sun was out, the air was fresh and I was arriving at my best friend's flat. I bounded up the stairs and rang the doorbell.

A silhouette loomed up through the frosted glass, the lock rattled and the door swung inwards. What met my eyes almost drew a gasp from my open mouth. Spliff stood wrapped in his silk dressing gown, wearing it like a corpse wears a shroud. His skin was pallid, beads of sweat dappled his forehead and stubble was encroaching on his normally neatly trimmed beard. "Hello, Sam," he managed, his voice barely a whisper and his eyes flinching as if the quiet words were hammering his brain. "Come in, please."

He shambled away from the door and left me to close it shut. I followed him into his living room and my nose wrinkled at the unmistakable smell of vomit masked by disinfectant permeating from the adjoining bathroom. "You look like shit. What's the matter?"

My best friend tossed Dante off the sofa and crumpled up into where the cat had been lounging. The feline considered this rude deposition for a moment but decided to wind his fluid, black body around his owner's legs rather than scratch out his eyeballs. "Nothing, Sam. It's my own fault..." His voice drifted off as he rolled his head onto the back of the sofa. His eyes drifted shut whilst his chest rose and fell in a slow rhythmic manner.

I raised an eyebrow. "You been at the lighter fluid again?"

This managed to procure a slight flicker from the

corner of Spliff's mouth – all he could manage of a smile. "It's just so tasty, you know?"

I smiled and sat down on the opposite armchair. Dante lifted his head and peered at my lap. I wasn't sure whether he was contemplating curling up there or pummelling my manhood to death so I took the sensible precaution and crossed my legs. The cat gave a superior sniff and decided to jump up onto the sofa next to safer territory. Spliff let a weary hand drape across his cat and Dante snuggled down, roaring loudly. "Seriously," I asked, "what's up with you?"

His eyes still closed, Spliff gave a non-committal shrug. "I enjoyed myself too much at the Borough last night. From what I recall, I was the life and soul of the party. There's probably humorous pictures of my jolly antics all over the Twittersphere by now."

I tapped my fingernails on my teeth. Something was not right here. I had known Spliff half my life and drink had never reduced him to this state of incapacity. "How much did you have?"

A vague, languid wave. "Too much. Can't remember." He forced an accusatory eye open and levelled it in my direction. "You just come here to make me feel even worse than I look?"

"I just fancied a chat."

"A chat?"

"Yep."

"Really?"

"That's right."

Dante lifted his head and watched our verbal tennis ball lob back and forth wondering which player would default first and give the real reason for their current situation. I gave him the pleasure of cracking first.

"Caroline showed up yesterday."

That got the weary priest's attention. He levered himself upright and both eyes were suddenly bright and alert, twinkling with unbridled glee. "Well, well. What grubby little rock did her ladyship crawl out from under?"

"She's not like that," I groaned. "She's..."

"A devious, manipulative, power-hungry little harpy." Spliff interjected, all signs of imminent expiration suddenly evaporating into the ether. "Please tell me you were going say that and not that she adores baking cookies and singing to the animals as she sweeps out the homes of seven diminutive miners."

I groaned and clasped my head in my hands. Spliff had never liked Caroline. He had always felt that she was using me as a means to resolve some sort of father issue. I had constantly needed to remind him that he was studying Religion and Politics *not* Psychology. "She came for help."

"Really?" He practically spat the word out. "What does she want *this* time? Someone to idolise her and tell her how wonderful she is? Oh, wait. She had that last time! I guess it must be something new." The frame of the sofa groaned as he heaved himself out of the chair and made to stalk off to the kitchen. "I need a glass of water."

"Her son's in trouble."

Spliff paused as he reached the door.

"She thinks he's involved with a cult," I explained

to his back. "I know the lad. I can't turn my back on him."

Spliff's silk shoulders rose and fell causing the dragons to dance slightly on his back. "Where do you know him from?" He still faced away from me, obviously trying to control his emotions on the matter.

"I met him at Saint Edmund's last week. He's a really nice lad."

"What does his father think about his mother going running to her old paramour?"

"There *is* no father."

"Dear God, don't tell me he's a child of the *Force*!"

I chuckled slightly. The Anakin Skywalker quip was a sure sign that he was calming down somewhat. "No. Nothing mystical there. His dad's just not on the scene."

"Probably had the good sense to get while the going was good," Spliff harrumphed as he turned to face me. "So what are you going to do?"

"Look into it, I guess," I shrugged. "Apparently he's involved with a group going by the name of Credete." I rummaged around in my pocket and fished out the leaflet. Spliff took it, wobbling slightly on his feet as he did so. I leapt up and grabbed him. "You really are rough. Sit down. I'll get you some water."

He nodded shakily and let me guide him back to the sofa where he lay down gingerly and closed his eyes, the leaflet forgotten. Once I had made sure he was not going to throw up or roll off the couch I went over to the kitchen and located a reasonably clean glass. As I filled it with water I saw a pack of pills next to the drainer. Placing the water on the counter I picked the box up and read the label: *Stemetil*. I was familiar with the product; it was a brand name for prochlorperazine, a prescription anti-nausea drug. I had used it myself for my tinnitus spins. I frowned as I read more. It was dated last Friday - the day that Spliff had been hunting for his elusive hospital appointment card. I glanced up through the door to my best friend dozing on the sofa. Why had he been prescribed an anti-nausea drug? Had he been expecting to feel rough? What was worse, why was he still being sick four days later? I placed the box back on the counter and carried the glass of water through to my patient. "Here you go."

He opened his eyes and smiled as I handed him the refreshing drink. "Thank you, nurse," he smiled.

"Small sips," I cautioned, knowing too well from personal experience that too much liquid would make the stomach cramp and regurgitate.

He took the tiniest mouthful.

"Keep the liquid in your mouth for a while. You'll rehydrate quicker."

Spliff did as instructed then, after swallowing, said, "My, aren't you the fount of knowledge today?"

I chuckled, my eyes not leaving him. I wanted to tell him about the deaths of my abductors, but there was no way that he was in any fit state to listen. "Look, I'll be off. Ring me if you need me."

"Okay," he nodded vaguely. "I'm actually a lot better than I was earlier."

Liar. I thought to myself.

"I'll feel like eating tonight. Want to meet up? Usual time?"

"You sure you'll be up to it?"

"Of course I will. Now stop fussing will you? Unless you're actually going to wear a nurse's outfit, of course..."

I smiled again, turned and headed to the front door. "I'll see you later, then. Seven o'clock."

He waved me off and I left him to his rest.

Amidst all the hustle-bustle of Luneside's campus there is one small corner that remains forever calm and restful: Spliff's rose garden. Spliff has one true passion in life (aside from gin, verbally abusing those in authority and committing numerous far-from-clergylike deeds that could get him sacked at any given moment), and that is gardening. Where he grew up, his parents had a massive garden. He took me there a few times when we were younger. There were rolling lawns, trellises, flower beds, pergolas and roses. Rose upon rose upon rose. It looked like something out of a Disney princess cartoon. The sweet scent pirouetted in your nostrils as you walked past them, and the velvet of the petals brushed soft against your fingertips. It was paradise.

When he moved away to uni, Spliff lost all that. He found campus life bleak and barren. I sometimes think that was what turned the young Mister MacIntyre into the man that he is now; he was looking for a way to escape the concrete jungle that he saw around him.

Anyway, when he took the role of chaplain at the university, he requisitioned a scrap of wasteland behind the chapel. It had been used as a dumping ground so nobody really minded when one day he was found digging out the discarded rubble and levelling freshly dug topsoil. Then, when the powers that be realised that wooden fencing was going up and stone seats were being set, they started to take notice. They claimed that it was all very well tidying up the rubbish, but construction such as was happening there was not in keeping with the surrounding area of the campus plan.

They even sent him a letter saying this.

Spliff sent the letter back telling them in which dark orifice they could insert it. Sideways.

They backed down very quickly. This was either because they did not want to upset their volatile chaplain or they just couldn't really be bothered with a noisy argument.

So Spliff carried on and, as the days turned into months, his little paradise started to evolve. First there were a few bulbs, then some lavender and shrubbery. Then came the roses. All manner of roses. There were red ones, yellow ones, white ones and black. He even has blue ones which I never knew existed. To this day I'm convinced that it's some sort of alchemy that he brews and applies to the soil. I also think it's this self same alchemy that encourages the roses to stay in bloom well past their natural flowering season.

So it was that after leaving Spliff's apartment I was sat down on a cold autumnal day drinking in the sweet smelling paradise of rose perfume. It was peaceful. It was quiet. It was Heaven. Just what I needed to clear my mind.

What was wrong with Spliff?

Was John Adamson involved in a cult?

How had those actors died?

I had answers for none of these questions so, for now, I was just going to push them to the back of my mind and take a breather.

There was crunch on the gravel path behind me. I turned and saw a young face smiling at me. "Hi there," I smiled back.

"Hey, Sam," Grace replied. "How ya doing?"

I waggled my hand back and forth. "So, so. You?"

"Okay," she shrugged. "I just came here for a bit of quiet thinking time."

"Oh, okay. I'll get out of your way." I made to get up, but her arm reached out and her small hand touched my sleeve. It hesitated there then snatched back to the rainbow-coloured shoulder strap of her bag.

"No. No, it's okay," she apologised glancing up and down between me and her hand. "Stay for a bit, please? I'd kinda like the company?"

"Okay," I nodded, settling back down. I shifted to one side of the stone bench and she came and sat down next me, shifting her heavy bag down to the floor. "That looks like a lot of reading. You here to ponder an essay?"

I caught the glimpse of a smile as she studied her vibrant red Doc Marten's. "No. Nothing like that. It's a bit more personal."

"Ah!" I recalled a conversation from the previous week and nodded sagely. "Spliff did mention last week that you were having," I used my fingers to quote him, "*man problems.*"

There was a stunned silence and a horrified look

on the young barmaid's face.

"What? What's the matter?"

"Well... what exactly did he say?" she blustered, her forehead creasing with worry underneath the brown beanie hat that she always wore.

"Just what I said. I was worried about you last week and he... said..." I trailed off as a look of total relief passed over her face. I fought to find the right words to say. I was definitely missing something here so I decided that the best course of action was to change the subject. "Spliff says he had a great night last night."

"Really? Where at?"

"The Borough, of course."

"Oh." Grace looked perplexed at this. "That's odd. I was on last night and I didn't see him."

Now it was my turn to frown. He had lied. That combined with the Stemetil really worried me. "I'm sure he was just confused," I covered. "He looked pretty hung over."

"Okay." Grace accepted my explanation with no argument which was just as well, I thought, I wasn't sure what was going on myself. So we sat there quietly for a moment, both of us with our own thoughts, mine juggling around deceit, murder and death, Grace's probably something far more pleasant. Eventually her voice drew me out of my reverie. "I think roses are like really romantic. Don't you?"

I leaned back a touch and regarded the variety of blooms and colours. "Sure, I guess. They certainly cost a fair bit on Valentine's day."

Grace giggled lightly.

I turned to face her. "What?"

"You always make me laugh, Sam."

"What can I say? It's the big feet and the red nose."

This induced another fit of giggles until, once she had brought herself under control, she carried on with her train of conversation. "Just look at them, so perfect. But what were they originally? A small tight bud, curled up so tight so no-one could see its potential." She turned and her green eyes looked up at me. "So no one could see its true emotions until it unfolds and blossoms putting all its heart on display. Do you ever feel like that, Sam? Or perhaps you know someone who needs encouraging to bloom? Could you be capable of unfurling someone's tightly closed bud?"

I looked down at her bright, young eyes and realised just how much truth there was in her words. There was someone who I needed to help blossom. There was someone who kept themselves guarded from me, but just needed some care and attention and they would open up to me. "You're right," I nodded. "You're so right!"

Grace beamed with delight.

'I'll ring her straight away." I rummaged around in my pocket for my mobile. When I found it I looked up to see Grace frowning. "Oh sorry, you don't know, do you? Caroline turned up yesterday."

"Caroline? Who's Caroline?"

I stood as I flicked through my contacts. "Old girlfriend. We knew each other back when I was a student here." I found Caroline's number and my finger hovered over dial as I had a quick thought. "Grace, could I ask a favour? Could you please make sure that no-one grabs my table tonight? I'll bring her in for a meal." With that I hurried away with the phone dialling the number. The curious thing was, as I turned the corner I was sure I could hear the sound of gravel being tossed at the rose bushes. I think my tinnitus must have been playing up again.

Caroline picked her phone up after only two rings. She was delighted to hear that I was making progress and would love to meet me for dinner at the Borough. Seven? Sure. Not a problem.

All I had to do now was actually make some progress before this evening. It couldn't be that hard, could it? I slipped my hand into my jacket pocket to pull out the Credete leaflet only to find fluff, a battered packet of Luckies and thin air. Where was it? I'd had it this morning. Quickly, I rummaged through my other pockets, succeeding only in looking like a crazy guy who has an imaginary friend leaping about his person. I'm sure some of the students pointed and sniggered at me. They do that to people over thirty, you know.

Then realisation struck me.

Spliff! I had left it at Spliff's! I cursed loudly and the staring students quickly averted their eyes as I stormed off the campus with my fingers continuing their knowingly futile search through my pockets. It was when they located something in my *chest* pocket that I paused. I drew the slip of paper out and read the eleven digits penned in fluid, feminine handwriting and smiled.

CHAPTER 5

"Well hello, bugle boy," chirped the sing-song female voice at the other end of the phone. "You're lucky to catch me. It's break time."

"Hi, Abalone. How's it going?"

The music teacher at Saint Edmund Campion chuckled mischievously down the phone. "All the better for hearing from you." Then, dropping her voice to a conspiratorial whisper, "You ready to educate me now?"

I was sure that I was blushing as I walked quickly through town, back towards Dalton Square. "Erm..." Words failed me. She was even more keen now there were no kids around her. "Actually, I'm sort of on a case and I could do with your assistance."

"Splendid! You gonna whisk me off in your TARDIS and take me on adventures through space and time or am I gonna be the stay at home secretary that flutters my heavy eyelashes at you every time you walk past?"

I actually pulled my phone away from my ear and stared at it in total disbelief. Was I really hearing this?

"Are you legally safe to teach," I eventually asked, "or do all teachers have over-active imaginations?"

Her chuckling rang not unpleasantly into my ear. "It comes with the job, trust me. After two hours of trying to get twelve-year-olds to stay in tune whilst playing *Ode To Joy* on glockenspiels, fantasy and a good dollop of humour helps to save the sanity."

My lips broadened into a smile. She certainly was infectious. "I can imagine."

"Anyway, *Samuel*, what is it that I can assist you with?"

I ran my fingers through my hair, unsure what to say right now with people walking past. "Could we meet up at lunchtime?"

"Sure, I can dodge out at one."

"Okay. I'll meet you just after that then. In Starbucks?"

"Sounds good to me, Mister Investigator. It's a date," she laughed as she hung up.

A date? Wow. Two in one day. Not bad.

One o'clock saw me dunking a ginger biscuit in my black Americano. There is, I consider, a subtle art to this practice. Not enough dunk and the action has been somewhat pointless – you still have a hard biscuit minus the coffee flavour. Too much dunk and... Well, I'm sure that coffee shops have gone from supplying teaspoons to these weird splintery stirrers just to provide amusement for harassed baristas. The highlight of their day must be watching unfortunate customers try to fish over-dunked ginger biscuit from the bottom of a mug

65

with the aid of something which looks like it should instead be used by Action Man as a splint.

I am a master dunker.

Not too much, not too little. Careful not to drip coffee on the table, or worse your shirt, then sit back and smile as the ginger and coffee do a little dance on your tongue.

Bliss.

Mind you, it's not like I can take my pick of any other foods that are on offer in these places. Salted Pop Chips, dark chocolate and the aforementioned ginger biscuit are the only vegan fayre on offer these days. There used to be a fantastic falafel thing which I treated myself to once a week but they ditched it and replaced it with a salad box! I mean, come one, not only did they plonk mayo in there, but the packaging... Really, Starbucks. That totally ruined my day.

Okay, rant over.

Back to the present.

Just as I popped the last of the ginger biscuit in my mouth the door opened and in breezed Abalone, her blonde hair escaping from under a large, furry hat. She looked around, saw me and waved as she made her way over. "Good God, it's freezing out there today."

"I'll get you a coffee," I said. "What do you want?"

Her blue eyes twinkled mischievously behind her glasses and the edge of her mouth turned up.

"I meant, *What type of coffee?*" I sighed, albeit with a touch of amusement.

She shrugged, "Well I suppose we are in public. A latte please."

I chuckled to myself as I went and ordered the drink. When I returned, she had discarded her hat and coat and made herself at home. "Thanks. So what was it you wanted to ask me about then? Why all the cloak and dagger?"

I sipped my coffee, silently judging my words. Like my ginger biscuit, this would take care and precision. "When I was at your school last week, I noticed that a lot of the pupils wear," I made a circle motion around the base of my hand, "wristbands."

"Sure," she shrugged. "It's not covered by uniform, so as long as they're not offensive, most things are sported as a kind of individuality."

I nodded. In my day it had been socks, bright luminous ones. There had been pink ones, orange ones, green ones. All sorts. Eventually schools had clamped down and black was now the only colour deemed suitable in many places. It was logical that something else would emerge as that little act of rebellion. However, teenager protest fashion was not what I was interested in.

I dunked a little bit more. "Tell me about the lilac ones."

In an instant the atmosphere had changed. The smile was instantly gone, her legs were crossed and the latte was held in front of her like a milky, caffeinated shield. "Bitch," she murmured through pursed lips. "I thought she didn't even like you."

"Who?" I frowned, genuinely confused. My metaphorical biscuit was now seemingly in danger of dropping messily into my drink.

"Wetherington," Abalone snapped. "I know she doesn't approve, but to try and get info this way..." She grimaced and shook her head. "Thanks for the coffee, but I need to get back to school." She picked her coat up and made to rise.

"Whoa! Whoa! What's going on? I'm in the dark here."

The young teacher paused mid-flounce and peered at me the way I imagined she peered at a child who said their dog had been fornicating with their homework. I could see her evaluating my body language, trying to perceive the slightest hint of deception. "Then why are you asking about them?" she finally asked.

"I've been hired by a client who is concerned about their son." The truth, plain and simple. I let it radiate from my face.

"Nothing to do with Ballcrusher?"

I chuckled involuntarily at the nickname. "Not a thing."

She waited a moment, still sizing me up, then lay her hat and coat back down next to her.

I withdrew my metaphorical biscuit intact, saturated to perfection with coffee.

"Thank you."

"So tell me more, then." Her voice was still quite icy, but I could sense the start of a welcome thaw. I tried to apply a verbal heater to push back the ice flow.

"Well, basically, a mother of a child at school has approached me with concerns that her son is involved in, as she termed it, *a cult*." I watched her face for the slightest reaction. There was none. I continued. "Personally, I think she's overreacting, but I promised her I would look into it." Still nothing. "So here I am."

Abalone sat quietly again for a moment, her lips pursed in thought until she picked up her drink, sipped it and said, "There's nothing wrong with Credete." Her words could not have been any more defensive if she had built a fort around herself first made from those little wooden stirrers.

"I'm sure there isn't." My tone was soft, placating. "I read one of their leaflets, all very harmless from what I can see. Can you tell me more?"

She looked down at her coffee, deep in thought, her fingers drumming pensively against the mug. "Sam, do you know what it's like to lose someone who was so close to you that they were your life?"

"Yes," I nodded. "My father died when I was younger. It almost destroyed me."

Abalone's shoulders rose and fell as she looked up at me, her crystal blues filled with utter sorrow. "You have my sympathy," she said, "but it's not quite the same."

I sat and waited quietly for her to continue.

"Last year, I was madly, deeply, *totally* in love with the man of my dreams. Russell was another teacher at Saint Edmund's. Geography." Her lips formed a melancholy smile. "Oh, he was so Geography. You know the sort? Corduroy jacket. Unbrushed hair. Totally scatty. Well he was all of these and more.

"And I loved him with all my heart.

"We were totally one body, one soul. We had the

wedding planned for earlier this year.

"Then a black saloon ploughed into him on King Street just after Christmas. My life died instantly, it's body crumpled up in a bloody mess on the side of the road.

"They never caught the driver."

Abalone paused as she sipped her drink.

"My life was ruined. I had no future, no reason to live. I went off long-term sick, never intending to go back. I barricaded myself in my bedroom. My housemate was going spare. She could not entice me out with anything. Not even Hob Nobs." The smile started to lose its melancholia as happier memories began to surface.

"Then, one day, I ventured downstairs and I saw a leaflet sticking through the letter flap. I was hungry by that point and thought it was a pizza menu or something. It wasn't and it changed my life.

"It was a leaflet from Credete. I read it with a scathing cynicism, poo-pooing all their wild claims, dismissing it as fodder for the desperate masses.

"But something inside of *me* was a desperate mass. Something inside of me was calling out to go to one of their meetings. Something was pushing me along a path that I had no idea of where it would lead.

"My life has never been the same since the first time I set foot amongst them."

"Why?" I asked, my throat dry from the inactivity whilst I had been fascinated by this young woman's tale. "What was it like?"

"It was... It *is*..." She held her hands up, lost for words. "Indescribable. You have to experience it just to see how wonderful it is."

I tapped my teeth with my fingernails and thought over her story. To lose someone so dear then fall into the welcoming arms of such a group... I was somewhat perturbed. Then I realised that she was looking at me expectantly. "What?" I asked, feeling a sinking feeling.

"Well? Will you?"

"Will I what?"

"Come to a meeting, tomorrow night at the Ashton Hall? Eight o'clock. See what it's like then tell your fussy mother that she has nothing to worry about."

Oh, this was not good. Nightmarish memories of smiley faces and blue jeans rose up in front of my eyes, but what could I realistically do?

Besides, it would mean that I got to spend some more time with Abalone.

"Okay," I gave in. "I will."

After Abalone left, I struck out from Starbucks and lit up a Lucky. All around me people were hurrying about doing this or that. As I made my way down Market Street and up Penny Street I gave room to wondering just what people were doing. What was going on in their lives? There was a guy wrapped up in a thick overcoat, a briefcase clutched tightly in a gloved hand. Was he a banker? A businessman? There was a young girl, early twenties, pushing one of those big HGV pushchairs which contained two kids screaming and wailing. Was she happy with her lot? Did she go home at night, put the kids to bed then cry herself to sleep with a bottle of vodka?

I had no idea. All these people around me. All going about their everyday lives. All so normal. Yet, what were they really like? How had their lives formed and shaped them? Now, I'm no psychologist, but I only have to look at my past to know that it has an influence. My hand latched onto my mobile. I drew it out, flicked onto the contacts and typed in *M.* There she was, in the list. My mother.

A lot of years had passed.

Too many.

I could press her icon right now. The phone would dial and I would hear her voice. That gentle voice that had soothed me when I had fallen and grazed my knee, sung to me when the night terrors had first come bringing the voices that spoke to me in the middle of the night.

The same voice that had scolded me for getting involved with a young trollop of a girl. The voice that had despaired at me following some faddy eating disorder diet.

I pushed the phone back into my pocket.

Yes we all had back history. We all carried our baggage in a very large back pack that weighed us down when we thought about it.

Why should the outwardly bright, sassy Abalone Morris be any different?

As I entered Dalton Square I cast an eye over to the Borough. What baggage would Caroline be carrying when we met tonight? I dreaded to think. I pushed that thought well out of my crowded mind and made my way to my office. My feet carried me up the stairs in a far more dignified manner than they had the previous day and I let myself in, checking for mail as I did.

There was none.

Good, no distractions.

I discarded my coat, my hat and my jacket then seated myself down at my laptop. I flicked it on and called up a web browser before navigating to Google. I had some time to kill before tonight and I had to spend it productively. That meant research.

I typed in "Divergence". My vision started to blur halfway into the first hit. It was rambling on about a mathematical term in vector calculus. Something to do with vector operators and sinks or something. I exhaled sharply and navigated back to the first set of hits. The next hit gave me the definition, "The act of diverging."

"No shit, Sherlock," I grumbled. This was ridiculous. There was nothing at all. Secret societies were not supposed to keep secrets secret! Someone was always supposed to leak juicy tidbits into the good old *Interweb*. For example, if you wanted to know the deepest, darkest secrets about a politician's sexual fetishes, all you had to do was Google it and there it would be, displayed on some forum in all its bare-arsed, disturbing entirety.

I tried a different tack.

"*The* Divergence" found me looking at the webpage for a rock band. Not exactly what I had in mind.

I leaned back in my chair and ran my fingers down my face. This was ludicrous. Surely there should be something out there? Some tiny little fragment? Or perhaps the vampires were just too good at their job?

Perhaps they kept an immaculate house and tidied up thoroughly wherever they went.

I shuddered at the thought of someone like Marcus "tidying up".

I needed a drink. I grabbed a bottle of Jack from my filing cabinet and poured myself a good thinking measure. Slumping down into my sofa I took a large swig and rested the glass tumbler on the coffee table where the pad lay with Caroline's number. I scooped up the pad and clicked out Mr Biro. It was time for a list.

Okay, so what was there rattling round in my head right now?

One. *Divergence*. Duly jotted down. Top of page.

Two. *Suicides*. Five names all in a row. I drew an arrow from these to Number One.

There was something else to go with these. I wrote *Dragon* along the arrow and next to that, *What does this mean??? Symbolic???* Let's face it, dragons aren't real. One of Lancaster's greatest showed that. Sir Richard Owen lived just off Dalton Square and was the guy who came up with the term *Dinosaur* – terrible lizard. He was one of the paleontological forerunners who obliterated the idea of fire-breathing creatures roaming the Earth. Well, for us sane folk, anyway.

However, I digress.

Three. *Children of Cain*. *Vampires*. They were involved in this so on the list they went. What were they exactly? I didn't think they were antagonistic. They came across as supernatural safeguarders; there to watch and wait then act when necessary. I tapped my teeth with my fingertips as I re-read their name. Cain? Which Cain? I scribbled down *The Cain?*

This brought me onto number four.

Werewolves. Where there were the Children of Cain, there was also the Bloodline of Abel. I wrote their title next to them on the list and sank into thought again. Cain and Abel. One brother murders the other. In biblical history, Abel was the good, faithful servant. His sacrifice was pleasing and Cain killed him in jealousy before being banished. This was odd. Very odd. How could the goody-two-shoes produce such crazed killers and the murderer spawn supernatural watchmen? I drew a large question mark next to this as I also pondered another thing. Did either of the Hawkins siblings mention the Divergence? I cast my mind back over both their rantings and drew a blank. No, it had only been Nightingale and Marcus. Only the vamps had talked about it. Did the werewolves even know about it? Perhaps they were just a side show, a rather hairy, sharply-toothed distraction? It seemed somewhat likely. Something deep inside me was twirling its fingers telling me to move on, guiding me to more relevant matters.

Five. *Credete*. I circled this one. Even before the creepy suicides and deaths, this had been my first matter at hand. Next to it I penned *cult?* and *who?* This was the thing. So far I had an entity with a name but no face. Every group had a leader. Who led this little shebang? There had been no name on the leaflet and I had stupidly forgotten to ask Abalone. This disturbed me. I don't like secrets; they never come to anything good. You can be walking along quite happily enjoying the sunshine, whistling away to yourself when suddenly a paving slab becomes an open man-hole and down you plummet into the dark. Not good.

I needed to know who Credete's David Koresh was. Was he some silent psycho, quietly feeding his adoring goldfish into an apocalyptic frenzy or was he just some charismatic wordsmith telling needy folk what they wanted to hear whilst laughing merrily as his current account sucked in their donations.

I seriously hoped it was the latter. Dear God, I did. I did not want another week like the last one.

I scribbled next to *Credete*, a note to myself that I needed to find out who ran the show.

I read down the list. Five neat jigsaw pieces that I needed to rotate, examine and slot together. There had to be a pattern, a common factor that drew them together. I was just about to lay the pad down and take a sip of the bourbon when there was a discreet cough at the back of my subconscious.

"What?"

"You *know* what."

"No I don't."

"Yes you do, Sam. You're just conveniently ignoring it."

"The hell I am."

"Really?"

Sulking silence on my part.

"You know you have to put her on the list."

"No I don't."

"Yes you do. She started this. She's a factor."

I sighed, downed the Jack and snatched up pen and pad. Underneath *Credete* I stabbed out another "C" word.

Caroline.

My inner voice had a point. She was the catalyst. Without her I would not be sat here writing this list. I could, instead be sat back enjoying a peaceful glass of whiskey. Okay, true, Philips and co. would still be dead, but that was not my fault, not my problem.

Apart from that Divergence business.

Okay, yes apart from that Divergence business.

And the dragons.

Yes, and the *dragons*. Sheesh, give a guy a break.

So apart from some crazed satanic abductors topping themselves and/or dying horribly after rambling on about unidentifiable events to do with mythical creatures, my week would be relatively normal.

Caroline always had a way of turning my life on its head.

Just as she had in her father's library.

It was the second day of my placement and I was taking a relaxing moment before bed after what had been a manic day of parochial duties. There had been parishioners to visit, services to plan, meetings to minute; all of which had seemed to blur into one, commentated on by the dour authoritarian monologue of Father Adamson.

He would instruct me as to how the parishioners were to be cared for but not molly-coddled. He would divulge intelligence on how services had to be succinct yet spiritual. He would stress that meetings were to be endured for the sake of those who felt that they benefitted from attending them but then casually disregarded as what was determined in them was as much use as a chocolate teapot.

In truth, I actually had a certain amount of respect for the priest but I needed a small time to myself where I wasn't being lectured on parish matters.

So I found myself wandering the vicarage and ending up in the library which was situated on the first floor just down from my bedroom. I let a surprised whistle squeak through my teeth as I gazed at the numerous volumes that lined the walls. It was just like being back on campus. I had never seen a private house so well stocked with books. There was high-brow literature, modern and classical poetry, academic texts, collections of bound newspapers. The list was endless.

I lingered by the poetry section and let my finger rest on one particular volume: *Blake's Poetical Works*. I smiled affectionately. I had always been (and still am) a huge fan of William Blake. In my teenage years, when others had been more concerned with fashion and love bites, I had been more inclined to curl up with a copy of *Songs Of Experience*. I flicked through the worn pages of Adamson's book and found the verse that I had read to myself over and over again.

There was a creaking noise that made me jump somewhat as the only window in the room swung open. I regained my composure when I saw that it was no burglar breaking their way in, just a blonde-haired, teenage girl. "A little help?" Caroline asked as she swung herself over from the huge tree that grew next to the house.

I grabbed my host's daughter under her shoulders and aided her unorthodox entry into her own house. It was a fairly fumbled attempt at gallantry as I still clasped the book in my left hand with my thumb marking where I had been reading. "I thought you went to bed ages ago."

"You and my father, both," she grinned as she settled her feet on the floor and quickly brushed herself down. "There are times I like to get out without him knowing."

"What, so you can go and lurk at some friend's house?" I mocked disparagingly, recalling my not-so-distant teenage years.

"Oh, I don't ever lurk," she grinned, her brown eyes gleaming mischievously. "I tend to be quite energetic. It depends who I'm with."

I am pretty sure that I went red at that little revelation. "But... but you're fifteen!"

"Sixteen next week," she pouted. "Besides, it's my life. I can do what I want with whoever I want." She noticed the book and there was a waft of patchouli and jasmine as she sidled up close to me. "What are you reading?"

"Words, words, words," I grinned.

"Oooo... educated." Caroline reached over my arm and plucked the book from my grip. "Tut tut. Wrong author. Don't quote the Bard when reading a metaphysical."

I turned and faced the cheeky grin that was twinkling up at me.

I swallowed at the sight of those deep, brown

eyes.

"Hey," I protested somewhat lamely, "it sounded cool."

Caroline raised a blonde eyebrow. "You stand here reading *The Tiger* and use a word like *cool?* You deserve to be shot."

"That's a bit drastic, surely? You barely know me." I reached for the book. She hid it behind her back and I suddenly found my face very close to hers.

"No, I don't," her smooth, teenage lips whispered. "But so far I like what I see, so that'll do for me." With that, she placed the book into a pair of hands that I was desperately trying to prevent from trembling, turned and walked out of the room leaving me breathless.

Yes, Caroline definitely had a way of turning things on their head.

CHAPTER 6

That evening saw me sat in my chair at the Borough, a faux leather-bound menu in front of me, a very large whiskey in my hand and a thoughtful frown on my face. For all intents and purposes I was just another would-be diner sat waiting for his friends to show up. In reality my was mind was running around in circles like a dog with a bone tied to its tail.

I was still turning over the list from this afternoon. I was missing something. There was a link. Or was there? Was I just being somewhat paranoid? Why on Earth should there be a connection between Caroline, Credete, the Divergence and the suicides?

Because my gut told me there was, that was why. There was a formless phantom sidling around just outside of my peripheral vision. If I could somehow grab the smoky tendrils of this elusive shadow then it would complete the jigsaw. There was something that linked the deaths to Credete, I knew it. I had no justifiable reason to think so, but it was there, the suspicion.

Perhaps it was last week being the week from

hell.

Perhaps two attempts on my life had left me somewhat jittery.

Perhaps a tree falling down in a forest when no-one was around *did* make a sound.

How was I to know? All I could do was hunt around until something struck me. Something that was hopefully not a large blunt instrument.

"The last time I saw a face like that, the vice-chancellor's dog had farted very loudly at an executive soiree."

"Pleasure to see you too."

Spliff settled down into his seat: gin in hand, grin on his face.

"I didn't hear you come in."

"I think you were too busy planning how to scurry off into Mordor," he observed before taking a large (make that disturbingly large) swig of neat gin.

"I take it your insides are feeling better?"

"Of course," he purred, settling the tumbler down onto a beer mat. "It takes more than a dodgy drink to floor me."

I thought about Grace's comment that he had in fact not been drinking and said nothing. There would be a time and a place for the truth. This was not it.

"Listen," his mercurial personality quickly flitting onto another subject, "are you doing anything this Saturday?"

I sipped my whiskey, my spidey-senses suddenly tingling. There was that recognisable twinkle in his mischievous grey eyes. My best friend would probably describe what he was going to suggest as a *jolly jape*. Through a more historically accurate perception of these sorts of events, I was more likely to describe it as an *embarrassing disaster*. "Can't say that I've got anything planned yet, although I can quickly find something depending on what you say next."

He ploughed on, totally ignoring my sarcasm. "Did you know that *What's It Worth?* is coming here? To the Town Hall?"

I shrugged my indifference. *What's It Worth?* is one of those programmes that just does not appeal to me. The idea of sitting in my armchair watching middle class pensioners pretending that they are not interested in the possible monetary valuable of their Great Aunt Maude's bed warmer is not my idea of an evening's entertainment. Apart from the news, if it doesn't involve lightsabers or laser guns, it tends to pass me by. "So?"

"I thought we could go."

I screwed my eyes up and peered over the top of my glass. "Okay, so I'm going to ask you, 'Why?' and, if you say that it's because you have some antiques that you want valuing, I will roll my eyes to the back of my head and groan in displeasure because I know that's not true and there is some other motive for this as of which I am yet unaware."

"I think you've been spending too much time with PC Plod up the road," Spliff pouted. "It was just a simple question."

"Spliff, with you, nothing is ever simple. Now, spill it."

He took a deep breath, steeled himself and

whispered conspiratorially, "*She'll* be there."

"*She*?"

"Harmony."

"Ah," and the penny dropped. Harmony Briers, how could I have not seen it? Spliff is totally smitten by those piercing green eyes and sophisticated Home Counties accent. She was his ultimate gay icon.

Personally, I have never really been able to get this whole *gay icon* thing. Sure, I can understand the likes of Freddie Mercury, Elton John and George Michael. They were and are gay, so for them to be idolised by people of the same sexuality makes sense to me. But then you get all the prominent women who, as far as I know, are or were straight. Liza Minnelli is one as is Gloria Gaynor. Dusty Springfield had been another and even ended up singing with the Pet Shop Boys. Was Carol Vorderman secretly worshipped in bars named *The Blue Lobster*? I had no idea. I mean, what is it that makes someone a gay icon? One of these days I must look it up when I have time.

For Spliff it is the purring Ms. Briers, former Shakespearian actor *par excellence* (her Lady Macbeth was the talk of 2012 apparently) and now the presenter of a programme where you hope to take your dead gran's lavender-scented hankie and find out it is miraculously worth an arm and a leg. Of course he would want to go to the filming on Saturday.

I resigned myself to my apathetic doom. "What time is it?"

"They're letting people in from eight, so I thought we could pootle along about nine?"

Begrudgingly, I nodded. Depriving him of this experience would be like depriving a young boy of ten a smelly little mongrel dog. It would just be far too cruel.

"Fair enough. Meet me at my place and we'll head over."

Spliff beamed and picked up a menu from our table. "Thank you, Sam. You won't regret it."

"Tell me that after the event," I sighed.

"Oh," Spliff continued, gesturing to the three menus on the table, "It seems that you've picked up too many menus. Lost the ability to count to two today?"

I steeled myself for the inevitable tirade of abuse. "We've got company tonight."

"Really? Who?" I could tell from the way that he was mumbling this whilst perusing a menu he already knew like an intimate lover that he was not really bothered as long as he got to eat and drink in peace.

That peace shattered into a hundred fragments when I told him.

"Dear God, Sam," he huffed when I had finally calmed him down. "What the hell do you think you're playing at? Caroline? Here? No, no, no! That's not good."

I sighed in exasperation. I knew he could not stand her but this was somewhat of an over-reaction even for my best friend. "I don't see what the problem is, Spliff. I'm working this case for her and I need to report back. Dinner sounded the most civil way of doing so."

His eyes pierced the air between us. "Civil? *Civil?* Whenever was that little bitch civil? She makes Joan Collins look like Mother Teresa on prozac!" He drained his drink and glowered at me across the table. "And *here*, Sam? Why here of all places?"

"Why not?" I shrugged, totally at a loss. "I always eat here."

Spliff started to do that goldfish expression that the fatally baffled get from time to time. "Because... because..." His eyes flicked over to the bar as Grace came over, pad in in hand. "Oh, forget it," he grumbled, slouching down into his chair, arms folded over his chest.

"Hi, guys," Grace beamed. "You would be, like, ready to order?"

"Actually, Grace," I smiled up at the young girl, "we're waiting for someone to join us."

She nodded, her beanie hat bobbing happily. "Oh, okay. Who would that be then?"

"That," came the silken female voice from over her shoulder, "would be me."

Three pairs of eyes turned to the immaculately dressed woman in her mid-thirties. I could visibly track the daggers flying from Spliff's. Grace's were their usual bright and jolly selves. "Oh, okay," she smiled, backing off, "I'll give you some more time then."

"You do that." I frowned at the tone of Caroline's voice. It sounded somewhat unnecessarily curt. I had no idea why. I guessed that perhaps it was down to the shield of ice that Spliff was rapidly constructing in front of himself.

"Thanks, Grace," I smiled. "Could you just give us five minutes?"

"No probs, Sam," she grinned and headed back

off to the bar. Caroline's eyes followed her all the way then turned round and lanced me to my chair.

"You don't change do you? Still chasing the young ones."

I sipped my whiskey and frowned at her. "I don't get you."

She raised a perfectly shaped eyebrow as she pulled a third seat up to our table and neatly lowered herself down. "Forget it," she said. "Obviously my mistake." There was a slight curl to the corner of her mouth, a sure sign that something had amused her. I had no idea what, so I let it pass for now.

Caroline picked up the spare menu and started to leaf through. I looked at Spliff. He looked at me. It was a *you are in such trouble* look.

"I didn't realise we would have a guest," Caroline finally said from behind the menu.

"Believe me, I only just found out," Spliff snapped back.

I suddenly felt like I was trapped between North and South Korea and that there were rather itchy fingers on the big, red buttons. "Spliff, behave," I snapped. "Caroline, I normally eat here with Spliff. He also helps out advising me on my cases. I went to see him this morning to ask his advice about Credete. So, please, just calm down."

The fingers edged back from the buttons and the Borough was saved a nuclear cataclysm as both parties went back to studiously poring over their menus. I did likewise, realised that I would order what I normally ate and tossed the booklet onto the table before downing my drink.

Silence pervaded.

This was ridiculous.

I wished I still had some more bourbon left.

It was Caroline who finally broke the impasse. "I'll have the mussels."

Spliff grumbled that he was having the fish.

I waved at Grace and she beetled back over. "Hi guys. You, like, ready?"

"Why yes, *like*, we are," Caroline smiled, her perfect teeth showing neatly between her lips. "I'll have the mussels."

"Surely these *mussels* won't be stiff enough for your tastes?" Spliff sneered.

I shot him a warning look.

He harrumphed back to his menu.

Caroline held her menu up and waited for Grace to take it which the young girl promptly did.

"Spliff?" I enquired, praying for a more civil answer.

"Fish please, little dust devil," he winked at Grace, passing her his menu.

"And, you'll have the veggie-burger, Sam?"

I nodded.

"Want a top up?" She nodded to the empty glass.

"Please."

"Okay." She went and reached over the bar, stretching on tiptoes to grab my bottle of Jack Daniels before coming back and topping up my glass with a more than generous measure. "Anything else?" she beamed.

"A sick bucket would be useful," said Caroline, "but failing that, a vodka and tonic, plenty of ice."

For a second Grace was quiet, just standing looking at Caroline, then eventually she replied, "Ice? I'd have thought you could have just snapped off your tongue and dipped it in the drink," before turning round and stamping off.

A muffled chuckle emanated from Spliff's direction as Caroline sat back in her chair and regarded me. "So, here's the deal, do you have any information for me, or shall I leave before your little *friend* thinks really hard in that little head of hers and gives herself a stroke trying to come up with any more witty comebacks?"

Oh, dear God. I ran my fingers through my hair. "Don't mind Grace. She's probably just tired and overworked."

Caroline sighed. "She a student?"

I nodded.

"Then trust me, she's not overworked. Now do you have any information for me or not?"

Another barmaid brought Caroline's drink over and after she had walked out of earshot I started to explain my meeting with Abalone. Caroline listened intently and I was pretty sure that Spliff did likewise although he was a doing a good impression of someone who was more interested in a solitaire app on his phone.

"So, as of yet, you have nothing?" Caroline did not sound very impressed with my progress, or lack of it.

"Nothing tangible, but I'm going to go along and see what this meeting is all about. See if they sacrifice any goats," I winked.

I'm not the confrontational type. To be perfectly honest I would do more or less anything for a quiet life. Spliff and Caroline, however, have both always been somewhat feisty in their nature. My best friend will rant for hours about the latest thing to wind him up whether it be doctrinal, bureaucratic or boringly mundane. Caroline was always one for chomping at the leash wrapped around her neck by her overbearing father. The two of them had only met once before but that meeting was one too many times for either party.

It had been the day after I had caught Caroline climbing in through the library window...

"So how's it going?"

Spliff and I were sat on the vicarage lawn enjoying the warm summer evening. My best friend was sneaking a quick cigarette and I was sipping some juice.

"It's okay," I said. "Adamson's a bit of a task master but I think I'm learning a lot of stuff."

Spliff peered up the garden path. "So I see," he murmured.

I turned to follow his gaze and my jaw dropped. Caroline was walking down the path wearing a skimpy polka dot bikini, a large sun hat and round sunglasses. She was all legs and midriff.

Spliff took a long draw on his cigarette. "Sam. Have you ever read *Lolita*?"

I was about to reply when Caroline sauntered over towards us. She looked at Spliff, cocked her head to one side and groaned, "Not another one. Father hates those things."

"What?" Spliff inquired. "Potential ordinands?"

Caroline came and stood close to me. *Very* close. "No. Cigarettes. If he catches you smoking down here, he'll kill you."

"Murder on the vicarage lawn," Spliff smiled. "Very Agatha Christie."

Caroline harrumphed and draped an arm around me. "I thought you were going to be alone down here."

"Oh, Spliff came over to visit," I told her. "He had the evening off too."

"*Spliff*? What sort of a name is that? Makes you sound like a junkie."

"Better than being jail bait," he shot back. "Haven't you got a street corner to go and stand on?"

With that, Caroline turned and stomped back off to the house. Spliff shook his head as he watched her march back up the garden path. "Malcolm was right about her. You'd better watch yourself, Sam."

The arrival of our food dragged me back to the present hostilities. As the waitress lay our meal on the table Spliff was berating Caroline for selling her soul to such a filth-feeding hack as Swarbrick whilst Caroline was protesting that Spliff worked for one of the most corrupt and controlling bodies on the face of the planet.

Somethings in life are a constant.

There was a truce as we started to eat. Caroline eyed my burger. "You still veggie, then?"

"Vegan, actually."

She popped a mussel into her mouth, chewed and swallowed. "Christ, you have got it bad. Whatever possessed you?"

"Just felt right for me," I shrugged. I put my burger down and looked across the table. "You okay?"

Spliff had eaten about two mouthfuls and was just pushing the rest of his fish around its plate. "I guess, I'm still a bit under the weather." He dabbed his mouth with his napkin and rose from his chair. "I'll see you on Saturday, Sam," he said.

"Sure. You want me to walk you back home? You look rough." He was indeed a disturbing shade of green around the gills.

"No, I'll be fine," he protested. "Fresh air and all that. Catch you later." He did not say a word to Caroline as he walked out of the Borough and she in turn said nothing to him.

The rest of the meal was actually quite pleasant. We chatted about this and that. I explained how I had ended up in my line of work and she enquired about previous cases. I told her about Satanic actors and Saint Edmund's. I left out vampires and werewolves. Some things did not need mentioning.

Eventually we had finished our meals. Caroline placed her empty glass down on the table and said, "Well I guess I'd better be off."

There was a moment when we just looked at each other. I do not know what she saw, but I saw the young girl in the polka dot bikini trying desperately to play the femme fatale and I smiled. "Why don't I walk you home?"

Caroline lived on Coulston Road, just along from

Williamson Park. As we walked side by side past the tall trees, the green dome of the Ashton Memorial glowered down at me, reminding me of the events of the previous weekend. I swallowed down the memories and the aching muscles. Dwelling on it right now would be something of a passion-killer.

Passion-killer? Had I really just used that phrase? Sure, Caroline and I were not at each other's throats right now, but that hardly constituted a romantic reunion, did it? I glanced over at her in the rising moonlight. She too seemed lost in some inner conversation or debate. I could tell by the way she kept sucking her lips back between her teeth as she walked, her head slightly down. Perhaps she was feeling old emotions, old passions, starting to resurface.

Perhaps.

Perhaps not.

"So how long have you lived down here then?" I finally ventured, interrupting the creaking sound of metal wheels within wheels.

"Oh, about five years. We used to rent a small place out in Galgate but as John got older we rapidly outgrew it and high school was on the horizon which would have meant him getting the bus every day after I had gone out to work."

"And that would have been a problem?"

She laughed gently as she shook her head. "I forget you don't know what it's like to be a parent. Teenage boys are far from organised, Sam. If I was to leave him at home to get the bus in the morning I would come home that night to find him in his room wearing nothing but socks and pants whilst playing some bizarre Xbox game and with no concept of the day having passed him by." By the streetlights I saw her lips turn up into a warm, motherly smile.

"You love him very much, don't you?"

"Yes I do."

We walked in silence along her street. It was totally quiet, there was no-one else about.

I stopped, took her by the hands and stared down into those, deep brown eyes. "I *will* find out what's going on with Credete. I promise."

"Really?"

"Really, really."

We both chuckled at the reference and I let her hands drop. She thrust them deep into her warm pockets. We both intently studied the footpath.

"Well," Caroline said eventually, "here we are."

"Here we are," I agreed.

"Outside my house," she pointed out with a nod of her head.

My heart started to hammer and my throat suddenly felt like the Kalahari. "Yes," I squeaked.

"And it's late." Those chestnut eyes had me locked completely in their sights. My bones had turned to putty, willing to be moulded to whatever shape the modeller wished. "I'd better get in. John will be fretting."

Okay, so no modelling tonight. "Sure," I nodded. "You'd better get inside. It's cold."

"Very."

"Very."

Our breath hung on the crisp autumn air under the

orange glow of the street lamps. Caroline took a step forward, stood up on tip toe and kissed me softly on the cheek. The scent of patchouli and jasmine was my entire universe for a brief second.

"Thank you, Sam," she whispered in my ear, then she turned and crossed the road.

I think my eyes were shut in wonder when she called out, "If you're not doing anything Thursday, why don't you come over for dinner? Six-ish? You can report back about this meeting you're going to."

I was nodding maniacally. "Sure. About six. I'll bring a bottle."

Caroline grinned and waved silently as she let herself in through her front door.

I turned and began to walk back down memory lane...

A few days after the incident between Spliff and Caroline, Caroline and I were walking down Penny Street. She had just stormed out of a stern lecture from her father about her upcoming birthday. She was not just spitting feathers; she was a peregrine falcon flossing its beak with a sparrow. I had decided that a trip into town would calm her down.

"How dare he? He always does this to me!" Passers-by were carefully avoiding the crazy blonde who was shouting at the top of her voice and gesticulating with arms that threatened to take out an eye should it stray within their flailing range. "I mean, it's my sixteenth, for God's sake!"

So much for an attempt to calm her down. Instead

all it had seemed to do was to give her space to vent a lava stream of sulphurous anger. She was ranting about her father's designs on her upcoming birthday. Caroline had apparently been planning it for months now. There was going to be a rented hall, a DJ, lots of cake, fun and frivolity.

Her father had disagreed.

"He wants to incorporate it into the Parish Summer Fair!" she wailed. "Can you believe it?"

When all I could manage was a sympathetic shrug, she craned her head back, stretching the neck muscles taut and emitted a guttural groan of frustration to the heavens: "Men!"

This was entirely new territory for me. What was I supposed to do? Was I supposed to tell her to calm down? That course of action looked like it would get my head bitten off in one vicious snap. Was I supposed to placate her? I had a feeling that reaction would end in me being scorned as weak and pathetic.

So I took what I considered to be the middle road. I kept my mouth shut and just let her continue to rant.

"Here's the deal," she grumbled. "I hate him. I truly hate him. He's controlling, possessive and cannot accept that I'm almost an adult. I can't wait to be rid of him. I can't wait. In a few years' time I'll be away from here. I'll be off somewhere like London. I'm going to be a journalist, you know? You'll see me on the telly presenting my own programmes. I'll be really famous and he won't be able to stop me.

"I'll be free of him.

"I want to hurt him so bad!"

This was perturbing to me. The idea that she wanted to hurt her father was incredibly alien to me. I thought about my father back home, lying in his sick bed awaiting the end and I shook my head. This girl was full of such anger. It was unhealthy.

Caroline was taking a breath between her verbal scourging of her father's soul when we passed Gorrills. Gorrills is one of those places in Lancaster where everyone has shopped at least once. This is because it magically seems to have displays in the window for the ideal gift that you need right at that moment in your life when you need to stop someone from thinking that either they are unloved, need to jump off a building or that Jeremy Kyle deserves a BAFTA. As the summer sun beamed down that day, a sparkling light caught my eye and I gently guided Caroline towards the window. She continued to ramble and rage as I peered through the glass and smiled. I knew what she needed right now.

"Just wait here," I managed between outbursts and I darted into the shop handed over some cash and came back out with a small gift bag and a big, toothy grin.

She paused mid-rant and half smiled, half frowned at the bag. "What's that?"

I handed it over. "Early birthday present."

Carefully, Caroline peered into the bag then extricated its contents which were wrapped in copious amounts of tissue paper. She looked up at me and her blonde eyebrows knotted together. "Sam?"

"Go on," I gestured. "Unwrap it."

Continuing with puzzlement and care, Caroline

peeled the layers back until she revealed the contents and gasped in fascination at the small glass elephant that sat on its haunches with its trunk blowing crystal water into the air. "Oh, Sam," she gasped, "it's beautiful!"

"Did you know that in Africa the elephant is regarded as a symbol of loyalty?"

She shook her head, unable to take her eyes of the small, glass model. Then slowly, she lifted up her face and I was aware of was her dark brown eyes drawing close to mine as she kissed me warmly and deeply before drawing away with an exuberant smile on her face.

"No matter what happens, Caroline." I said with earnest seriousness, "I will always be loyal to you. I will never leave you."

How wrong I was.

A small cough dragged me back to the present. "Good evening, Sam."

I was half-way down Wyresdale Road, heading towards East Road. I had not even been aware that my feet had been moving, let alone that I had acquired a companion.

"You."

The teenage boy nodded. "Me."

I groaned. "Please tell me that this is a coincidence."

"I don't believe in such things," Alec shrugged, "and you should be careful when you paint the past with sepia."

"And why's that?" I quickened my pace, hoping to

leave him behind.

He just quickened his step. "Because she's hiding something."

"Oh, really?" I turned the corner onto East Road. "You of all people should know that everyone hides things, Mister Now-You-See-Me-Now-You-Don't."

"True, but her's is a real killer."

I stopped, threw back my head in frustration, grunted and turned on him. "So what might this big secret be then?"

"Sorry. Can't tell."

"Oh, really. And why might that be?"

"You'd get upset."

"I'm upset already."

"Okay. You'd get *more* upset." His eyes flicked down to my fists which were rapidly clenching and unclenching. "*Violently* upset."

"Right now, I don't need to get upset to feel violent, so why don't you just tell me?"

Alec made to speak then for a split-second his eyes glazed over before he was back in the room once more. "Sorry, Sam. I can't. Just be careful."

And he was gone.

One second he was there in front of me, the next he had vanished.

It was a good job that the street was still deserted as my choice of language at that moment was not really for polite ears. I stomped off down East Road back into town.

CHAPTER 7

Lancaster Town Hall is quite an impressive building. It was completed in 1909 and dominates Dalton Square with its domed clock tower rising like an all-seeing eye above the city. As well as housing the city council offices it also has a large venue around the back where various concerts and large meetings are held. This is the Ashton Hall, named after James Williamson (Lord Ashton) who had financed the construction work.

The next evening saw me hovering nervously just down the road from the large doors that led into Lancaster's prestigious auditorium. With my hands thrust deep in the pockets of my trench coat and my collar turned up to keep the cool air away from my neck I looked like a decidedly dodgy character. I know that my preferred choice of clothing is not what would be called "everyday" for most people, but I'm just not a fan of denim jeans and brightly coloured t-shirts. Someone once told me I was a typical only child of older parents. I replied that he was the typical product of a whore and a sociologist.

I am just me and I will dress how I want and live how I want. End of story.

However, I cannot help but feel a bit odd when passersby give me that, "Are you for real?" look every now and then. Hey ho. Their loss.

"Boo!"

I think I screamed, just a little bit, as I was snapped out of my reverie.

"Sorry," Abalone apologised, trying hard not to laugh, "I couldn't resist it. You were miles away."

"Quite," I remarked, raising an eyebrow. "How's a man supposed to contemplate the inner mysteries of life on a street corner when people scare the living daylights out of him?" I peered down the road at the doors that led up into the Ashton Hall and sighed, "Are you sure about this?"

"You want to know all about Credete?"

"Yes."

"You want to be reassured that we're not bug-eyed, green-scaled, child-eating monsters?"

I grinned. "Fair enough. Lead the way."

So she did. We walked down towards the large doors then came to a sudden stop. "Oh will you look at that?" Abalone was referring to graffiti that had been scrawled across the doors, although *scrawled* was hardly an appropriate description. *Neatly penned* would have been more accurate. "Spud was here." She read out loud shaking her head. "Vandals."

I frowned. This was not the first time I had seen the slogan. Just the week before I had come across it whilst queuing outside the Sugar House. The words were identical along with the correct grammar, spelling and punctuation. "Curious indeed," I murmured as Abalone opened the door and led me inside. My mind filed the odd graffiti away for later as my heart started to palpitate at the thought of what I was about to endure.

As those of you who have read *The Case of The Vexed Vampire* already know, I 'm not keen on attending large, noisy venues.

First, there's the social side. I will inevitably feel like the proverbial fish flopping around out of water gasping at cruelly asphyxiating air. While others dive in and submerge themselves in the apparent glee of mingling, I will be sat or stood rather awkwardly at the edge of the venue like the poor sap who did not get the message that the party was no longer fancy dress and the latest Klingon fashion would no longer be appropriate for the funeral.

Then, there's the matter of my ears. Both the tension of the new experience and the volume of a large crowd play havoc with my tinnitus. My anxiety always rises, increasing my internal tintinnabulation and not only making it hard for me to hear what is going on around me, but actually causes me to feel disorientated and dizzy.

Inevitably I end up looking like some poor sod that has been dragged in off the street and is desperately trying to make out just what is going on around him whilst smiley, happy people are off partying and generally enjoying themselves. There have even been instances in the past where I have passed out or collapsed and have been driven home in embarrassment. Needless to say this makes me rather nervous about such functions.

So it was that when I arrived at the staircase leading up to Ashton Hall, the butterflies in my stomach were trying to create a tsunami off the coast of Africa.

"You okay?"

I looked the pretty blonde in her bright, blue eyes and the lepidoptera's wings slowed slightly.

"I will be, I guess. I'm just not too much of a social animal."

"You make it sound like a student rave," she giggled. "I can assure you there won't be a drop of hard stuff in sight."

Shame, I thought to myself as we headed up the stairs. Right then I could have murdered for a bottle of Jack. My heavy feet climbed the marble stairs which took us up to the hall and my mind ran over and over what would be the forthcoming scenario.

Guitars. There would be guitars - lots of them. Some of them would have rainbow-coloured straps. Or was that just found within the province of happy-clappy church groups? I shrugged. There would be a tambourine - probably one of those 1980's George Michael affairs, a semi-circular contraption that says, "'Hi, I'm hip with rhythm," as opposed to a Salvation Army version which is circular and says, "Donate for the poor, tight-wad, because you can't take all that cash with you when you go." Oh! There would be a flute. Just one of these and it's player would be young, female, slight and willowy. Probably with wavy red hair - and she'd be Irish. She would be the quiet type who didn't say much, but when she placed those sweet lips on the end of that long instrument she always brought tears of joy and pleasure.

Hey! Cut it out smutty! That's not what I meant and you know it. Jesus! Some people have filthy minds.

So, enough of your sordid imagination, back to the Ashton Hall. We reached the top of the stairs and paused outside the doors that led inside. Abalone pushed one and motioned, "After you."

"Uh uh," I replied. "Ladies first."

She smiled, leant in so that her mouth was next to my ear and whispered, "Whoever said that I was a lady?" then, grinning as she entered, she passed the door to me, her slender fingers brushing my hand. What greeted us when we went inside made me nearly jump out of my already tense and blushing skin. A man about six foot tall with spiked blonde hair was stood inside the door. Nothing wrong with that you might say - just a bit taller than average. However, it was his face that almost caused the loudest girlie scream you have ever heard shriek from my contorted lips. It was covered in black, stylised tattoos. My eyes instinctively did a check on his legs. They did not appear to be robotic, therefore he was not Darth Maul and was most likely not a Sith Lord.

Still scary though.

"Hi, Matt." Abalone bounced up to the tattooed doorman, her lightweight skirt flowing behind her as she gave him a warm hug. Yep. definitely not a Sith. A force choke would have been more appropriate.

"Hi, Abs. How's it going?" Matt had the kind of voice that matched his face: deep, husky and spoke of long nights drinking and smoking in biker bars. I could see under his long-sleeved t-shirt that muscles rippled and flexed as he hugged her back. A little green-eyed monster in the back of my head snorted in disgust. "Showoff," it spat.

Abalone stepped back and introduced me. "Matt, this is Sam. He's just visiting us tonight."

"Cool, Dude," Matt grinned as he crushed my hand to a pulp in his oversized paw. It was okay. I always kept a spare set of phalanges at the end of my other arm. "Good to see you. New blood is always welcome."

Blood? Blood? I knew what the guy meant, but all the same, he was not allaying my nerves.

"Thanks. I'm just here for the show, so to speak," I replied, carefully massaging the damaged muscles at the base of my swollen fingers. "Perhaps have a chat with a few guys afterwards?"

"No probs. We'll make sure you get to talk to the head honcho, too. He'll blow your mind."

Yeah. Far too many biker bars. Smiling politely I followed Abalone to the rows of chairs that had been arranged facing the stage area. I held back as she confidently made her way towards the front. When she reached her preferred row and noticed I was still hovering at the back, she cocked her head to one side and made a beckoning gesture with her index finger. I shrugged in response and tentatively inclined my head to the back row. She smiled and walked back up to me. "Nobody here bites, you know."

"I know that, it's just..."

"That's okay, sweetie." She placed a hand on my arm and everything felt sort of okay again. "Let's just slide in here, then."

So, in we slid, taking our seats and I started to observe our surroundings. The first overwhelming thing which struck me was the banner at the rear of the stage. It was a huge representation of the T-shaped motif with descending symmetrical swirls that I had seen on the wristbands and the pamphlet. Atop it danced the legend "Anything Is Possible" in bright, lilac lettering.

I frowned somewhat. Lilac was everywhere. Not only was the logo lilac, but there were lilac coloured drapes, lilac coloured streamers, and lilac coloured t-shirts on group members milling around whilst setting things up.

Someone had quite the penchant for this subtle shade of purple.

My stomach knotted somewhat. This was all rather too familiar. I recalled my dream from the previous week where I had been captive once more at John O'Gaunt Media and there had been a lilac banner with a golden version of this logo.

Coincidence? I surely hoped so. I looked over to Abalone who smiled back at me. "God, you look so nervous, Sam. Chill, okay?" She squeezed my hand and grinned as the music group started up some sort of cheery number.

And so it was that, for the next aeon-like hour, I sat and endured my own personal little bit of hell. Rousing choruses were interspersed with thoughtful readings and heart-rending statements of personal salvation and achievement that were all centred around the phrase for the day, children: "Anything is possible".

Want that promotion? Go out and earn it. Anything is possible!

Need extra cash to pay that credit card? Randomly choose winning numbers on the Lottery. Anything is possible!

Think your living room could do with a new rug? Just wait until Granny dies and get hers. Anything is possible!

I sat and politely cringed inwardly as speaker after speaker rose to the podium and revealed more and more ludicrous examples of chance occurrences that they fervently believed to be manifestations of their own will. I didn't know what was worse - that they believed it themselves or that their audience was lapping up this hokum.

Once again I was starting to wonder what on earth Caroline was worried about. These sorts of shenanigans have been around in many forms over the years, normally at a time when society has lost faith in itself and can see no way out of the hole that it has dug itself into. People desperately want answers and solutions to the mundane that constantly drags them down and, when they find none in the normal day-to-day, they start looking under metaphysical rocks for a gem of insubstantial knowledge.

This was daft, yes, but dangerous? I didn't think so.

I was more concerned that Abalone was totally suckered into it. She was a bright, sparky individual who seemed, on the surface, to have no need for an emotional crutch. Appearances, however, can be so very, very deceptive. What was it that was dragging her down into the mire of society? I recalled her tale of the late, great Russell, Geography teacher supreme. Grief and despair can make people perfect targets for emotional manipulation. Had someone done a Jedi mind trick on her and told her that these *were* the droids she was looking for?

I was pondering this when Matt the Tat bounded up onto the stage. "Okay, people," he announced from behind a huge, male Dathomiri grin, "here it is! The moment you've all been waiting for." He paused and nodded like a deranged chipmunk as members of the audience gave way to involuntary whooping normally found at Wild West rodeos and semi-finals of the X Factor. "The man of the moment," Matt finally continued. "The reason we're all here..."

I stifled a yawn.

"The man who has shown us how *anything* is possible..."

I peeked surreptitiously at my watch.

"Malcolm Wallace!"

All those around me jumped to their feet and started to scream and shout out whoops of joy. I stumbled up, knocking my chair back as I tried to see the stage. Surely I had misheard? It couldn't be, could it? But as the crowd quietened and started to drift back down into their seats bringing with their attention an awed hush, there he was, standing calmly and quietly at the podium.

My old university friend: Malcolm Wallace.

My list of stupefaction had just grown even longer.

I was stunned, flabbergasted, shell-shocked and all the other corny descriptions one might want to use to illustrate the state of mind one is in when the least likely person is stood in front of you.

I had last seen Malcolm back in the days of my university studies. As I said in *The Case of the Fastidious Phantom,* he was responsible for landing a ghost called Gerald in my care before swanning off into the night with his *benefactor*. This was an action that I had far from forgiven him for.

As I sat pondering how I had not noticed his return to Lancaster, I cast my wary eyes over him. He had certainly aged, but in a way which suggested maturity rather than decrepitness. His hair was now pure white and long enough to be smoothed back over his head, framing his curious orange eyes that held the audience enrapt. He wore a plain canvas-coloured suit and sported a simple tie in the eponymous lilac around the neck of a crisp, white shirt. He had leant against the podium a highly polished walking cane and under the lights of the hall I could see a dress ring glinting on the little finger of his right hand.

For all intents and purposes, Malcolm looked like he was doing alright for himself - more than he would have done had he followed his original plan and entered the clergy.

As the crowd settled, he waited, patiently, not saying a word. His orange eyes drifted over the excited throng in front of him as if seeing all and knowing their each and every hidden thought. Gradually, the hushed chattering and breaths of awe subsided into a silence which hung in the dusty air of the Ashton Hall and framed the still personality of one man. Time passed, it was just seconds, minutes at the most, but it felt like, days, weeks, years as Malcolm just stood passively at the front of the hall, his hands lightly clasped together in front of him. His face betrayed no emotion and he half-closed those curiously coloured eyes as if he was straining to hear the slightest sound. Then, when he was sure that he had the complete and undivided attention of absolutely everyone in the room (myself included), he spoke one word:

"Friends."

He opened his eyes and a smile spread across his face. He held his arms out to his sides, now holding the cane in his right hand. "Welcome," he greeted them in his quiet, well-spoken manner. "Welcome to our time together. Time where we know that anything is possible.

"It is good to see you all here, today." Slowly, he walked up and down the front of the stage, his eyes scanning every face in the congregation whilst his cane tapped a steady, pulse-like rhythm. "It's good to see faces new and old." My heart skipped at that; had he seen me? "We are all here for one purpose and one purpose alone: we want to know where we are going. We have lost our way, our map has been drenched in the downpour of life and all those little B-roads have blurred and smudged into one big sticky mess. Many people are shouting at us, telling us that their way is right, that we should listen to no-one but them." He shook his head sadly. "Poor, misguided fools. They are so full of their own petty insecurities that they feel they have to impress us with vain attempts at self-idolization. They harangue us from that goggle-box in the corner of the living room while we eat our meals. They bombard us from the radios when we drive to our places of servitude. They never let us be. Over and over they tell us that their way is best, that they have all the answers. But they are wrong, oh so very wrong. For there is but one truth that shines down on us this and every day, if only we acknowledge it and embrace its purity.

"And what might that be, my friends?"

"*Anything is possible!*" came the roar in unison.

Malcolm's face beamed with joy. "Indeed it is. Indeed it is, and you, yourselves, are witness to that very fact. You see it in your lives. You do not need the pop stars and media moguls to tell you what to do. You do not need politicians domineering your lives. You do not need your brains pulping by the billboards and flashy images of advertising nazis. No! You *know* the truth in your heart. You see it there when you sleep. It visits you in your *dreams*. It whispers in the dark at the base of your subconscious.

"Anything is possible.

"Anything is possible.

"Anything is possible.

"Whatever you want, you can achieve. Whatever you desire, you can do. It is there inside you, buried under a mountain of detritus that has been heaped upon you by modern society. They have ground us down, friends. They have told us that, without them, we are worthless – lower than the smallest, little earthworm.

"Well, I tell you this, you are so much better than that. You can stand proud like this symbol behind me." He pointed with his cane to the large T on the banner. "You can grab the diverse factors of reality in your hands and bend them to your will, for *nothing* is stronger than the desire you have within you to create a better life for yourself. Nothing can stand in your way, however impossible it may appear."

Malcolm paused, his chest heaving as he took in much needed air after his monologue that had grown steadily in passion and intensity, then he turned to Matt the Tat who stood waiting at the edge of the stage. "Matt, could you bring the Watts family onstage, please?"

It was at this point that I realised I had stopped breathing. This was not the Malcolm Wallace that I remembered. The twenty-something from my distant past had been shy and painfully quiet, withdrawn from his peers and concerned only with his studies both academic and personal. What had caused this transformation? As a young family were ushered onto the stage I was aware of footsteps entering the hall and someone settling themselves down into a spare chair behind me. I glanced quickly at Abalone. She had not heard the late-comer. Instead, her eyes were transfixed at what was playing out on the stage in front of us. The young family consisted of a man and a woman in their late twenties with a girl of about ten who was sat slouched in a wheelchair.

"This is Melanie," Malcolm informed us as he crouched down next to the little girl. "She is visiting us here today with her parents, Sue and Keith." He looked up to the couple, his body language a living sculpture of concern and heartfelt sympathy. "Tell us, Sue, what is wrong with Melanie."

"We... we don't know," the young woman stammered. "Neither do the doctors. Mel was fine. She was a happy, smiley little girl, then... then three months ago..." A heartfelt sob stole the rest of the explanation.

Malcolm lowered his eyes and shook his head.

"The doctors don't know," he whispered. "The doctors don't know." Rising to his feet, his orange eyes burned bright with anger. "In this modern, scientific world where great minds are happy to devise bigger and better weapons to bring civilisation to the brink of annihilation, not one of those minds can tell these poor people what is wrong with their little girl. Not one of those supposedly respectable doctors thinks it is *possible* to heal this child."

There were murmurs of discontent from the audience.

From behind me I could hear a humming so soft and quiet that it almost fell under the radar of human hearing. The hairs on my neck prickled and I felt blood rush to my face.

"*Anything* is possible!" shouted a man over to my right.

"*Anything* is possible!" shouted a woman near the front.

"*Anything* is possible!" shouted Abalone next to me.

"*Anything* is possible!"

"*Anything* is possible!"

"*Anything* is possible!"

Around and around it circled the room, like an eagle hovering ready to strike, growing louder in volume, greater in passion. Faster and faster the shouts came as individuals rose to their feet and shook their fists in sheer, unadulterated anger.

"*Anything* is possible!"

"*Anything* is possible!"

"*Anything* is possible!"

This was the mantra. This was the *truth*. As the humming behind me took words in a lilting tongue that I did not understand, but in a rhythm that cried out to every cell in my body, I too was calling out, "*Anything* is possible! *Anything* is possible! *Anything* is possible!"

The wings of the swooping eagle were now a violent storm, a whirlwind and there, at its calm epicentre stood the white-haired Moses of this new age, ready to lead his people through the stormy seas of the violent, modern world.

Raising his cane in one hand, he placed the other firmly on the shoulder of the young girl and, with one word brought a shuddering silence to the clamour:

"Rise."

And she did.

As the little girl who had been a shell of her former self and bound to a wheelchair for three months rose to her feet and ran laughing to her parents, the singing behind me abruptly ceased and the congregation erupted into whoops of applause. I turned in time to catch sight of a slim, dark-clad figure slinking out of the doors through which I had entered. I had to follow her. I needed to follow her. My entire body craved to hear that song once more and my libido was busily styling its hair with the finest Brylcreem to achieve that possibility, but to leave now would be to turn my back on someone else that I desperately needed to talk to.

Malcolm Wallace.

As the congregation dispersed a short while later, I rose and made my way with Abalone to the front. My heart was pounding and my palms were sweaty. I rubbed the offending skin on my jacket and prayed to God that I did not look a mess. Wallace was stood in the middle of a small group of followers. He was paying complete attention to their every word and consoling them where needed, encouraging as necessary and generally sending them off in a much better frame of mind than they had been just a few minutes previously.

The Watts family were also stood nearby, chatting to members of Credete. Little Melanie looked over at me and smiled. I wandered over to the child as it was plain that Wallace was going to be tied up for a bit.

"Hello," she said to me.

"Hello," I replied, not quite sure what to say to a child who has just been faith-healed. "How are you feeling now?" I asked as I crouched down to a more child-friendly height.

"Much better, thank you. Look!" She giggled as she wiggled her fingers in front of her. "I couldn't do that this morning. Actually, I couldn't do a lot of things this morning."

"You must have been really scared."

She nodded vigorously. "It was like being stuck inside a lump of clay and it stopping everything from moving."

I frowned. "What happened? What caused your body to," I looked for the right words, "stop working?"

The little blondie shrugged. "Don't know. But it was after the dream."

"The dream?" This piqued my curiosity. "What dream?"

"I was playing in the road outside our house," Melanie explained. "It was dark, but warm. Then suddenly it got very, very cold and someone was stood behind me. I wanted to turn to see who it was, but my body couldn't move. I tried to call out to Mummy and Daddy, but my mouth wouldn't work. All I could do was cry. And that's what they found me doing in bed the next morning: crying. It was all I could do apart from eat sleep and, you know..." She leaned up to me conspiratorially and whispered in my ear, "*poo.*" She giggled again. "But now I'm better thanks to nice Mister Wallace. Cool, isn't it?"

"It certainly is," came a quiet, male voice from my side. I turned and there he was, smiling gently at me. "It's good to see you, Samuel."

I straightened up, my knees creaking ominously. "Good to see you too, Malcolm. How's it going?"

"Surviving," he smiled. "Keeping myself busy."

"So I see. You're looking well."

"Thank you." His orange eyes looked me up and down and he frowned slightly. "I believe you have something that bothers you. Something with your ears."

I kept my surprise in check. There was no need to be a psychic to know I suffered from tinnitus. People with long term conditions have certain mannerisms and tells that give the illness away. Obviously I had one that I was unaware of, plus he had been around me at university. True, he had not exactly been a close friend so I had never spoken to him about my condition, but he had always been the quiet, observant type. "I have Meniere's disease."

Wallace raised a white eyebrow. "And you're here to be healed of it?"

"No, no," I laughed nervously. "I'm just here with a friend."

He nodded slowly, knowingly. "That would be Miss Morris, then." It was most definitely a statement, not a question. "I believe you met her at her school last week. There was a bit of paranormal trouble, it seems."

Okay, now I felt threatened. Someone had been talking. I shot Abalone a quick glance. She was off to the side, chatting and laughing with a group of other very cheerful members of Wallace's congregation. "It was something and nothing," I managed through a forced smile.

"Really?" Wallace's voice oozed concern like a politician oozes sincerity. "I would have thought a poltergeist would be most troublesome. I believe you vanquished your foe in the end."

"Something like that."

"So you come face to face with a poltergeist yet you refuse to believe in the power of one's own mind," he mused, his thumb slowly caressing the two snakes that decorated the head of his ornate cane. "Most intriguing."

"If you say so." I was nowhere near able to string together any long, civil sentences. My hackles were up and I had buckled down into defence mode.

"So, again, I ask myself as to why you are here..."

Wallace's musing was cut off as a man I had not seen before interrupted him. "Mister Wallace..."

My old acquaintance turned quickly to the newcomer. The man was mid-fifties, grey-haired and seemed to favour one leg as he walked. "Ah, Mister Flint," Wallace beamed, all warmth and welcome, "so good of you to join us. Is it that time already?"

The man nodded nervously.

"Samuel, this is Mister Flint, caretaker of this fine hall. Mister Flint, this is Mister Spallucci, a very dear old friend of mine who has decided to make my acquaintance once more out of the blue."

Mister Flint shot me a confused smile. I politely offered him my hand. His touch was wet and clammy. This man exuded a primal fear that was almost palpable. After the shortest of handshakes he stuffed his hand back into his coat pocket and said, "Mister Wallace, I'm afraid I have to be asking you to leave right now. You know you're only booked for the three hours."

I started and pulled my shirt sleeve back in a fast manner. Three hours? Sure enough it was eleven o'clock. How the dickens had that much time passed without me noticing? Okay, there had been the waffle and prattling about how life-changing Credete was but that had not lasted that long, surely? Then Wallace had spoken. That had been what, five minutes? Fifteen at the most? Then there had been the healing followed by a few more choruses and it had been time to finish.

Where had the time gone?

My mind's eye recalled the slender figure leaving the hall and my libido shuddered.

"We will pack up shortly and be out of your hair soon, Mister Flint." Wallace smiled warmly as he said this, but there was a chill to those weird eyes of his.

"I'm sorry, Mister Wallace," the caretaker persisted, "but this isn't the first time that you have overrun. There will be a surcharge."

Wallace sighed as he turned back to me. "I do apologise, Samuel. I have to sort this little matter out. Why don't we catch up later? I have your phone number."

I cringed. Damn it! How much did this guy already know about me? "Sure. Ring me when you have time. I'd like to catch up."

He nodded, placed an avuncular arm around the nervous caretaker and pulled him away, talking closely and quietly into his ear. I let out a deep breath and made for Abalone.

"So, what did you think?"

We were walking up from the Town Hall towards the Moorlands area of Lancaster. Abalone lived there in a small two up two down on Dunkeld Street with her housemate. "It was *enlightening*."

Her light voice sparkled with laughter in the clear evening. "Oh, I'm so glad you think so. Isn't Malcolm amazing?"

Well that was one word for my former university acquaintance. *Creepy* was another. As we walked up Quarry Road I cast my mind back to a hall full of people, myself included, stood on their feet crying out the three word mantra.

Anything is possible.

Had he really cured that little girl? The cynical side of my mind said, "Surely not," but there was that little niggle scratching away at the back with a marker pen and sheets of A4 paper. It was drawing pictures of werewolves, fairies and vampires. If they were real then what was a casual bit of faith-healing?

What about little Melanie's dream? It obviously had something to do with her illness, but what? I sighed, deep in thought.

"Penny for them?"

"Sorry, just getting my head around everything." Then something struck me.

"Abalone, do teenagers go to the meetings? I think I'm right in saying that was fairly much an adult affair, so to speak."

She stopped walking, placed her hands on her hips and locked those blue eyes on me. "Is this to do with that client of yours?"

I shrugged. "She's paying the bills. I have to be thorough."

"Fair 'nuff. Sure there's a teenage group. The kids from school go to that one. I'm not sure what day it meets on." We resumed walking up the hill. "Malcolm could tell you." She paused and shot me a sideways grin. "I think he was really pleased to see you."

"It was very weird seeing him there after all these years," I said truthfully. "The sight of him up on that stage commanding such respect and love almost bowled me over. He was a total mouse at uni. Hardly ever spoke to anyone."

"People change."

I nodded. "I guess they do."

We skirted round the corner and headed up Aberdeen Road. Terraced houses flanked our right as we climbed the steep hill. I could see Dunkeld Street just up ahead.

"So then..."

My heart skipped a beat as my ego started to smooth down its hair and check its breath. "So... what?"

Abalone grinned again as we reached the end of her street. "I really enjoyed tonight. I'd like to do it again."

"Me too. Although without all the crowds. Somewhere a bit more private, perhaps?"

"Sounds good to me, Mister Investigator." She reached up and ran a finger along my cheek. My ego started to somersault and juggle flaming clubs at the same time. "Why don't you give me a ring this weekend and we'll arrange something?"

"Will do." I paused then called out after her as she

turned to go, "Just confirm one thing for me."

"What?"

""You're not the sister of a deranged werewolf."

The blonde beamed from ear to ear. "Goodnight, Mister Investigator." She blew me a cheeky, little kiss then turned and headed off to her house. I stood grinning on the street corner for a few minutes before heading back down into town. It had been a rather nice end to a rather peculiar evening.

This could actually work, I thought to myself. *This could actually work.*

CHAPTER 8

The next day found me feeling decidedly chipper. I had a beautiful, intelligent woman interested in me who, as a bonus, was not a homicidal maniac. Nice one! Perhaps life was turning a corner and fortune was starting to favour the not-so-brave? I do believe I actually started to whistle to myself as I poured soya milk on some sugary cereal. If my life had been a Disney movie, cartoon blue birds would have been sat on the windowsill waiting expectantly for me to burst into song.

Munching away through my tasty bowl of potential tooth decay I flicked on the goggle box and settled down into the comfort blanket that is breakfast television. Friendly faces wearing cuddly cardigans smiled up at me telling me what a wonderful world I lived in and how bright and sunny the future was.

For once I was inclined to agree.

I sat and devoured this morning panacea, lapping up every jolly morsel. They were just getting to an interview with the famed Professor Robert Richmond, who was going to fill them in on his latest archaeological dig in the Indus Valley, when my mobile piped up. I glanced at the display. "Unknown," it informed me. I frowned but clicked the *answer* icon.

"Hello?"

"Samuel. How are you this morning?"

I flicked the television onto mute and set my bowl on the coffee table. "Hello, Malcolm. I'm well. You?"

"Very good indeed," came the cultured voice. "It was marvellous to see you last night. I thought you might like to meet up today, if you're not busy."

"Sure. What time?"

"About ten?"

I glanced at one of my clocks. That was okay. It gave me just over an hour. Plenty of time. "Okay. Ten it is. Market Square?"

"Very good. I'll see you then."

We said our goodbyes and hung up. I turned the television off just as the renowned Professor Richmond was pointing out details of an image of a horned man sitting cross-legged surrounded by animals.

I picked up my bowl and finished off the cereal before taking the empty dish back through to the kitchen. As I washed and dried it I wondered to myself how had Malcolm achieved all this? How had he gone from being the bookish outsider at university to the magnetic focus of last night's Credete meeting? It seemed as if he had undergone a personality transplant. Perhaps our meeting would shed some light on this incredible transformation.

Malcolm was sat waiting outside the Starbucks in

Market Square. He appeared a picture of refined calm in the hustle and bustle of Thursday morning. He wore a light coloured suit over a lilac coloured shirt and dark purple tie. His long white hair was loose but neatly groomed. His cane was clasped between his hands as he surveyed those who hurried past him.

"What do you make of them, Samuel?" he asked without even turning his head. Until that moment I had not realised that he was in fact aware of my presence.

I approached my old acquaintance and sat next to him on the bench. "What do you mean?"

"Look at them all, scurrying from this place to that, their heads down, eager to avoid even the slightest bit of eye contact with anyone be it stranger or friend. Are they even aware that we watch them?"

"I guess not," I shrugged, unsure where this was leading.

"They are selfish, Samuel, every one of them and that will ultimately be society's downfall. It has turned inward, away from its friends and neighbours." The street philosophy continued as I frowned at the somewhat harsh tone: "Tell me, does the ant see the elephant just before the poor insect is crushed under the pachyderm's mighty foot?"

Okay. This was weird, but I went with it. "I'm sure it does. It must feel the coolness of the shadow." I was rather pleased with that response. Very deep.

"Or does it just think that the path of the wind has changed?" Malcolm turned to face me watching for my response with his curious orange eyes. "Samuel, people never truly realise when disaster is imminent. They may

125

have a gut feeling that something is intrinsically *wrong* but they ignore it as they scurry hither and thither with their dull, mundane and," he turned back to watch the fair folk of Lancaster, "ultimately pointless lives."

We sat there in silence for a minute or two, he pondering the deepest philosophies of the universe and me wondering what the hell was going on. Eventually he broke the silence. "So where would you like to go for refreshment?"

Like I have already mentioned, I have been told a number of times that caffeine is really bad for my tinnitus. Apparently it increases the heart rate which in turn makes the ears pound more or something such. The thing is, by the time doctors have extolled the virtues of decaf coffee or tea that tastes like it was picked from under a cow pat I have normally lit up a Lucky and swigged down a glass of Jack.

Quite frankly I consider coffee to be the least of my vices. It seems fairly pointless trying to pick away at a mountain with a drawing pin so, until I've given up the fags and the booze, the three shot, black Americano will be my drink of choice.

It was not, however, the desired beverage of one Malcolm Wallace.

"You actually enjoy this?" He was stirring around in his drink as if expecting a kraken to rise from the brown depths and grab him by the throat.

"It keeps me awake." I downed a warm sip feeling the wonder drug start to kick in. "I have a habit of not sleeping well. Bad dreams."

Malcolm raised a white eyebrow. "Really? Anything in particular?" He lay his wooden stirrer down and sat back expectantly, the coffee forgotten.

"Work stuff." That was all he was going to get. This little fishy was not hungry.

His orange eyes bored into me over steepled fingers, his golden ring glinting in the sunlight that streamed through the window. "Some feel that poor sleep is down to an unfulfilled lifestyle, Samuel. Would that be true with you?"

An sarcastic laugh escaped my lips. "No, it's more likely that my tinnitus is just playing overtime while I'm sleeping giving my brain too much night-time entertainment."

"That doesn't sound like fun."

"You can say that again," I shrugged. "it seems to have gotten worse as I've gotten older and it's been particularly bad this last week."

"That must be awful, Samuel." Concern practically dripped off his tongue. "I imagine you'd do *anything* to be rid of it."

At that moment a goose jumped up and down on my grave whilst playing a sousaphone. I moved uncomfortably in my chair. "Almost anything. I don't think I'd sell my soul just for a good night's sleep."

I laughed nervously.

Malcolm did not.

"Besides," I coughed, rapidly trying to change track, "It's most likely just work. My first week was somewhat *eventful*."

"Indeed," he nodded. "Apparently you were

abducted, so the news report said."

"And apparently everyone has seen it apart from me," I grumbled.

Malcolm smiled serenely. "It was most *informative*. To be honest, I was wondering when our paths would cross."

"Really?"

"Indeed. Tell me, Samuel, why did you *really* come to Credete with young Miss Morris? I'm guessing it was neither a first date nor genuine curiosity. A case perhaps?"

I shifted even more uneasily in my seat. Oh crap! He was *good*.

"I see," Malcolm observed, obviously amused at my embarrassment. "May I ask what my devilish *cult* has been accused of?"

I let out a deep sigh and drank up some more coffee before answering, "I have a client who is concerned about their son. Apparently he has joined your merry band and she is worried."

Malcolm nodded sagely and rubbed his ring between his finger and thumb. "That is understandable. Mothers do have a tendency to fuss somewhat. It would have been nice of her to contact me first, though. I might have been able to allay her fears."

"He wasn't there last night."

"No, we have a teen group that meets every other Monday. The next one is next week. The numbers vary, such are the vagaries of adolescence."

I smiled. "Are they the same format as last night?"

"Good grief, no!" he exclaimed. "I keep the

younger group far more light-hearted and lower key, so to speak. It tends to be games and activities. I'm sure you know the sort of thing."

I did. The staple of youth groups all over the world: table tennis, board games and intense discussion on the latest, greatest computer game or television programme. Hardly life-threatening or soul-destroying. "Tell me about the wrist bands."

A warm smile filled Malcolm's face. "Pure marketing," he admitted. "The teenagers love them. They get something that creeps through their uniform regulations and I get a walking advert for Credete. It's a win win situation."

I nodded. That did make sense.

"May I ask who the concerned mother is?"

I pondered this for a moment, drumming my fingernails against my teeth. Should I tell him? I had to say that so far I could see no real harm in Credete. Sure they were a bit driven and charismatic but in the last week I had certainly come across far worse. However, what if I was wrong? What if there was more; dark secrets lurking in the shadows? Also, what about client confidentiality?

I shook my head. "Not just yet. It wouldn't be proper."

Malcolm nodded understandingly. "I see. Don't worry yourself about it. Tell her to contact me and we can have a chat. I imagine it's all a misunderstanding. Besides I'm sure she would listen to you."

My mind drifted back to a time that I had been the one listening to Caroline...

It had been a warm summer's night and we had snuck away from the madding crowd of the summer fair that had doubled up as her sixteenth birthday party. We exited quietly through the kitchen of the vicarage and found a secluded spot under the full moon. Her hand gently clasped mine, leading me through her garden. I still remember the sweet scent of some sort of lavender and rosemary that lined the winding path. As we ran our fingers through the foliage the aromatic scent enveloped us in its embrace.

Eventually we arrived at the foot of the garden; the hubbub of the party was just a dull, distant hum - a world away. Caroline sat herself down on the curved stone seat that nestled underneath a large tree and she patted the surface next to her. I obliged and sidled up. Her eyes shone beautiful and dark in the moonlight, contrasting against her fine, blonde hair which my fingers were itching to stroke the same way that a small child cannot help but stroke a pet cat or a crazy person their stuffed raccoon. She must have been reading my mind as she took my hand in hers and rested the side of her head into my palm, closing those dark eyes.

"This is nice," she whispered. "I could stay like this forever."

"You might get a crick in your neck," I grinned.

She sat up and giggled, holding my hand in hers. It felt so small. "Oh, I have something for you." She stood up and felt around in the pockets of her tight jeans before fishing out a small, neatly wrapped package. "Here."

I took the proffered gift and looked down at it, bemused. "What's this for?"

"I saw it and thought of you," she shrugged. "Go on, open it."

I smiled and set to unwrapping the small package. A brass Zippo lighter tumbled into my lap. It was adorned with a pyramid atop which was an all-seeing eye. "Cool."

"I know I hate those wretched things you smoke, but if you will insist on torching your lungs, you might as well do it in style. Turn it over. There's an engraving."

I thumbed the lighter over and saw there in curling script: "Nil illegitimi carborundm." I chuckled. "You know that's not a real Latin phrase, don't you?"

"But it sounds good." She nodded up towards the vicarage. "I'm sure if the Romans were in your position, then they'd say that all the time."

I grinned. Her father had been constantly on my case all week. At times I feared that he knew about us but then logic stated that I had not yet been turned out of the vicarage on my backside. "Thank you," I continued to beam. Standing next to her I took her in my arms. "Thank you so much." Then we were kissing: me stooping down, her tiptoeing up, my hands stroking her flaxen hair, her arms wrapped around my back.

When we pulled away, there were tears trickling down her cheeks. "What's wrong?" I asked.

She shook her head vigorously, the back of her hand wiping the tears away. "Nothing, nothing at all."

"Then, what is it?"

For a moment she just stood, staring up at me,

those dark eyes surveying all that I was, all that I had been, all that I might be, then she said the three words I had been longing to hear all week:

"I love you."

My heart was probably skipping a few beats, but my brain didn't notice as it was too busy reeling the audio track back to make sure that it had heard right. When it was sure that it had, I asked:

"Really?"

Caroline smiled. "Really."

"Really, really?"

Her arms linked up behind my neck. "Just kiss me again." So I did.

It was paradise.

The next day was hell.

"Samuel?"

The gentle, enquiring voice snapped me back out of my reverie to the present day. "What? Sorry. I drifted off a bit there."

"So I noticed." Malcolm's cup was empty. I had not even seen him touch it. I must have been well away.

"Like I said, last week was rather tiring."

"I think it's more than that." He leant forward and gripped me with his strangely-coloured eyes. "Tell me, Samuel. Just how much do you trust this woman?"

I remained silent as, in my heart of hearts, I could not find an answer that I truly liked the sound of.

"Look, enough of such things." Malcolm's voice was now much lighter and convivial. "I think we have so much to catch up on, don't you? I'm going to the Grand tonight. I have a box reserved. Why don't you come and join me?"

I thought about my dinner date with Caroline and John. "I'm afraid I can't. I already have plans."

Malcolm regarded me silently.

"Otherwise I would love to come."

"Very well," he said. "If you change your mind or if you feel you need to, I'll be in box number one from seven thirty. I would most enjoy your company." He lifted his arm and checked his watch. "Now, however, I must be off. Things to do and people to see, as it were. It has been most illuminating catching up like this."

We stood and shook hands before he headed off out into Market Square. I resumed my seat and finished off my almost cold coffee. *Most illuminating*? How could that be? I did not think that I had told him all that much about me. I got up and headed out of the café feeling somewhat disturbed.

CHAPTER 9

I arrived at Caroline's half an hour early, bottle in hand. I stood in front of her yellow front door and took a deep breath. I could do this. Yes, I could. It was just a meal with a client and her son. That was all. There was nothing special about it whatsoever.

Liar, liar. Pants on fire!

Who was I kidding? This was such a big deal for me. Caroline was my greatest mistake of all time. We had been entwined in something beautiful and it had gone suddenly, rapidly sour. One minute she had loved me deeply and completely, the next...

There had been nothing.

What had I done wrong?

Had it been something I'd said? Something I'd done?

To this day I was still in the dark.

And here she was, suddenly back in my life, begging for my help. I could not refuse. I had to make amends for whatever it was that I had done even if that was just telling her that John was not in mortal peril.

Then, of course, there was Abalone. Damn you, bad timing! Something was developing there, I was sure of that and I did not want to prune that particular rose before it had flowered. It was a far too beautiful and delicate thing.

So, what to do?

Well, for now there was only one thing that I *could* do. I knocked on the door. My knuckles rapped three hard pulses and I took a polite step back as my heart pounded in my chest and bells rang wildly in my ears. There was that age long silence that always follows as you wonder to yourself whether the person in the house has heard you knock or not. You stand in front of the door, rocking back and forth on the balls of your feet trying to decide whether you should knock again or not. You glance at the windows and try to see if you can discern whether there are people inside without appearing to be a peeping Tom. Next you have to decide whether you knock again or not. Has it been long enough? If you knock now, will it have been too soon and will they answer the door whilst making some sarcastic comment about you being impatient. So you raise your hand and quickly lower it again a number of times, unsure what to do. You look like a worried marionette with a cruel puppeteer lifting and dropping your hand over and over. Then, just as you are about to knock one more time, you hear footsteps approaching and you smile with relief as the door opens.

"Hi, Sam," John beamed as he swung the door open. "Great to see you."

"You too," I smiled.

"Wanna come in?"

"Sure. Sorry I'm early."

"That's okay." He led me down the short hallway through to the second door on the right which took us into the dining room. The smell of cooking reached my nose and my stomach rumbled noisily. "You sound hungry," he laughed.

I grinned, "Apparently I am."

There was a doorway on the other side of the room which led through to the kitchen. Caroline appeared, framed by the light of the kitchen which appeared to be a hive of industrious activity. I could see pans boiling, something baking in the oven and copious amounts of flour. In fact it looked like a snowstorm had happened through there, she even had streaks of white through her chestnut brown hair.

"Everything okay through there?"

"Mum doesn't entertain much, but when she does she gets creative," John informed me, much to the embarrassment of his mother whose cheeks flushed bright red.

"Does she indeed?" I raised a knowing eyebrow towards Caroline as the double-entendre flew straight over her son's head as soon as it had bounced out of his mouth.

Ever the professional, Caroline cleared her throat and greeted me. "Hello, Sam. Why don't I put that," she motioned towards the wine, "in the fridge?"

I nodded and followed her through into the den of creativity. As I walked behind her, the aroma of patchouli and jasmine drifted up to meet me. "Something smells nice."

"Thank you," my host replied, slipping the bottle into the door of the fridge. "It's a tart."

"Pardon?"

"In the oven. Hence all the flour," Caroline explained. "John's right. I don't entertain much and I tend to get in such a flap." She bit her lower lip as she surveyed the white drifts that lay piled up around the room. "Oh God, it looks like I had a fight with Mister Kipling."

We both laughed at that. It was nice.

"Do you need any help?"

"No." She shook her head and a cloud of flour billowed out from her hair. "Believe it or not, everything is under control. Why don't you go chill out in the other room while I finish off in here?"

"You sure?"

Her head bobbed up and down emphatically as she shooed me out of the kitchen. "Go. Talk boy talk or something."

I conceded defeat and gave up the role of Good Samaritan as I ambled back into the dining room where John was busying himself setting the table and not watching what was going on in the kitchen, honest guv. I shed my hat and jacket before picking up some cutlery and finally managing to make myself feel useful as I placed knives and forks around already positioned place mats. "So, how are keeping?" I asked.

"Same old, same old," the teenager shrugged non-committally. "You?"

I chuckled quietly to myself. "Oh, rather busy."

"Ghosties and goblins?"

"Ghosties and goblins."

"Cool."

My chuckling intensified.

John frowned. "What is it?"

"Nothing," I smiled as I lay the last knife on the table. "I just love how you're so enthusiastic over things. It reminds me of when I was your age."

He appeared to ponder this for a moment then asked, "Don't you get excited about things these days?"

I stood and regarded the young lad as I pondered this. When was the last time I had truly gotten excited over something? I wracked my memory for some glimmer of an image but nothing was forthcoming. If there was a book, a film or even a curiously shaped potato that had made me jump up and down fanatically then it had been buried beneath images of vampires, fairies, satanists, dragons and werewolves. "I guess work's just getting in the way a bit at the moment." I looked up and gave an involuntary shudder as I caught sight of the picture that hung on the wall above the fireplace.

"You okay?"

I forced a smile. "Sure. I'm good. That's quite a picture."

John turned and followed my gaze. "Oh, yeah. It's great."

Great was not the word that I would have used. There, dominating the dining room, was a large print of the Ashton Memorial. It was a Chas Jacobs – a local artist. I could tell by the bold, striking colours and lack of shading that were his trademark. A very popular artist, his work could be found framed in every art gallery in town and on greetings cards in every newsagents. His style was described as "simplistic" and "childlike". I had no simple, childlike feelings as I stood staring at the dark green trees that lined the stone staircase up which I had fled not long ago to escape the slavering Hawkins. There framed against the night sky was the very stonework from which the murderous beast had leapt in an attempt to kill me. All it needed was a full moon hanging watchfully behind the green dome and the nightmarish image would have been complete.

"I used to play there as a kid."

"Sorry?" His words snapped me out of my nightmare. "What did you say?"

"I said that I used to play there as a kid. When I was young, mum didn't have much cash so she'd take me up there every weekend. It was a very special place where I ran up and down those steps fighting imaginary battles with monsters and stuff, you know?"

My mind saw Hawkins stalking up the stone steps after a younger version of John. My stomach lurched. If my face was showing any of my horror, he did not seem to notice. The boy was transfixed, staring up at his infancy. This was incredible. How could a place that had been hellish for me be so paradisiacal for someone else.

"We used to pretend it was a palace. We would hold court for imaginary nobility." He smiled softly as he continued; "People would look at us gone out as we sat on the steps addressing our lords and ladies. It was all very daft - a queen and her prince – but truly wonderful.

"Once, I asked Mum a question." His voice took on a softer, more melancholy tone. "I asked her why there was no king. Every royal family had to have a king, I said, so where was ours?

"I remember Mum going very quiet. For a moment I thought she hadn't heard me, but then she turned to me and said that ours had run away and left us.

"It was the saddest moment of my childhood.

"That night I crept out of the house and snuck up to our palace. In my eight-year-old head I must have reasoned that our king was really hiding there – perhaps playing hide and seek. So I toddled up to the park and hunted through," he pointed to the swathes of dark green on the picture, "those trees, but the king wasn't there. I decided that perhaps if I waited for him, he would come and find me.

"So I waited and waited.

"But he never came.

"However, my mum did. Needless to say, she was not very happy. No, not at all. I don't remember too much, but I do remember her crying lots as she brought me home. She made me promise never to do something so stupid ever again and she took me into her bed and curled up with me so we went to sleep together."

He turned and grinned at me. "The things you remember."

I heard a noise from the kitchen doorway and turned to see Caroline watching us. Her eyes said it all.

The things you remember, indeed.

The food was great. Caroline had excelled herself.

It was a red pepper and tomato tart. She had found the recipe on, as she put it, some lentil-eating, hippy website. There was a great deal of conversation, albeit not from the adults. A number of times Caroline had to scold her son for talking with his mouth full. As I watched the young lad eating his food and whiffling away about this thing and that thing, I couldn't help but smile. He had a truly infectious enthusiasm for life which radiated from him like light from a candle. *If the world is in the hands of a generation like him*, I thought to myself, *then it is in very safe hands.*

After the meal, Caroline told John to tidy the plates and wash the dishes. I was amazed at how agreeable he was to get on with the chores. He just scooped them up and headed off into the kitchen, whistling to himself. "He's a good lad," I said.

Caroline's eyes followed him out of the room. "I know. That's what worries me so much about this Credete business. He's a soft touch. He'd do anything for anyone."

"Well, that's something I don't think you need to worry about," I said, leaning back in the dining chair, my stomach contentedly full. "I checked them out. Apart from being a bit free and easy with the happy vibes, they don't strike me as any sort of threat. My guess is it will run its course and dissipate." Caroline said nothing so I carried on. "I went to one of their meetings and it was all about self-confidence and faith healing – not exactly sinister. Then I met with the group leader and he said that if you had any concerns you should get in touch with him." I paused. Her brown eyes were staring off across the table into the middle distance. Something was wrong, something I was missing. "Caroline, you okay?"

She shook her head. "No, that can't be right. It can't be. I was sure there was something." Her manicured nails drummed impatiently on the dining table and she turned to face me. "Here's the deal: you're wrong. You have to be. There must be something."

Okay. So I was *definitely* missing something here. I dialled it back a bit and trod cautiously. "Sorry, Caroline, but I really don't think there is."

"No." She shook her head vehemently, causing her brown hair to swing violently from side to side. "There is. I know there is. It just appeared from nowhere overnight. How did Wallace manage that? How could he afford it?"

I frowned. How did she know Wallace's name? Had John told her? Had she mentioned it before now? I recalled Alec's mysterious warning that she was hiding something. "Caroline, is there something I don't know?"

"You guys alright?"

Both our heads snapped to the kitchen door. John was stood there holding a red and white tea towel, a look of consternation on his face.

"It's fine, sweetie," his mother reassured him. "Nothing to worry about."

It was obvious that he did not believe her as he twisted the damp cloth anxiously between his hands.

"Your mum's just a bit concerned about you, that's all," I explained.

"Why?"

"Sam, we really don't need to..."

I held my hand up, cutting off the protest. "Actually, I think we do. John, Your mum's really worried about the group you're hanging around with. Credete."

Confusion crept into his blue eyes. "Really?"

"I know. I've just been explaining to her that they are not so bad and she should not be worried about you having joined a cult or anything."

"I should hope not." The corner of his mouth turned up as he started to laugh. "I mean, after all, she was the one who suggested that I join them."

Next there was a stunned silence.

Then there was shouting.

"So you set this up? You made your own son join a group you were suspicious about just for a scoop?"

She tried to explain, she tried to be reasonable.

I was not for listening.

"It wasn't like that, Sam. It really wasn't." Caroline's voice was starting to take on a thin and reedy petulance which was really starting to get on my nerves.

"So what was it like then? Why don't you tell me?" I had abandoned my chair, all post-dining contentment flushed down the drain, and was pacing back and forth like a trapped lion. Right now I felt like biting someone's head off and Caroline's was the obvious choice. "Come on, Wondermum, enlighten me."

Caroline tore her eyes away from me to John who was still stood in the doorway silently watching us fight. She opened her mouth to say something to him but shook her head and let her lips snap shut before turning back to me. "Sam, look at me," she begged. "Just look at me. I'm a failure, a bloody failure. I was supposed to go off and become a hotshot journalist but instead I'm stuck in a backwater city writing garbage for a *What's On* section in a local rag. To make matters worse, I'm shunned by my family and alone with my son."

"My heart bleeds for you," I sneered.

"Hector Swarbrick was on my back," she continued. "He said I wasn't pulling my weight and my section was going to be cut. My neck was on the block if I didn't get him some juicy stories for the paper. So I hunted around, all over the place. I scoured everything: bars, courtrooms, the net. Then I came across Credete and I thought, *Bingo*. Here was a group that had sprung out of nowhere and was offering its followers the world.

"They had to be dodgy.

"So I told Hector that I going to get dirt on them and he asked me just how I planned to achieve this. Then it hit me that I had no idea. If I walked in they would see right through me as a reporter. So I said the first thing that came into my head."

"You said you'd send me." John was slouched against the door frame, all traces of joie de vivre expunged from him. Poor kid.

"You willingly sent your own flesh and blood into what you expected to be a nest of vipers?" I shook my head unbelievingly. "And I'm guessing you got nothing."

Caroline hung her head and kept silent.

"You didn't realise that the teens had their own meetings which were effectively just a youth group. You needed another strategy. You needed someone who could get in with the adults."

She nodded, sullenly.

"So," I continued, "what should happen but your employer and your son have chance meetings with an *old flame* of yours. Not only that, but said person actually went to university with the very founder of the group you wanted infiltrating. It couldn't have been planned better. You turned up on my doorstep full of sob stories and heartache and lured me in to do exactly what you wanted.

"Only, you've not got what you wanted, have you? It was a waste of time. Credete is harmless. Creepy, yes, but totally harmless." I shook my head and grabbed my hat and coat. "I'm leaving." I turned to John. "I'm sorry about this. I really am."

His head gave a set of small, nervous nods and he returned to the kitchen leaving us alone. My heart broke for the poor lad. I turned on Caroline. Her wet eyes looked up at me through her dishevelled hair and I felt nothing but anger. "Don't you ever contact me again," I hissed. "I'm through with you. We have no connection. None whatsoever."

As I grabbed the door handle, a small, pathetic voice whispered, "Yes we do. We have our son."

CHAPTER 10

I stormed into my flat and opened the bottle of Jack that I had purchased on the way home. My head was pounding and my ears were screaming. I needed something to silence them both. On my way to the kitchen I took three deep swigs from the bottle and, as the liquid heat spread down my chest, I half-filled a whiskey glass I'd snatched up from a table.

Breaths, deep breaths. I stood clasping the kitchen counter as I tried to control the rhythm of my gasping lungs. It was no good. I drank some more bourbon, this time from the glass.

I should have known it.

I should have seen it.

It had been there in front of me all the time, hidden in plain sight. There had been the crystal elephant, my secret gift to Caroline just before her sixteenth birthday. Then there was the age of John, for crying out loud! How could I not have noticed that one?

Perhaps I had not wanted to.

Perhaps I had subconsciously been in denial.

Perhaps I had not wanted to suffer rejection once more.

I had a son.

I had a son, and I had screwed up once again. I had just turned and walked away. I thought back to the last time I had walked away.

The day after Caroline's birthday party, I woke refreshed and renewed. I was a different person: alive and joyful. The pain of my father's imminent death had been transported somewhere else entirely – a different planet, galaxy or universe. Right now I was invulnerable; nothing could hurt me.

I lay in bed looking dreamily out of the window at the morning sunshine and wistfully touched my fingers to my lips. Caroline had kissed me there. Lots.

That had only been the start of it.

We had made love down at the bottom of the garden. It had been so sweet, so tender. Hidden away from prying eyes in our own paradise we had become one body, one soul. An intimate union had occurred that nothing could ever split asunder.

I clambered out of bed and dressed hurriedly, eager to face the coming day, excited at our lovers' secret. We had something that was truly ours and no-one else knew. There would be knowing glances, snatched kisses and more love making.

But right now, breakfast.

I practically skipped downstairs and when I entered the dining room Caroline was already sat there, toying with a grapefruit.

I grabbed some cereal and plonked myself down next to her. "Morning, you!" I beamed.

"Hi." She continued to prod the flesh of the fruit with her spoon.

"How are you?"

"Okay."

I leant across to kiss her.

She drew away. "Sam. Don't!"

"Ah, right. Okay. I understand." I glanced out the door of the room and saw no-one but it paid to be careful. I poured some milk on my cereal.

Caroline sighed and pushed the grapefruit away, uneaten.

"You okay?"

She shrugged.

I reached up and ran a finger through her blonde hair.

She reached up and drew my touch away. "Please don't."

It was about this time that I realised something was wrong. "Caroline?"

She sat staring at her discarded breakfast.

I was also starting to feel less than hungry. "Please. Talk to me. Have I done something wrong?"

Slowly, she shook her head.

"Then what is it?" I glanced over at the door again to make sure we were still alone and whispered, "Are you having regrets about last night?"

No response.

"Caroline, it really meant something for me. I love you."

She turned. Her brown eyes rimmed with tears held mine as she said, "But I don't love you." She stood, slid the chair back under table and dumped the discarded grapefruit in the bin. "I could never love you." She turned away from me. "Father wants to see you. You'd better not keep him waiting."

And she walked out of the room.

I sat there for a moment, crushed and deflated as a dark void began to rise inside my chest and crept up inside my ears causing bells to toll. I fought the darkness down and pushed my inedible breakfast away before rising to go see Father Adamson.

Caroline's father was stood looking out the wide window behind the fastidiously tidy desk of his study, his hands clasped tightly behind his stiff back. The sun was bright outside and he cast a long, foreboding shadow across the room.

"You wanted to see me, Father Adamson?"

His shoulders rose then sagged in one fluid motion. "I do not *want* to see you. I *need* to see you. There is a difference."

It did not take an idiot to realise that I was in deep, deep trouble. Surely he did not know. I swallowed nervously then asked, "Is there something the matter?"

He continued to stare out of the window, down the long, grassy lawn as he spoke in a low, threatening growl, "Could you not keep your filthy little hands to yourself?"

Okay, so he *did* know.

I tried to offer an explanation. I tried to volunteer some logical fact that would prove my innocence, but all that came out was an unintelligible stutter. I was screwed.

"I took you into my house. I fed you and gave you somewhere to sleep. I provided you with experience for your chosen career path – a career path I must say you will now *never* follow." All the time he kept his back to me. He was a dark silhouette in the bright summer sun.

"But, I can explain..." I finally managed. "I..."

"Enough!" Adamson roared, whipping around and slamming both his hands palm down with a thundering crash. I took an involuntary jump back. It was not just the sudden noise; his face was a study of terror. He looked like a creature from the lowest pit of Hell. I had never seen such a scowl, such a grimace of sheer fury. "My daughter has told me everything. I know all that I need to know. I know how you two..." His face contorted as if he was tasting the bitterest poison on his tongue. "I know enough," he repeated, finally bringing his bilious wrath under control.

She had told him? Why on Earth had she done that? A large part of me wanted to curl up and wither right there. I had been rejected and betrayed by the girl that I had given my heart to. The delicate little ember of my unrequited love had been ground under foot into the dirt and pulverised into extinction. However, a tiny voice at the back of my head screamed to be heard. "Don't you dare!" it yelled at me. "Don't you give her the satisfaction. This is not your fault."

So I pulled my shoulders back, took a deep breath and said, "I'm not the only one."

For a terrifying moment Adamson said nothing. He

just stood there, hunched over his ornate wooden desk, his dark brown eyes glaring at me. I was convinced that if he had been in possession of a gun he would have mown me down and spat on my rapidly cooling corpse. However, something else happened. Slowly, he lowered himself down into his padded leather chair and, as he did, the mask of malevolence slid from his face revealing a look of haunted despair. His eyes lost all their wrathful fire and turned dim as he said quietly, "I know, Sam. I know.

"Now pack your things and get out. You are no longer welcome here."

"That's okay. I no longer want to stay."

And I left.

The crystal glass smashed against the wall. Shards splintered off around the room and golden liquid cascaded down. The bitch! The absolute bitch! How could she do this to me? She had waltzed back into my life, tugged at my heart strings as if it was a marionette for her cruel amusement, and played me for all it was worth.

She had used me once again, just as she had used me before. Last time I had been blinded by young love; this time my mature eyes had finally seen through the vicious little game that she had been playing. Last time she had wanted to strike out at her over-domineering father; this time she had wanted to improve her career by getting a trashy inside story on my old friend.

What a bitch!

I stood panting heavily in the middle of my office, my shoulders rising and falling in a ragged rhythm. My broken heart banged in my aching chest and scalding tears of rage welled from my between screwed up eyelids. I screamed out loud in an incomprehensible roar, sank to the floor and pounded my balled fists into the carpet. Over and over they struck the synthetic fibres which burned against my skin. I relished the feel of the pain; it was real, unlike Caroline's affections for me.

I had been such a fool - a bloody, stupid fool. She was chip off her boss' old block, selfish through and through. How had she produced such a nice lad in John? Heaven alone only knew.

The thought of John made me bring my carpet thumping to a halt. Instead, I rested my forehead on the floor and rocked back and forth. The poor boy. It was just not fair that he had such a conniving little cow for a mother. What must have been going through his mind right now? Had he overheard her little revelation? If not, would she tell him?

I sighed and rocked back onto my rear, sitting cross-legged on the floor, staring at the shards of glass and rivulets of Jack Daniels. The initial tension was leaving now, but the anger was still there, simmering away in the pit of my stomach like an over-cooked stew of bile and remorse. I had refused to believe Wallace when he had said, categorically, that all humanity was doomed because of its blind selfishness. Now, however, I saw his point entirely. He had spoken truthfully; possibly the most truth I had heard in a long time.

I glanced up at the station clock. He had told me

that he would be at the Grand from seven-thirty. I still had time to clean up this mess and freshen up. I needed some truthful company.

Insistent, chilling rods of October rain hammered down from darkened autumnal skies onto my wide-brimmed fedora as I stormed my way across town. My feet sloshed in pools of muddy water that congregated down Great John Street and probing headlights flashed across my eyes as I drew my collar up close to prevent the worst of the weather from penetrating my clothing.

It was a vile night and I was in the foulest of moods. I had been used, betrayed and spat upon. I felt abandoned and alone. I needed someone who would listen without judging me, someone who had been right from the very beginning.

I needed Malcolm Wallace.

He had warned me; oh, how he had warned me. People of this day and age were users. They were selfish to the core and had lost all respect for those they claimed to love. They were blind to those around them and their own fate. I too had been blind but now I could see clearly. You could not rely upon anyone else. You had to draw upon your own convictions and pursue them to the fullest.

Anything is possible.

The trouble was I was scared to trust my newly reborn vision. I needed guidance.

I darted across Moor Lane, dodging more puddles in the worn, cracked cobbles and made my way over to Saint Leonard's Gate. This had once been the site of a leper colony. The pariahs of society had been rounded up and locked away from sight of the general public. They were afflicted and different, made to fend for themselves as best they could with little resources. I knew how they felt.

The rain was coming down so hard now that it was actually getting difficult to see through the precipitation. People scurried past me, barely visible; spectres in the night. They were not real to me. They had no purpose in my life so I paid them no attention. I had to focus on what I wanted now. I had to take charge of my life and pull back together the fragments that Caroline had smashed apart.

The smell of take-away food assaulted my nostrils and my treacherous stomach rumbled. How could I be hungry already? Caroline had fed me before her deceit had been revealed. Besides, it was irrelevant. I had to ignore the want of my body and concentrate on what my mind and my soul longed for.

Truth.

The Grand Theatre is one of the older buildings of Lancaster. It has stood since the late 1700's and suffered from such fates are fire, flood and local planning. It has the ubiquitous hauntings of dead actresses and the even more numerous groups of local am-drams who step to the stage in whatever play takes their fancy from time to time. I've never really been a theatre-goer; my attention span is far too short and, besides that, sci-fi never really translates well to the stage. I mean, can you imagine *Star Trek on Ice*? I rest my case.

I stepped through the main door, out of the downpour and indeed out of the twenty-first century. Middle-aged men in black tie stood amongst the bustling theatre-goers, showing them to circle or stalls. The décor of the foyer was mainly of a deep red wallpapering and dark wooden furnishings that one would expect from the era of pre world war two. I half expected young flapper women to bustle in swinging their bead necklaces and babbling on about the Charleston or some other such care-free whimsy.

I removed my hat and a flood of rainwater drenched the carpet at my feet. I grimaced as I saw a dark-suited man approach me. He was about six foot five, had short-clipped grey hair and a pencil thin moustache crowning an incredibly stiff upper lip. A muscular physique rippled under his evening attire and from his posture I could tell at an instant that he took no crap. Ex-military I surmised; typical Sergeant Major type. He probably excelled at barking underlings into an ear-bleeding submission and then firing shells out of a Freudian cannon onto ramshackle villages of helpless natives.

I didn't think we were going to be good buddies.

"You look lost." The voice was sharp, clipped and to the point. What the words actually meant were, "Piss off out of my theatre you scruffy little urchin."

I drew myself up and met him in the eye as best I could, and by *eyes* I actually mean *chin*. "I'm here to meet a friend," I explained.

The towering Sergeant Major's immaculately groomed eyebrows rose with military precision. "Oh, really?" His piercing blues slowly appraised my drenched and bedraggled attire as if trying to locate a target. "A *female* friend?"

I sighed. I had endured enough crap for one night and I made to push past the jumped up dictator of the theatre foyer.

His arm shot out and a vice gripped my arm. "And, where do you think you're going, Sonny?"

"Like I said, to meet my friend," I spat, my contempt now very vaguely concealed. Anger was boiling up and I seriously wanted to lash out at this pompous arse, but I had somewhere to be and someone to see.

"You got a ticket then?"

"No."

"The street's that way, then," he pointed with a fat finger on the end of a rigid arm.

"My friend is waiting for me in box number one."

The grip slackened on my arm and I saw hesitation creep into the man's eyes. "Box one?" he repeated, his mouth suddenly sounding dry and his voice less sure that the world was actually round.

I nodded, my eyes narrowing with caution.

It was when I saw the ultimate tell of his adam's apple bobbing that I knew I had won the battle and he could only fire duds. His hand dropped to his side and he motioned up the stairs with his head. "It's up there on the right hand side of the circle, sir." He paused, awkwardness dancing merrily between the two of us. "Sorry about the fuss, sir. It's just... well..."

I didn't give him the opportunity to finish his half-baked apology and made my way through the crowded foyer, up the stairs and into the theatre. It was as I politely squeezed passed people down the side of the circle that I realised I didn't even know what the play was. I looked for someone selling programmes, but couldn't see anyone and just gave up, walking over to the doorway of box number one.

For a moment I paused outside the box, looking up at the gloss-red door. Should I just walk in? No. I raised my knuckle to knock when the door swung inwards and there he was sat in one of the two padded chairs that overlooked the stage: Malcolm Wallace, the bringer of truth. He turned to me and smiled warmly. "Samuel, you came. Wonderful! Do come in and could you close that behind you, please?" He motioned towards the door.

As I closed it behind me, the fact dawned on me that I had not touched the door and Malcolm was sat over the other side of the box.

Anything is possible.

But surely...

I dismissed the notion. This was an old building; perhaps I had just stood on a loose floor board which had caused the door to swing inwards.

Well, that's what I wanted to believe for now, anyway.

There was a row of hooks on the back wall of the box. Malcolm's overcoat occupied one of the pegs. I hooked my mac and my hat up on the other end of the row so as not to dampen the material of his finely tailored outerwear then I made my way over to the spare chair and seated myself.

So, here I was, the eager student ready to learn from the wise master. Questions, so many questions, but how to pose them without looking like a complete muppet? I drummed my fingers against my teeth and words stumbled and stuttered over each other in my head. They would not behave themselves. They were all there, every one that I wanted to say, but they would not form themselves into coherent phrases.

All the time Malcolm just sat calmly, his meticulously neat, white hair framing his pensive, orange eyes as they peered out over the theatre and surveyed the members of the audience as they clambered into their seats.

"Do you think they know we watch them," his low voice suddenly cut into my awkward silence, "those people down there? Do you think they realise that we sit here high above their heads, gazing down and watching their every insignificant footstep? Why should they? We are not part of their mundane lives. We are not their TV dinners or their soap operas. We are not their *Jeremy Kyle Show* or their *X Factor*." If the names of the shows had been liquid they would have been potent enough to stun a blue whale. "Look at them, Samuel. Really *look* at them."

I turned and followed his gaze out over the stalls beneath us. There, down below sat a young couple, he with his arm around her shoulders, her with a face like thunder. Further along sat a family: man, woman, three kids. The kids were bouncing and yammering whilst the mother had the weary look of, "Oh, dear God, not here," on her face whilst the husband idly played on his smart phone. Then there was the young woman bending over to sort out her handbag completely unaware of the old man behind taking great interest as her skirt rose rather too high.

"Do you see them, Samuel?" Malcolm asked. Even without looking at him I knew that those intense eyes were now fixed on me as his hand grasped his ornate, serpentine cane. "Do you see them for what they really are?"

My broken heart shrivelled in my aching chest and wept with no control. "Caroline..." I eventually whispered as I turned to face him.

"Caroline, the girl who broke your young heart after university," Malcolm soothed, his face full of sadness. "Caroline, the woman who walked into your life and played with you as if you were a yo-yo on a string or some sort of cat's toy to bat around the floor until it falls apart from the savaging of her claws." The sage words from my new master continued. "Caroline, the trashy rag reporter who sent you into my midst to find as much dirt as you could for her to plaster over her little provincial newspaper."

My jaw fell.

A hint of a smile formed at the corner of Malcolm's mouth. "Was she worried about that nasty cult, Samuel? Was it going to snatch her beloved baby from her? I am not a fool. I knew the boy was her son from the moment I laid eyes on him." He shook his head and turned to look out over the darkening theatre. "Do I really look like a man who would kill a child?"

"No... no," I said. "You don't." And the thing was, at that point, he really didn't.

The play was fairly dreadful. I can't recall its title as my mind was racing with all the stuff that was bombarding it about Caroline, Malcolm and everything. I just seem to recall it was some depressing little number about these guys who take a tramp into their care and end up shouting at him lots. I think I must have yawned at least half a dozen times during the first act. Malcolm, however, was totally caught up in the piece and hardly shifted position as his eyes remained fixed on the characters on the stage, his left hand clasping the head of his cane and the thumb of his right hand twiddling his ring which bore two snakes. I decided that he really had a thing about snakes.

Eventually my boredom was relieved by the interval. The curtain lowered and the house lights came up. Malcolm gave a small sigh of satisfaction. "Fascinating," he murmured, lifting his right hand and caressing his lower lip with his ring. "Fascinating."

"Yes," I said, surreptitiously flexing my shoulder blades, "it was."

My companion turned to me and raised a white eyebrow as there was a tentative knock at the door. "Enter!" he called out, his orange irises not drifting from me for a second. A young woman entered carrying a tray with a silver tea pot and two china cups. She set them down on a small table and left without a word. "Tea?" Malcolm enquired of me, lifting the pot and pouring himself a pot of steaming, hot liquid. "It's Earl Grey."

"Thank you." I gratefully took the second cup after he had filled it and sipped slowly. The aromatic flavour danced soothingly on my tongue. "I didn't realise the theatre provided such a service."

"They don't. At least not to anybody else." Malcolm sat back in his chair, saucer in one hand and cup in the other. He looked for all to see like a gentleman at home in his study. "I have an... *arrangement* here. I have been very successful financially and as a result I contribute greatly to the Grand. As a result, there are certain," he gestured around the box with the tea cup, "benefits."

There didn't seem to be much to say on that matter so I kept quiet and tried not to appear stupid. I was totally out of my depth here: theatre, luxury box, expensive tea, incomprehensible dramatics. Definitely a time to keep schtum.

Malcolm finished his beverage, placed the cup lightly on the saucer and smiled at me in a way that a genial uncle regards an inept nephew. "You don't attend the theatre much, do you Samuel?"

I sighed deeply. I had been sprung. "God's honest? I think the last play I saw was a rendition of *The Very Hungry Caterpillar* by Miss Harper's class back in primary school. I seem to recall it was very well received by the critics. Well, Danny Clough said that Amy Johnson looked "well fit" as the piece of cherry pie."

Malcolm smiled as his thumb rocked his ring back and forth. "And we all know how harsh a critic a child can be, don't we, Samuel? Let's face it, Caroline wasn't much more than a child when you first met her, was

161

she?"

At once the tea in my gut turned to bile and I felt anger start to boil within me once more.

Malcolm nodded in appreciation. "Yes... yes... she makes you so angry, doesn't she? And quite rightly so, Samuel. That little tramp ruined your life. She lured you in like a sweet smelling flower draws an unsuspecting insect, then just when you were all warm and cosy, her jaws snapped tight around you like the Dionaea muscipula she is and she devoured your future, snatching away all confidence that you ever had in yourself. You've blamed yourself for so long now," his soft voice soothed. "Poor, poor Sammy, devastated that he could never love another soul without getting hurt, yet eternally doomed to punish himself for taking advantage of a sweet, sixteen-year-old girl."

There was a loud *crack* as his cane rapped the floor between us.

"Well enough is enough, Samuel." Malcolm's voice was low but penetrating; commanding and forceful in our enclosed, private space. "Enough is enough. Caroline was no shrinking violet. She used you then and she used you now. You know that to be true or you would not be here tonight."

My head drooped as I nodded in mournful agreement.

"The question is, Samuel," he pondered, absentmindedly stroking his cane, "what are you going to do about it?" The lights dimmed and the audience hushed down below. "Well for now, I think that we should watch the second half of this play." He smoothed down his lilac-coloured lapels and turned towards the stage. I rubbed my hand across my forehead and did likewise. The actors shambled out and meandered messily around the stage. I really had no idea why people paid to come and see this sort of stuff; it did absolutely nothing for me. I felt that it was just pretentious twaddle; a collection of longing stares and pregnant pauses mixed up in a solution of heartfelt monologues and diatribes. The words drifted over me as I sat there occasionally glancing at my watch. As the play dragged on, I began to feel that this had been a mistake. Yes, Malcolm had been somewhat sympathetic, but had he really been the help that I had expected? Had he given me any real answers?

A gleeful chuckle bubbled up from my companion as his thumb played once again with his snake ring.

"What is it?" I whispered, daring not to be heard.

"Oh, this is just marvellous," he crowed, his eyes darting about the stage in frantic animation. "The things, one learns."

"Really?" I asked, somewhat perplexed.

Malcolm turned and looked at me, his orange eyes twinkling mischief in the half light. "Oh, not the play, Samuel. That is utter," he waved a hand dismissively, "balderdash and piffle - especially in the hands of rank amateurs. No, it's what one can learn about the actors. Most fascinating."

I frowned. "What exactly do you mean?"

"You see the tramp?" Malcolm gestured with a tilt of his chin. "He is so desperate to improve himself. The actor that is, in real life, so to speak. So much so that he is looking for a way to leave this little troupe. What's more he's intending to do it by stealing an upcoming part from his best friend, the young chap there."

I looked at the two men arguing on the stage, their arms waving like windmills and their mouths flapping like castanets. "Did you read that in a magazine or something?"

Malcolm shook his head. "No, Samuel. The best of it is though is that the third chap down there, the one who keeps fiddling with the plug, knows about the older chap's designs and has already informed the young fellow, who is seething with such rage. Oh, such *delicious* rage. In fact, he is fit to explode and any second now... any second..."

Smack!

The audience gasped as the younger actor floored the older man with a vicious right hook. The tramp collapsed to the floor. The look of absolute disbelief painted on his face was soon replaced by terror as the younger man fell on him and started to pound him around the head with clenched fists. I saw a commotion at the side of the stage as the third actor dashed into the fray, trying to drag the younger man away from his victim. The attacker was having none of it; he screamed and cursed as his fists connected with the face of the tramp, one after the other. The last thing I saw before the curtain quickly fell down sealing off the carnage was the sight of the older man's nose exploding in a spray of blood.

"I'm guessing that wasn't in the script." I turned and looked at Malcolm who was sat back in his chair smiling as if he was the proverbial cat with the cream or the estate agent with the gullible newly-weds.

"Not the script of the play, perhaps, Samuel. But it was certainly inevitable. It was there for all to see as long as one believes one can."

"You're saying that you had no knowledge of that before you came here tonight?"

He shook his head. "Nothing. Not a jot."

"I find that very hard to believe," I protested. "Okay, perhaps you could read their body language and see where it was heading. All this stuff about the old man snatching the young one's role, well that could just be speculation." I ran my fingers through my curls. "I can't really believe you know what is actually playing out in their lives."

The satisfied look did not leave Malcolm's face as he gave me his full attention.

Suddenly, I felt distinctly nervous. "What? What is it?"

"Tell me, Samuel," his words were low and seductive, "what was it like?"

"What was *what* like?"

"Killing her? Gunning her down in cold blood?"

I felt as if the floor of the box had been removed and I was tumbling arse over tit down to the floor of the stalls below.

"How?" My voice cracked. "How?"

Wallace leaned into me, his unnaturally coloured eyes dancing like fire. "Samuel, Samuel, *anything is possible*. You are in such a dark place right now. Your life is at its ebb and you know not how to proceed. Life has been such a trauma for you. There is blood on your hands and guilt in your broken heart. But do not worry, I am sure most of us would have done the same. You had no idea who she would tell, did you? And those ravening beasts... that," he spat the words, "*despicable* Bloodline... you could not have them pursuing you, hunting you down.

"But it can all go away now. It can all be made better."

The world was spinning. I could feel nausea rising as the ringing started to scream in my ears. I could not stop my hands from clasping at the side of my head as they tried to rip out the very noise itself. I shut my eyes to try and steady my other senses. I had no way of knowing which way was up and which way was down. I needed my clocks, my comforting, ticking companions, but they were not here.

It was all going wrong.

It was all going wrong.

Then, amidst all the chaos of the senses, a cool pair of hands covered mine and a soothing spring breeze drifted through my ear drums and into my inner ears. I felt it stroking at my terrified cochleae and an intoxicating aroma of spices and scent filled my nostrils. An overwhelming feeling of peace and serenity washed over me.

Then there was nothing.

There was no noise.

My ears were quiet.

"It's okay," Malcolm said as I opened my eyes to my new life, "I am here to save you."

CHAPTER 11

The soft warmth of autumnal sunshine bathed my face as I strolled down Market Street with my mentor on Friday morning. It was one of those rare moments of seasonal beauty that the weather graces you with before the bitterness of winter starts to bite. Around us the folk of Lancaster hurried about their business: teenagers huddling in groups, mother's dragging demanding children or perplexed husbands, suited office workers nipping out on a coffee break.

And I could hear every word around me.

I had not stopped grinning since the previous evening. A lifetime of incessant, high-pitched noise gone in an instant. Instead, there was the normal humdrum of the everyday world. It was bliss. I could hear the chatter of children discussing the latest electronic toy. I could hear the cantankerous moaning of an old couple berating the proposed building work down on the quay. I could hear birds.

I stopped outside Morrisons and gawped up at a sparrow perched in a tree on the edge of Market Square.

It was sat there, chittering away to its little heart's content. I could hear every single, sweet note. I could not help but grin.

"Wonderful little chap, isn't he?"

"Not a care in the world," I agreed to Malcolm. I turned and faced him. "Right now I know how he feels."

Malcolm nodded and sat on a nearby bench. I followed him and did likewise. He gripped his ornate cane in his hands and let his eyes wander around the square. "Tell me, Samuel, who do you think is the most blessed this Friday morning? This mass of consumers with all their gadgets and wealth, their overflowing shopping bags and their comfortable houses or your little feathered friend up there in the tree who does not know where his next meal will come from or whether he will survive the night safe from a predator's hunger?"

I groaned audibly. "Don't go all Yoda on me, okay? I know you want me to say that I think the people are better off because they won't get eaten tonight, then you'll jump in and say something like, 'Aha. Blessed the sparrow is for unburdened with pressures of consumerist society is he.' Am I right?"

My white-haired friend smiled, "Know me well, you do, my young apprentice."

We both chuckled. Then quiet settled between us before he asked, "But tell me, Samuel, which life would you choose for yourself? Safety and the tedium that it brings with it or total happiness and freedom with the constant risk of death?"

"Well I can't say that my life has been very tedious, recently," I snorted. "If it carries on the way it's going, I'll soon have as many white hairs as you."

Malcolm nodded in agreement. "True, true. But consider this fact; these shoppers do not really know where they will be this time next week. They assume that they will be living their monotonous little lives, day in, day out, the usual routine. But how can they be sure? What if some great predator swooped down and devoured them? It could happen. Look at the Twin Towers."

"I hardly think that Lancaster is the same political target," I scoffed.

"People thought that about the London underground and a shopping centre in Nairobi. Terror can strike anywhere, Samuel. It doesn't even have to be political. What if an asteroid struck us?" He hammered the tip of his cane down on the floor between his legs. "We are totally unprepared! The politicians of this world are far more concerned with lining their own pockets than planning for possible futures. We need to take a hold of our existence and shape a future that suits us. Sacrifices have to be made to ensure this happens."

I frowned at him. "Sacrifices? What do you mean?"

Malcolm gave a deep sigh, composing himself back to his normal, unruffled self. "Enough of this talk for now. Let us go for a cup of tea, or, if you prefer, some of that hideous coffee you drink." With that he stood up and led the way. I followed, a touch perturbed by his little outburst, but willing to follow all the same.

When I was a kid in the seventies tea in a café

was served in a light green mug topped up with milk. You drank it at a table that had an easy clean surface of laminate or melamine upon which sat the usual condiments of salt, pepper and vinegar along with tomato ketchup and brown sauce in their individually coloured squeezy bottles. In some establishments the ketchup bottle was actually in the shape of a tomato.

However, things change. These little retreats from the stresses and strains of everyday life gave way to fast food restaurants with their shakes and fries which, in time, retreated from the relentless product that was the infinitely versatile coffee bean. So the High Street became dominated by ubiquitous coffee shop chains such as Costa and Starbucks with their Cappuccinos, Lattes and other such socially recognisable beverages.

However, in the back alleys and dusty arcades of our towns and cities, a silent revolution has begun to take shape. Small establishments have started to provide journeys into other times and distant lands. Yes, they still provide a range of coffee-based drinks for the less adventurous, but their star turns are birthed from the leaf not the bean. Here you find Darjeeling, Assam, Ceylon and the lord of them all, Earl Grey. They are served in china cups that come atop a saucer and they have fresh, home-made cakes of all shapes and sizes depending on your budget and your appetite.

These are the tea rooms and there is not a tomato-shaped ketchup bottle in sight.

Such an establishment was *Guy's Café*. Tucked away down Sun Street, the humdrum of the main trawl passed it by, letting it revel in all its neo-Victorian splendour. The thing that struck me, as the rather overweight proprietor effused over Malcolm and thanked him for his patronage, was the doilies. The place was overrun with them. Every cake stand stood atop one. The condiments on the polished tables rested on them. Was there even one poking out from under the till?

"Pardon?" I snapped out of my doily pondering when I realised that Malcolm had asked me a question.

"I said, 'Shall we sit here?'" he smiled, gesturing to a small table in the corner of the room next to a parlour palm.

"Sure."

The proprietor saw us to our table and beckoned for a young waitress to come over and serve us. She took our orders (mine was a black coffee, Malcolm's was an Earl Grey) as the middle-aged man hovered behind her, watching her every move. My companion, in turn, was intently watching the man and the girl. As they headed off to prepare our drinks he nodded silently to himself. "Well, what did you make of that?"

Make of what? "Sorry?"

Malcolm smiled and shook his head as the young waitress brought our drinks over. "Thank you, my dear," he said.

The girl smiled nervously and headed back off to the kitchen. Malcolm nodded again then turned his attention to me as he sipped from his aromatic tea.

"Tell me, Samuel, why are there so many things in the way?"

"In the way of what?"

"Life, Samuel. Life." His eyes watched the steam

rising from the hot drinks as if it was a troupe of dancers on a stage, his orange irises tracking every twirl and pirouette. "You know the sort of things that I mean. There will be things you want to do. Say, that holiday you wish to take, that book you want to read or," he paused to sip his tea once more, "that girl you want to woo."

I swallowed as my thoughts crossed their arms and let out an irritated snort.

"All these things you want," he continued, "yet time after time the mundane, boring, little day to day things get in your way. Your house needs a new roof so no holiday that year. Your neighbour has lost their dog so you spend the day hunting for Fido rather than curled up with Jane Austen. The girl you wish to woo..." He sipped his tea. "Well, we both know how that one ended don't we? Work got in the way. The need to further herself was far more important to her than your emotions.

"Imagine if there was a way to remove those barriers. Consider, if you will, a life without barriers, a world where you can achieve your dreams.

"All people need is to be liberated and then anything will be possible.

"All the world needs is change."

I frowned. "Surely the world *is* changing? Look at all the new technologies we've created in the last century. The world is changing all the time."

Malcolm gave me a small, knowing chuckle. "You actually think that the world is any different now to how it was in the Stone Age? Sure, we have all our nice, shiny toys, but is humanity actually any different? We may have evolved intellectually but do we actually know what we should be doing with all our electronic marvels?

"Tell me Samuel," Malcolm settled his fine china cup onto its saucer with a delicate *clink*, "if the world was to end tomorrow, what would people do?"

I sipped from my black coffee and instantly countered, "What sort of end are we talking about: supernova sun, nuclear bomb? What? It would affect things, surely?"

He nodded, sagely. "Good point. Indeed it would. To clarify then – something apocalyptic, something out of this world. An event so unlike anything that humanity has seen the like of. An event of singular cataclysmic significance. What then?" He placed the cup and saucer precisely on the table, leaned back in his chair, and awaited my reply with steepled fingers.

As I pondered this, my eyes were drawn to his ornate ring. Two serpents entwined around each other, one with a red jewelled eye, one with black. I shuddered involuntarily and shrugged, "I guess it would not make much of a difference. There would be widespread panic. People would hide as best they could. Some would pray to their god, others would seek out their families. Some..." My words drifted off into obscurity as I saw him chuckling quietly to himself. "What? What is it?"

Malcolm's oddly-coloured eyes twinkled over his steepled digits. "Tell me, Samuel, how would they possibly know? How could someone in Africa seek shelter in his village hut if this event had occurred right here in Lancaster? How could someone scaling the sides of the Grand Canyon know if a cataclysm had occurred?" He slipped his mobile phone out of his jacket pocket and lay it purposefully between us on the table. "This is how, Samuel. This is how. Should an event causing the end of the world occur, two things will indubitably come to pass. First, all those in the vicinity will reach for their mobile phones, their little umbilicals to the rest of the world, and begin to tweet away or start snapping photos for Facebook. Then, shortly after that, they will most certainly start to complain that they have no phone signal." He stared intently at me for a moment until a clap of laughter thundered from his mouth. When he had brought his mirth under control, he dabbed at his eyes with a handkerchief. "You know that I tell the truth, Samuel. These things *will* come to pass."

And, unfortunately, I knew he was right.

"The earliest evidence we have of *Homo Sapiens* is from about two hundred thousand years ago, give or take, since then we have stopped evolving. We have become dependent on these little gadgets," he stated, waving the phone around before popping it back in his jacket, "and other similar niceties. We started with stone axes, worked our way through bronze and iron receptacles, onto plastics and circuitry always passing the hard work onto another little toy whilst shrugging off our own responsibilities and consuming more and more of the planet's finite resources. We think we are so clever to have made all these wonderful discoveries to make our life *easier*, more *comfortable*." He sneered the words as if they soured his tongue. "But what is life without evolution? Where will we go? We will stagnate, that's what!"

I shook my head. "So what, you think we should follow Pol Pot's nice little idea of going back to a Year Zero and wiping out all the intellectuals? We both grew up with those images of mass burials in Cambodia."

"Not at all, Samuel." Malcolm's voice had taken on the gentler tone once more of a patient uncle explaining a hard subject to his less than bright nephew. "What I am saying is that change is inevitable, no matter how much we, as a race, seem to be slowing down in the evolutionary process. It is all down to sheer logic. As we continue our lifestyle we consume far more than this planet can produce. Our lifestyles are bleeding creation dry. They are totally unsustainable. We have nothing entering our system. We are consuming all around us like ravening beasts hungry for more and more. The time will come when there will be nothing left."

"And you feel that will be the end of the world?"

"Oh no. The end will arrive before humanity has had a chance to wallow in the toxic detritus of its entropy. The end will come when some right-minded individual stands up, says, 'Enough is enough,' and brings the whole thing to a surgically precise end.

I downed the rest of my coffee and sat back in my chair. I wanted to counter him. I wanted to say that I had faith in humanity, that everything would work out okay. I desperately wanted to say that we would turn things around and make it all better.

I just couldn't.

Right there at that moment, after all that Caroline had put me through, my broken heart knew that he was right. We were devouring our world at a cataclysmic rate whilst ignoring the wars and poverty that raged on around us. They were an inconvenience that we did not wish to see; a huge elephant trumpeting its trunk in the corner of a room where everyone wore earplugs of reality television and viral clips of cats doing stupid things.

We had become blind to our fate and steeped in a selfishness that drove us to use our planet and our friends as we saw fit.

The young waitress came back over to our table and asked us if we needed anything else. Morosely, I shook my head, not wishing to meet her happy, little face.

"One thing, my dear," Malcolm said. "A bit of information."

My ears pricked up as the girl replied, "Sure. What do you want?"

"Are you happy in your job?"

The shrugged, "I guess so. I haven't been here long, but it seems nice."

"*Seems* nice?"

"Well, yes. I guess."

Malcolm nodded quietly, his orange eyes not leaving the girl and his thumb casually rotating his ring around his little finger. "But you're not too sure, are you, my child?" he whispered, his conspiratorial voice not audible to anyone out of our circle of three. "There are little things, aren't there?"

The girl shuffled back and forth on her feet. This was clearly making her uncomfortable.

"It's okay, my child," Malcolm purred seductively. "You're among friends. You can tell us."

She gave a quick, furtive glance around the tea room, at the lacy doilies, the fresh flowers and the decidedly middle-class patrons. All the time her fingers were playing with the smartly cut blouse.

"Ah..." her inquisitor sighed. "I see. It's like that, isn't it? He makes you feel uncomfortable. The way he *looks* at you." He almost sang the word as his voice rose in knowing emphasis. "And you really don't like it, do you, my child?"

The waitress snapped her head from side to side, her dark fringe bobbing across her eyes which were now tightly shut as she fought to hold back the tears.

"You hate the way his eyes follow you around the room," Malcolm continued, relentlessly pursuing the matter, "always studying your figure when he thinks you're not looking. He insists that you wear the smart clothes and spray yourself with seductive scent. Your make up has to be just so. 'It's for the customers,' he says. 'We have an image to present.' But you know different, don't you. He just likes to watch you. He *lusts* after you."

"Malcolm..."

He waved a hand to cut me off, his eyes never leaving the poor girl, who was now close to exploding. "You feel trapped, don't you, my child? Your employer is keeping you trapped underfoot. It makes you feel worthless."

She nodded vigorously, a single tear escaping her tightly shut eyes and tracing down her impeccable make up.

"You need the money. *Desperately* need the money because..." He closed his eyes and seemed to concentrate for a brief second. "Because of your *child*."

She gasped and her eyes flashed open in shock, causing a stream of tears to waterfall down her cheek. "How?" Her voice was cracked and hoarse. Other customers started to crane their necks in our direction.

"Anything is possible, my dear," Malcolm crooned. "Once you understand that, then you are truly liberated. He looks at you with his lustful eyes, wanting you for himself. You allow that so that you can scrape a meagre crust together to feed yourself and your little one, all the time dreading that he will find out about your secret infant. A single mother would not sit comfortably with his doilies and his chintz. But anything is possible. Anything is possible. All you have to do is decide to take the first step." He rose from his chair and placed our payment on the table. "You can stop him from abusing you with his gaze, from holding you and your little one to ransom. You truly can."

And with that he walked out of the tea room, oblivious to the gaping and gasping that followed him.

I grabbed my hat and my coat, stumbled out of my chair, made to say something apologetic to the girl, failed miserably and ran after him. By the time that I had caught up with Wallace, he was already out of *Guy's Café* and heading back into town. I grabbed him by the arm and span him around. "What that hell was that about?"

My companion silently fixed his eyes on my tight

178

grip and waited patiently. I withdrew my hand and took a step backwards. "Thank you," he said before continuing to walk down the road.

I huffed in exasperation and followed behind him. "Well?" I demanded. "Are you going to tell me or do I get the silent treatment now?"

Wallace's cane clicked rhythmically on the cobbles. "I would have thought it obvious, Samuel. I just liberated the girl."

"Liberated?" My voice had slipped up a register with disbelief. The arrogance of the man! "Humiliated, more likely. Did you see the way the other customers looked at her? You reduced her to tears!"

"That is of no consequence. The opinions of others do not matter. She now knows that she has the power to control her own destiny. She will do what needs to be done."

We emerged onto Market Street and into the hubbub of the weekday business. "Oh? And what might that be, I ask?"

Wallace turned, his strangely-coloured eyes fixed on mine and stated simply, "That is for her to decide." With that he casually walked off into the crowds leaving me stood seething and bubbling over with contempt.

I stomped off in the opposite direction through Market Square. What the hell was the man playing at? Was this the same guy who had made a small girl walk and had healed my infernal ringing? How could someone I had gone to for solace in my darkest hour suddenly turn round on a sweet kid and reduce her to tears like that? My mind was racing as I barged my way through the mass of shoppers. Had I been played with once more? Had my emotions been batted around like a ball of string in a game of cat and mouse? It just did not make sense. What did I actually know about Wallace? Where had he been all these years and what had he been doing?

I needed answers.

I headed for Cheapside.

"Hey there, Sam. You hungry?"

"Sure am, Bob. What you got for me?"

The street vendor idly flipped some onions over on his griddle. "Depends what you're after, I guess."

I looked around in a somewhat furtive manner. I was the only one in the queue, which was something of an unusual occurrence. "Information."

Bob nodded. "Hawkins? 'Cos I got nothing else on him."

My stomach lurched at the thought of a slavering beast bearing down on me up at Williamson Park. "No. That's dead. Buried."

"'Kay. What you need then?"

"Someone's walked back into my life. Someone I haven't seen for many years. Name of Malcolm Wallace. Heads a society called Credete. You heard of him?"

The smell of grilling onions drifted up to me as Bob chewed his bottom lip for a moment. "Can't say that I have," he finally volunteered as he deftly assembled a veggie burger in a bun. "Name doesn't ring any bells. He local?"

I shook my head. "He studied at uni with me and

now he's back in town all successful and something smells wrong."

Bob handed the burger over. "I'll listen out for you. If I hear anything, I'll let you know. That one's on the house."

I smiled. "Cheers, Bob." I gestured to the lack of customers behind me. "Quiet today?"

The vendor scowled across the other side of the street. "Too bloody right. She's off on one today. Driving them all away with some depressing dirges. Bring back bloody Abba, I say."

I chuckled slightly and looked over at Betty. There she was, as immaculate as ever, just selecting a track on her CD player. A low drone emitted from the speakers followed by a laconic male voice; "It begins with a blessing and it ends with a curse. Making life easy, making it worse." She stood with her eyes staring up into the ether and swayed slowly from side to side as heavy guitars and drums pounded out a beat.

"She's been like that all day," Bob grumbled. "Don't know what's caused it. Don't *want* to know. I just want her to bloody well stop. It's ruining business."

I stood and watched Boombox Betty, away in her own little world. She raised her arms in the air and looked all the bit a charismatic preacher caught up in the ecstasy of the spirit as she remained in her own private little world, absorbing the music. Passers-by gave her just the quickest of glances before hurrying past.

"Now people are watching, people who stare," continued the singer, "Waiting for something that's already there."

I smiled. It seemed somewhat apt.

The next line, however grabbed my attention to the full.

"Tomorrow I'll find it. The trumpeter screams, then he remembers that he's hungry and he drowns in his dreams."

The trumpeter.

Dreams.

"Sam. You okay?"

I snatched a glance back to Bob. "Yeah, sure. It's just... It's just a bit weird." I finished off my burger and walked across the street to stand before Betty. Smoother music was playing now from the track, the sort you would find in a neon-lit dive bar, it drew me in as the singer sang about his head being a night club with glasses and wine. Then the song exploded: "Get out of my dream...!"

I couldn't move. My feet were set in the paving stones of the street and people I was oblivious to jostled past me. Betty opened her eyes and looked straight through me as she sang along to the music: "Once I awakened, my eyes filled with tears. I had been sleeping for thousands of years, dreaming a life full of problems and sadness, endlessly turning in spirals of madness."

Then, suddenly, as if I had slapped her, her eyes focussed sharply on me. She gasped, her hand flying to her mouth and she stooped down, deftly flicking off the CD player and scurrying away.

It actually took me a few seconds to wake up to the fact that she had gone. She was hurrying down towards Damside. I pursued her. "Wait!" I called out.

"Betty!"

She ignored me and continued tottering as fast as her high heels would permit her with the boom box cradled protectively in her arms like a new-born infant. Eventually she reached Damside, just as a double decker bus pulled round. It blocked her way and gave me the chance to catch up. "Betty, please wait. I just want to talk."

She turned to face me and worry was written over her face. I pointed to the CD player. She pulled it as close to her chest as was physically possible and gave a vigorous shake of her head.

I hold out my hands placatingly. "No, it's okay. I don't want your player. I just want to know about the song you were singing. What was it?"

Warily, she cocked her head to one side and had the look of a child that doesn't really believe you when you say you you're not going to break their favourite toy.

"Please, Betty," I begged. "I think it's important."

She leant forwards over the top of the CD player until her nose was almost tip-to-tip with mine and she stared intently into my eyes. I stood there, playing along, ignoring the stares and sniggers of passers-by. Finally she pulled back, nodded and ejected the CD from the player. She held it out and gestured for me to take it. "Dream," she said, turned around and walked off towards the bus station.

I stood where Cheapside meets Damside and looked with great interest at a CD I had just been given by probably the craziest woman in town. It was bright yellow with green writing. "Kevin Ayers: The Confessions of Dr Dream and other stories" it read. I pocketed it and headed back up to Dalton Square. I had some music appreciation to undertake.

I dropped my newly acquired CD next to the pile of my usual listening material and went through to the kitchen to make myself a coffee. The kettle boiled, I poured the boiling water over the granules and trudged back into my living room where I slouched down onto my old sofa.

My shoulders ached with tension and I could feel the beginning of a headache starting to niggle away in my head. I closed my eyes and breathed deeply to try and relieve the symptoms. I smiled as the aroma of the coffee drifted up to greet me. It's flavourful vapours wafted up into my nose and danced lightly with my senses.

I actually started to relax.

"Hello Sam."

I damn near jumped out of my skin as the two words snapped me out of my stupor. "Jesus!" I cursed. My hot coffee sloshed down my front, scalding me through my shirt. "Bollocks!" I swore. Instinctively I grabbed my hankie from my pocket and started to dab at the searing, brown beverage.

After a few dabs my brain caught up with the fact that I was not alone.

"I've so got to get a new lock on that door."

"Indeed."

It was a female voice: quiet, clipped and precise. It made me think of long, hot afternoons spent toiling in the local library with a middle-aged harridan patrolling the stacks on the hunt for comics, contraband porn or, even worse, food and drink - horror of horrors!

Slowly, I stopped rubbing my crotch with a damp hankie and looked up at the source of the voice. It was the woman from my dream about the first day my ears had decided to hear things that weren't there. She was the definition of *demure*. She wore the same light green woollen two piece skirt and jacket over a light blue blouse along with polished, flat-soled, sensible shoes. Her dark hair was again positioned atop her head in a neat, precise bun (there was not a single stray hair out of place) and she wore dark-rimmed glasses that twenty years ago would have been totally unfashionable but nowadays screamed (albeit very politely in this case) *retro*. Definitely librarian material, but looking younger than I remembered from my uni years - or was I just getting older? Policemen, doctors, dentists - did librarians start to look younger too when you neared the magic forty?

"Although, I have to say," the librarian continued, "that no lock could have kept us out."

I frowned as something hit me. "Wait a minute. I'm not dreaming." I pointed an accusing finger straight at the woman who had previously taken me back to my childhood. "So you're real, then, and not some weird Jungian archetype of my deepest fears?"

There was a soft, familiar, fluttering of tiny wings and she was gradually surrounded by things that I was sure no other librarian would have been accompanied by.

"Fairies," I whispered, feeling myself slump further back into the warm, safe embrace of my threadbare sofa. This was getting worse.

My guest seemed slightly amused by this. "That term will suffice for now. It serves our purpose."

I let my eyes wander around my room and I counted about ten of the little folk bobbing up and down, looking around inquisitively. One was even typing something into a search engine on my computer. "I'm guessing that this isn't a social visit. Hey! Leave that alone!"

I lunged out of the sofa and bolted across the room to the mantle clock. One fairy had opened the glass and was about to turn the hands... backwards!

"Get off that you little sod!" I bellowed, swatting it away with the back of my hand. "Don't you have any manners, you trumped up luminous gnat?"

The fairy scowled and buzzed around my head, crossly twiddling its tiny fingers at me. I swished my hands around in an inanely futile gesture as if I was trying to swat an annoying insect, but it kept lithely dodging away out of reach before darting back in and poking at me. I could hear a tinny high-pitched whistling which I surmised to be its voice displaying annoyance.

There was a polite cough and my assailant flew away, perching itself on the woman's shoulder. It continued to scowl at me and its diminutive lips were moving in a manner that suggested it was mentioning very un-fairylike words under its breath.

"My companion," the woman explained in her smooth, matter of fact manner, "was just fascinated by your obsession with time."

"Obsession? What obsession?"

She just raised an eyebrow.

"Okay, so I have a few clocks. It's not like they control me. I don't go out and buy them all the time. I don't *need* to look at them. They're just there for... *recreational* use." God, that sounded lame. "Damn it! It could have broken it, that's all. Besides, you've made me jumpy, just appearing here like this and that. I thought you had gone off and left us."

Casually, she walked around the room, looking from clock to clock. She closed her eyes and appeared to be reading something that was only apparent to her. "These timepieces are your solace, Sam. They bring you comfort in your darkest moments, when the creature that rages inside your head threatens to break free and consume you."

My throat suddenly parched, I stood and listened. I thought about lying flat out on the floor, eyes closed ears open to the all-pervasive ticking as it calmed me, soothed me.

"You draw on their ability to tell the time to centre you in this reality," she continued, running an immaculately manicured finger over a cheap carriage clock. "From the smallest to the biggest, each of them plays its part in subduing that monster within. You depend on time to chain the beast." Her fiery eyes snapped open and snared me with the precision of a finely tuned animal trap. "What if time was not what you expected it to be, Sam? What if it went wrong? What if it were to split in two? What if it were to... *diverge.*"

I tapped my fingernails against my teeth. There it was again. That word. "I'd need twice as many clocks," I quipped, ignoring the growing panic in my gut as I imagined something snarling and squirming within me. Something brutal, primal.

She shook her head. "No," she said, her voice brimming over with sadness, "you wouldn't." Then she lay her hand on my shoulder and everything shifted.

It was a ruin. There was rubble everywhere. Buildings were either fallen or in the process of decay. Wild grass grew up through pavements and moss clung to broken brickwork.

"I know a builder who could fix this up. He'd be done by next Friday, if you're interested?"

Lighting up a Lucky, I blew cigarette smoke over towards my existential abductor before sitting down on the creaking remains of a park bench. It wobbled ominously as the rusted joints shifted under my weight. She remained standing whilst the fairies (or whatever they were) flittered around us, their little faces looking like puppies that had lost their favourite chew toys. Bless.

"What is it with you people? I mean, why do you have to drag me away from the same old same old to places of devastation and universal depression? I can be just as depressed at home, you know? Why didn't you leave me there? You could have come on your own and sent a postcard or something. You know the sort of thing: 'Wish you were here - instead of me!' or 'Happy Sunshine Apocalypse in Morecambe.'" I took another puff from my Lucky. "Christ I don't even know where we are. Are you going to tell me?"

There was no immediate reply.

I scanned my eyes around through the detritus and ruins. "At least there's no bloody wolves this time. Tell me, you're not related to a young lad by the name of Alec are you? This is one of *his* party tricks."

"Friend of the family." The woman neatly lowered herself down on the bench. There was no shifting of metal or scraping of rust. It was as if she were weightless.

I shivered. It wasn't just a bit nippy; I was chilled to the core. The sun was out high over the ruins and there was no breeze, but I felt as if a gale was gusting around my bones. This place felt like a pleasant little New England village in the hands of Stephen King; it was just *wrong*.

"Okay," I sighed, "so here we are, happy as can be and there's nothing I can do about it. Can you at least answer two questions for me?"

She sat quietly, her eyes of fire inspecting the devastation. I took that as a *yes*.

"First. What is your name?"

"Sophia."

I chuckled. "Nice one. *Wisdom*. I like it. Is that for real or do you just treat *this*," I gesticulated to her impossibly neat form as ash dropped off my cigarette, "librarian getup like some sort of virtual avatar?"

"It is my name," she replied succinctly. "Second question."

"Well if you are *Wisdom*," my voice was heavily

laden with sarcasm, "shouldn't you already know what the question's going to be?"

"Wisdom is not the same as all-knowing, and there are certain things that even we cannot foresee."

"Such as?"

Her head twisted and her steely eyes locked onto me. "Who is *Kanor*?"

I recalled a night from the previous week and the reaction of Marcus and Nightingale to hearing that name for the first time, not to mention the abject terror in Dave's description of his nightmare.

"Apart from from some badass vampire killer? I haven't got a clue. But we're skipping ahead here. My second question."

She nodded slightly.

"Where the hell are we?"

"We are in a place where things have gone terribly, terribly wrong, Samuel. Where time as you know it was supposed to proceed down one path. Something prevented the physical realm from heading in that direction. Instead it diverged and ended up here.

"We call it the Divergent Lands."

I shivered in the cold. "So what caused this?" I looked down and saw that all the fairies were now sat at our feet. They were enrapt and listening intently like school-kids around a teacher at story time. Now children, let's all listen to the tale of the Happy Apocalypse.

"Not a *what*, Samuel. A *who*."

"So?"

She dipped her head slightly. "We don't know. Our viewpoint does not extend that far. The Divergence obscures it. All we know is that it is near and," her eyes locked on me once more, "*you* are involved."

I jumped to my feet and windmilled my arms in disbelief. "You think that *I* caused this? Jesus, I don't even eat meat!"

"But you are a killer, Samuel. You have taken a life in cold blood."

I stopped mid-rant.

She sort of had me there.

"It wasn't cold blood," I mumbled. "It was self-defence."

They were silent and just watched me.

I squirmed. People knowing my darkest secrets was becoming an unsettling occurrence.

"It *was*."

Sophia sighed and stood up. "That is beside the point. All we know is that the Divergence will come about and that it will occur near you. You may not be the cause but you will, however, be intrinsically involved. You cannot avoid it. Perhaps it may be someone you know. Has someone entered your life recently? Someone with great power?"

Instinctively my hand tugged at the lobe of my silent ear. Sophia saw the tell for what it was.

"There is, isn't there?"

"No," I protested rather feebly.

She crossed her arms and peered at me over her dark-rimmed glasses. It was fifteen years ago and I had forgotten to bring Kinsley's *Hindu Goddesses* back on time. People were muttering behind me as I meekly handed over both the book and the appropriate fine.

"Name."

"But he couldn't do something like that." My voice was high and whiney. It had that *it's not fair* quality to it. "Yes, he's odd and he's creepy, but so are the *Addams Family* and everyone loves *them*."

"Samuel, I need his name." the voice was like ice, penetrating.

Damn it! I'd had enough. I was going to grow a back bone and stand up to my demons. I gave her my best *Paddington Bear* glower.

Sophia sighed and nodded to her tiny companions.

I realised that I had made somewhat of a miscalculation in my time to grow a spine. Paranormal creatures had no time or respect for rigid vertebrae. They darted towards me and, as I ducked, throwing my hands over my head, I felt them not only hit me at full tilt, but actually slide into my skin. My body started to jolt and leap all over the show as the fairies rummaged around inside, making their way up to my brain. It was not really painful as such, just somewhat awkward and intrusive. Then, as they reached the top I saw images of the last few days flash before my eyes. There was Caroline, the lying little bitch, pleading for my help in my office. There were Brande and Philips just before they both died. There was Spliff looking god-awful in his flat. Finally, there was Malcolm Wallace. Malcolm Wallace in front of the adoring masses. Malcolm Wallace sat in the shadows of the box at the Grand Theatre. Malcolm Wallace reducing the waitress to tears at *Guy's Café*.

I heard a schlurping noise as the little dervishes

extricated themselves then reported back to Sophia. She listened intently to them before lancing me with her attention once more.

"And you think that this man is not capable of great destruction?" Her voice was quite incredulous.

"He healed me," I protested. He's given me back my life.

Sophia shook her head and waved a hand in front of us. An image of Wallace appeared. She pointed at and it focussed in on his right hand. "Do you see that?"

I shrugged. "It's his hand." I was feeling rather peeved and uncooperative after having been interfered with by fairies.

"His ring," she glowered. "Look at it."

The image enhanced and the two coiled snakes were crystal clear: one with a red eye, the other with a black. I felt sick. I could see where this was going.

"You studied mythology, Samuel," the crisp librarian tone berated me. "You know what snakes represent."

"Dragons," I sighed.

"Dragons," she agreed. "What's more, there is something about this man. Or rather some one. He is not alone. I am sure of it. He has someone behind him. Someone old and powerful. I can smell her on him."

I thought back to the lilting voice singing at the back of the Credete meeting but kept my mouth shut on the matter. Instead I asked, "What now?"

"You distance yourself from Mister Wallace as soon as you can, Samuel. He is Death. He is Destruction. He is a danger not only to you but also to all those you love. His mistress is a jealous being and she will stop at nothing to get what she wants."

"And what do you think she wants?"

"To put it simply? Devotion or death."

I surveyed the wasteland around me and felt sick to the pit of my stomach. Everything was gone. Everything was destroyed. I could see no sign of life; not human or animal. Perhaps there was some somewhere, but here, where people had once bustled about their normal, mundane existences, there was nothing. Not a breath of vitality.

It was a barren land.

A divergent land.

Then a thought struck me and I turned to Sophia. "Another question. What was it supposed to be like? If the Divergence hadn't happened, what would have been here instead?"

She cocked her head to one side and I could tell that she was formulating a response that would be easily understood by a mere mortal like myself. After a small pause she said, "The Lord your God would have descended from Heaven on a throne of winged beings. The last trumpet would have sounded after which Heaven and Earth would have converged into one. The dead would have woken from their dark slumber and all pain would have ceased. The angels would have walked alongside their human cousins in a realm of perpetual bliss and harmony."

I closed my eyes, tears blurring at the edges. "You mean Paradise."

"Paradise," she said.

I opened my eyes. I was alone in my living room. A discarded coffee cup lay on the floor and rain beat against the dirty window on a cold, autumnal evening.

"Shit."

CHAPTER 12

Saturday morning crept up on me like a flea-infested, worm-ridden, three-legged dog. I kicked hard at it from under my bed clothes but it refused to leave me alone and eventually I surrendered to its tenacity and crawled out of bed. I showered, shaved and had just finished my breakfast when there was a resonant knocking at the door to my flat. I glanced at the carriage clock on the nearest bookshelf: nine o'clock. An early visit for a Saturday morning. I instantly began to worry but tried to reassure myself that at least they were knocking and not just appearing in the middle of my living room.

However, when I opened the door, my worry upgraded itself to panic. Jitendra stood there with a uniformed officer. He saw my eyes clock the bobby and said, "Good morning, Sam. May I come in?"

I stood back and gestured for him to enter. He did so on his own, leaving his companion stood with his back to my door. "Your friend not joining us?"

"I sincerely hope that he won't have to."

Oh, this was not good. I eased the door shut and stood facing the DCI. "What is it?"

"Yesterday afternoon, a young waitress at *Guy's Café* decided that she'd had enough of her employer. Now, whereas most would just hand in their cards and offer up a bit of verbal, she went a bit further."

My stomach was starting to sink. I could see where this was leading, and not to a happy ring of pixies in a forested glade where children go to drink ginger beer on long, hot summer afternoons.

"She went into the kitchen," Jitendra continued without even consulting a note book, "propped the door shut with a stool, picked up the nearest knife and stabbed her employer twenty times in quick succession before plunging the knife deep into her own stomach. Customers and other staff tried to intervene, but the jammed door prevented their access to the kitchen. By the time the paramedics arrived, both employer and employee had lost a drastic amount of blood. He died on the scene; she passed away in the ambulance."

I staggered over to the sofa and collapsed like a limp bag of bones and disconnected tissue. In my mind's eye I still saw the young girl dissolving under the acid touch of Wallace's tongue. "Dear God."

"When we questioned the witnesses, they stated that just prior to the act, the girl in question had undertaken a rather curious conversation with a pair of customers who had just left. One was described as a refined looking gentleman with striking white hair and orange eyes, the other was said to look like something out of a Mickey Spillane novel." He raised an eyebrow and awaited the inevitable response.

There was no point denying my being there. "I'd had a coffee there yesterday afternoon."

"Obviously." Jitendra gestured towards the mac and coat draped over my sofa. "You are somewhat *distinctive* in your attire. Care to tell me who your friend was?"

"An old uni friend."

He waited for more information like a heron waits quietly before spearing a minnow.

"His name's Wallace. Malcolm Wallace."

Jitendra nodded. "You have his address?"

"No."

"Phone number?"

"No."

"Not much of a friendship then," his voice loaded with sarcastic disbelief. "How are you supposed to meet up every now and then in order to encourage young waitresses to go psycho?"

"Now, hold on!" I surged from the sofa and started pounding my finger in his chest. "How dare you suggest that? I had nothing to do with what went on yesterday. Wallace dragged me along and all seemed fine until he just *turned.* One minute he was sweetness and light, the next he was turning that young girl's life upside down. And you know what? I think he was enjoying it. There was a look of total relish on his face as she realised that she was never going to come to anything. It was horrible to watch." I stopped, realised that jabbing a finger in the chest of a policeman was tantamount to assault and lowered my hand to my sides. "Please find him, lock him up and throw away the key. I'm done with him." I stomped off to the kitchen, yanked a cupboard door open and took out a bottle of Jack. I sloshed a good measure into a tumbler and marched back into the living room.

Jitendra was still stood waiting for me. "Anything else that you want to add? If I take him into custody will he inexplicably die under questioning?"

I snorted my contempt at the cheap shot. "Trust me, right now I'd see that as a blessing." I threw back half of the bourbon; it added extra heat to my ire. "Wallace is toxic! I was employed to investigate a little group that he runs. He tells people that anything is possible and they, in turn, treat him like some sort of Messiah."

"You mean Credete?"

That struck me like a fish across the face. "You know of it?"

"Of course we do, Sam. What do you think we do all day? Watch television? We've known about that little group for some time now and I don't like having a cult on my doorstep, trust me. I've tried to get it infiltrated before now, but to no avail." He paused, thinking. "Did you get in?"

"Yes," I answered carefully, worried about where this conversation was going. "I went to a meeting a few days back with a friend, Abalone Morris. She's a music teacher at Saint Edmund Campion. That's where I met Wallace, at the meeting. I didn't even know he was around here until then."

Jitendra slowly paced around my living room, his

polished shoes making next to no noise on the cheap nylon carpet. His eyes wandered from clock to clock in a carefree manner, but I knew that his mind was honed like the sharpest scalpel and he was about to make a critical incision close to the heart of the matter. "I want you to get in touch with Wallace again and gain as much information as you can on him: what he's up to, how he holds sway over people, where he's been before he set up this little shebang of his."

I shook my head violently. This was all I needed. I was not only being manipulated by paranormal entities but now also by the mundane and corporeal. "Not a chance. No way. I'm done with Wallace and I'm certainly not going all James Bond for anyone else. I'm forgetting the whole sorry mess and getting back to my ghouls, ghosties and goblins. I'm sick of people or entities pressing my buttons or tugging on my heart strings. I'm finished with it!"

Jitendra stopped his pacing, stood square in front of me and locked his eyes on mine. "Really?"

"Really." Although part of me was now having serious doubts on the matter.

He nodded to himself. "Right now, we are the only two people who know what really happened in Williamson Park. The constable outside is a new lad, a bit green one might say. Also, he's very eager. He's not nicked anyone yet. I'm sure he'd bring his granny in if there was so much as a whiff of trouble about her. I think you'll do this little favour, just for old times sake." He walked up to me, took the remains of my drink and downed it in one. The bastard had me exactly where he wanted me. "I'll be in touch next week for my information."

After the door swung shut and the footsteps of Jitendra and little boy blue retreated down the stairs, I slouched down into the padded comfiness of my sofa to consider my lot in life. Had I done something truly evil in a previous existence? Had I been a ruthless dictator or, even worse, a banker? What had caused me to be the butt of so many people's machinations? All I wanted was a quiet life. A few DVDs, the television remote and a decent bourbon. Was that too much to ask for? Instead, my life was rapidly spiralling into the plot of a Dan Brown novel – intrigue and conspiracies teasing and trailing the hapless hero as he stumbles his way through a repetitive series of dastardly dangerous events.

I had hoped that my first week on the job had been a hiccough, a blip on an otherwise sedate and calmly satisfying career. However, it was becoming apparent that it was to be the norm.

Perhaps I could just run away, leave it all behind? What would I do? I would have to live off cash only, no tech lifestyle so that Jitendra's boys would never find me. Yes, that was doable. I could manage that... for about a week! Then I would realise that I had no perceivable life skills to earn said cash and that I was missing my television with such devastating force that I would come crawling back and have to face the music.

How about if I found somewhere quiet where I could just go and *be*? There was a Buddhist retreat centre up in the Lakes. Perhaps I could spend my life there in peace and solitude. The food would not be a problem. Buddhism was compatible with veganism. But was it compatible with sci-fi? How would the monks feel when I started making lightsaber noises during morning classes of Tai Chi? I didn't think they would be too impressed.

No, I was stuck here, not through any third party keeping me here, but through my own inability to actually make do with the things that made my life fun. What was the point of a life on the run if it was miserable? A life without the comforts of home would be no life whatsoever. I would just have to stay put, grinning and bearing it.

"Hello, Mister Rock," I said to a point of space just to my right. "I'd like to introduce you to my friend here," I gesticulated to a space on my left, "Miss Hard Place. Now, I know she looks like a cold-hearted bitch with a face set in granite, but I assure you that she's quite the party girl. A few vodka martinis and she'll be on the table boogieing away to *Dancing Queen*. What's that, Miss Hard Place?" I turned to my left. "You think that Mister Rock is a rather fetching young man, but he really needs to pull his trousers up because he's showing far too much of his Calvin Klein underpants? Well I must agree, he does need to do something about his attire, but I'm sure you'll be able to whip him into... What the hell am I doing?" I yelled to my empty room. There are times when your sanity can be pushed just that little bit too far.

Fortunately, at that moment, my mobile rang. I fished it out, saw who was trying to contact me and smiled. Perhaps today was going to get a bit better after all?

"I'm just coming down Penny Street. I hope you've got some coffee brewing."

Good old Spliff, straight to the point, no messing around.

"To what do I owe this impromptu visit?" I switched my mobile to speakerphone as I started to prep the coffee machine in the kitchen. "It's not even ten. Isn't this early for you?"

There was silence.

"Spliff?" I yelled across the kitchen. "You still there?"

"You've forgotten."

Uh oh. "Forgotten what?"

"Oh, Sam. How could you?"

I started to wrack my brains as I poured the water into the coffee maker. What the hell had I forgotten? It wasn't his birthday; that I was sure of. It sounded important though. I switched the coffee maker on and picked the phone up as I wandered back through to the living room. As I did, I couldn't help but notice the unusual amount of people milling around Dalton Square in front of the Town Hall – people and a great, big outside broadcast van.

"Oh no," I groaned.

Spliff did not even bother to knock on the door to my flat; he never does. Instead, he barged in and did what he always does upon entering my alleged Fortress of Solitude: he complained bitterly. "I can never understand why the hell you have to live up so many stairs? It's worse than going for a stroll up Kilimanjaro."

"Good morning to you too," I smiled. "What's that?"

My old friend beamed from ear to ear as he thumped a parcel which had been hastily wrapped in dog-eared newspaper onto my coffee table. "This," he proclaimed dramatically as he unveiled the layers of some trashy tabloid, "is our ticket to get to see *her.*"

"That?"

"Yes. This."

"It's a dog."

There on my table was the scruffiest piece of chinaware that I had ever had the misfortune to lay my eyes upon. It was a black china dog, a terrier of some kind with wiry hair and squinty-looking eyes. I felt that if anyone from the Ming Dynasty were to lay their eyes on it they would have gone away and taken up metalwork.

"It's bloody awful!"

Spliff gave me a *look.* "What do you mean?"

"Oh, come on, Spliff," I laughed, fishing out a Lucky. "It's just... It's just..." I lit the cigarette and drew on the nicotine for help in searching for the right form of criticism. "It's just so *scruffy.* It's all black and wiry and looks like it hasn't seen a good clean for at least twelve months."

"Well, it's just like your scrotum, then," he snapped back. "Anyway," he sulked, picking up his supposed meal ticket, "I only just bought him from Oxfam. I saw him in the window and thought how cute and adorable he looked – perfect for getting me onto the show. All he needs is a little cleaning up."

I shook my head and continued to draw on the

Lucky. "He needs something, that's for sure. Perhaps a flea treatment?"

Spliff's icy silence slapped me in the face.

"Okay, okay. If you want to clean him up before we go over the road, help yourself."

Spliff swept past me, muttering something about bloody useless friends and stomped off into the kitchen. I heard the water run as he started to bathe his china dog. I followed behind, chuckling quietly to myself, then the image of Jitendra and his boy in blue drifted into my head. I opened my mouth to tell Spliff about Wallace and the waitress just as he turned round, drying his beloved pooch in a tea towel. "What's up with you, now? Catching flies?"

Slowly, I closed my gaping mouth. I would keep things to myself for now. I would tell him later.

"No. Nothing's wrong. Let's go see your beloved Ms. Briers."

The Ashton Hall was quite different in atmosphere from my last visit. The happy, smiley faces of enthusiastic group members had been replaced by expressions that were a mixture of concern and excitement as owners of antiques carefully ferried themselves about from queue to queue in the hope that their great-aunt's hand-embroidered silk bloomers (which they had no intention of selling whatsoever) would gain them five precious minutes on prime time television.

The lilac-coloured banner adorned with its stylised logo had been replaced by mobile studio cameras, bright lighting and boom microphones. I couldn't help but smile. The transformation was quite extraordinary.

"So where do you think she is?" Spliff asked, raising himself up on tiptoes to peer over the crowds.

"If you mean the wonderful Ms. Briers, I have no idea. I guess she's cozying up with some photogenic little old dear ready for her next, greatest photo shoot."

He shot me a withering look. "*Harmony's* nothing like that at all. She'll be mixing with the masses, bringing them joy in their otherwise dull, dull existences."

I shook my head. He was totally smitten.

So, for now, we were pursuing Spliff's own personal little piece of icon-worship that made him go all kittenish and trembly at the knees: Harmony Briers demurely sexy actor of the Shakespearian stage and champion of old people's even older bits and bobs. He waded through the mass of individuals carrying their great aunt's china urns or whatever it was they had and stood on tiptoe again to try and gain a sighting of his quarry. I contented myself to shamble along behind him.

I glanced at my watch. How long was this going to take? I was supposed to be finding a way to reingratiate myself with Wallace. It crossed my mind that I hadn't told Spliff about my morning visitation. Was there a reason? Was I being deceptive? Was it that I felt like I was being used as a spy by Jitendra? I ignored the questions and just followed my antique-laden friend.

"Damn it!" he cursed, gaining himself a reproachful look from an elderly woman in her seventies, "I can't see her. Oh, Sam, what am I to do?"

I was about to suggest giving up and heading over

to the Borough when I heard a silky smooth voice say from behind, "Can I help you, Reverend?"

Spliff turned, about to launch into some diatribe about stuffing one body part up another when he clocked the man's ID badge, marking him as part of the production crew. "Why, young man," he effused, all sweetness, light and buttered crumpets, "I certainly hope you can. We have come here, desperate to have my grandmother's china dog valued." His arm that wasn't clutching the hastily-wrapped dog bear hugged me to his side. "Could you possibly point *us* in the right direction. It would mean so much to both of *us*."

"What?" I gasped.

"Oh!" exclaimed the runner. "Of course, I can. Why don't you follow me?"

He turned and headed off towards a corner of the hall. Spliff made to follow him but was jerked back violently by the grasp of my hand. "What the hell are you playing at?" I hissed under my breath. "*Us*?" I demanded, my eyebrows threatening to shoot off the top of my forehead.

Spliff rolled his eyes. "Oh, come on, Sam. Everyone knows that the gay demographic is so vitally important on the Beeb these days. You should know that being all sci-fi and what not. Look at Doctor Who and Torchwood. I'm surprised they haven't painted the TARDIS pink yet."

There are times when my best friend causes words to fail me and the only sane response I could give would be with a very sharp machete. This was one of those moments. My mouth flapped open and shut as

Spliff wrapped his arm around me, bundling me off after the runner. "Come along, *darling*. We mustn't keep the good man waiting, must we?"

As we made our way through the crowds of antique holders I noticed a face in the crowd. There, at the edge of the room was a grey-haired man whose eyes seemed to follow me. I strained to get a better look at him, but a rather large lady wearing a horrendously flowery dress and carrying a parlour palm in an art deco vase sailed in front of me. By the time she had finished eclipsing the light from the windows, the man was nowhere to be seen. I frowned. He had looked familiar, but for now I needed to keep up with Spliff.

We were led directly to a table that was set up with an expert, a camera man and someone who, judging by the large headphones, appeared to be a sound technician. A number of people who had obviously been waiting in the queue for quite a while chuntered and murmured amongst themselves. If looks could kill then the antiques mafia would have been taking out a bounty on our heads. Spliff, of course, was either totally oblivious or just didn't give a monkey's bottom. I lowered my head and tried to avoid the glares.

"Trevor! Trevor!" the runner called out to the seated expert. "I have a perfect one for you. This is Reverend..." he turned to Spliff who was beaming jovially from ear to self-satisfied ear, "I'm sorry, I didn't catch your name."

"MacIntyre," he provided. "Reverend James Francis MacIntyre. I'm the chaplain at Luneside University."

"Marvellous," the runner simpered. "Reverend MacIntyre and his partner..."

"Actually, I'm not his... Ow!"

"... have brought an item in for you to look at."

"Jolly good!" Trevor was a rather red-faced man in his fifties with the sort of moustache that normally deserves a good twirling. He leaned over the table and shook hands vigorously with both of us. He had something of a perspiration problem and I had to resist the urge to wipe my hand on my coat. Spliff was now in full flow and slid onto the empty seat next to the man without even being asked. "So what is it you chaps have for me then?"

I sighed in resignation and dropped down next to my best friend as he dug his china dog out of his shopping bag. "It's this little fellow, Trevor. I inherited him a few years back when my dear mother died. She in turn had inherited him from her mother, so he's been in the family for quite a while now. We're all very attached to him."

I had to admire his balls. As far as I was aware, Spliff's parents were still alive and kicking north of the border. I wondered what they would make of this if it was aired then I decided that after almost forty years of him, they were probably used to his various shenanigans by now.

Trevor took the dog from Spliff and turning it over in his hands started to comment on such things as its glaze, its colour and its markings. I, in turn, started to tune out the event and let my eyes wander around the room. There were huddles of onlookers surrounding us, peering over each others' shoulders and pointing at the charity piece that Spliff had brought along. *If only they knew*, I thought to myself. Then, through the undulating current of the crowds, I caught sight of the grey-haired man once again. He was stood off to one side and, when he saw me, began to walk slowly in my direction. As he did so, I saw that he was limping and realisation struck me: it was Mister Flint, caretaker of the Ashton Hall, the man who had annoyed Malcolm at the end of the Credete meeting on Wednesday. I smiled at him and he nodded a silent acknowledgement.

"Well this is interesting." These words from Trevor The Expert, caught my attention and I swivelled back to see what was going on. He was carefully examining a marking underneath the china dog. "My, my, I don't get to see many of these at all."

"What is it?" Spliff was perched on the edge of his chair, rapt. "Is it good?"

"It most certainly is. This mark here," the expert leant over with the dog and pointed to a series of blue smudges on its base, "tells us where it was made and indeed by whom. It was cast right here in Lancaster, by none other than Robert Gillow."

I frowned. "Correct me if I'm wrong, but wasn't he a furniture maker, not a potter?"

"Indeed he was," Trevor beamed, "but just after his marriage in 1729 and before he set up shop the year after, he experimented with china wares. Some say it was boredom, some that it was a failed business venture. Personally I think they were gifts for his new wife, but then I'm an old romantic at heart."

There was a pause as the unasked question circulated the table. Robert Gillow. Chinaware. How much?

It was Spliff who voiced what we were both thinking. "So, not that I'm ever thinking of parting with it, but, you know... is it at all valuable?"

Trevor stroked his chin and motioned for the runner. "I think we need Harmony on film with this one."

I thought Spliff was going to explode, not only was his bit of tat seemingly valuable, but he was going to meet Ms. Briers as well. I chuckled quietly to myself then saw Mister Flint beckon to me with a sideways nod of the head. I leant over to Spliff and whispered in his ear, "Listen, I have to go."

"What? Oh? Okay." He was in shock. I decided to leave him there. Patting him on the shoulder I made my excuses to the television crew and made my way over to the caretaker.

"Hello again," I smiled.

"Not here. Too public. Follow me." He limped off through the crowd. I shrugged and followed him.

He led me away from the masses of tat-laden hopefuls to a small corridor off the main hall. Carefully, he closed the door behind us and looked up and down to make sure that we were alone. "I saw you here on Wednesday," he said.

"That's right. A friend dragged me along."

"A friend?" He shook his head in disbelief. "No friend would bring you to that... that..." He searched for the right word. "Monster."

I arched a somewhat shocked eyebrow. Harsh

words indeed. "You mean Malcolm Wallace? I hardly think overrunning a bit for a few weeks makes someone a monster."

"That's not what I mean. He's evil. Perverse."

I drummed my fingernails against my teeth. This was getting rather high on the weirdness factor. "Okay, friend, you'd better explain what you mean."

"You saw them. You saw what they were like. They all went off their rockers. You did too. I saw you. You were all standing up yelling his little slogan over and over again. It's not right."

"He also healed the girl. You saw that? Made her get up and walk."

Flint nodded his head quickly, nervously. "Sure he healed her. He healed her good and proper. But tell me this, how d'you think she got sick in the first place? Hmmm?"

"She told me it was after a dream."

"A dream? A nightmare more like," he shouted then snapped his head left and right scared witless that he had been overheard. "Since when did dreams start to make people sick? Really, you believe that's natural?"

He sort of had me there so I let him continue.

"Don't you think it strange that a man who can turn a group of normal folk into a bunch of gibbering loons is presented with a little girl who was crippled by a dream? Don't you think it's possible that he had something to do with her illness? Don't you think he was responsible for that dream, that nightmare? If he fixed her, then perhaps he was the one who broke her?"

My stomach churned. I had not even fully

considered the girl's story. Wallace had interrupted us before I could ask her anything. "Tell me, what other sorts of healing have there been?"

Flint opened his mouth to speak then, as if a breeze had brushed his face, he shuddered and his eyes glazed over. "I... I have to go," he murmured and he dashed past me back into the hall.

I swore under my breath and chased after him. I caught a fleeting glimpse of the caretaker diving into the crowd of people and made to follow him. Unfortunately the same woman as before walked in front of me and glared across her ample bosom as I almost knocked her parlour palm out of her hands. I apologised and dodged around her only to feel a hand close on my arm. I spun around, my fist raised instinctively and stared down into the cringing face of the runner. "Oh God, sorry," I apologised. "Somewhat on edge."

He backed off slightly, nervously watching my fist as I lowered it down and thrust it deep into a pocket. "I thought you might like to see this." He motioned over to the table where Spliff was still sat, only now he was accompanied by the demure Ms. Briers.

I glanced around the hall. Flint had disappeared. There was no way I could catch him now. I would ring the Town Hall on Monday morning and arrange to meet him. For now, the sight of Spliff sat smiling like Tinkerbell on Prozac would be a much welcome diversion.

"So," Harmony Briers purred, "I believe we have quite a find here."

"Indeed we do." This was Trevor The Expert, hamming up his time in front of the camera for all it was worth. "This charming little dog came in this morning with Reverend MacIntyre here."

"It sure is a curious little piece." I had to admit there certainly was something about her. Was it her eyes, her voice or just her mannerisms; I could not tell. What I could tell thought was that Spliff had it bad. Oh, *so* bad.

"It was my mother's."

"Really?"

"Yes. I call it Scrotum."

I slapped my palm over my face and did my best not to laugh, I really did. Peeping through my fingers I saw a perplexed Ms. Briers shoot a look at the cameraman. He twirled his fingers: *carry on.*

Ever the professional she turned to Trevor The Expert and asked, "So what makes this little chap so special?"

Trevor puffed out his chest and entered into his little spiel about Gillow and his wife as Spliff just continued to sit and stare in awe at his own object of wonder.

"So, Trevor," Harmony Briers smiled, "this begs the question, *how much is Reverend MacIntyre's Scrotum worth*?"

Did she just say what I think she said: I wondered, open-mouthed. Trevor The Expert was also exhibiting an expression of jaw-dropping shock, but the words that came were nothing to do with Spliff's valuable china dog.

"Dear God!" he gasped, staring up behind the camera.

I turned and followed his gaze. There on the

balcony level, overlooking the hall stood Flint. He had a noose tied around his neck. There was a rush of feet as a number of people dashed out of the hall towards the stairs to the upper level. I manoeuvred myself away from Spliff and his moment of joy. The fat woman in the flowery dress got in my way once more. This time I just shoved her and ignored the complaints and abuse she poured onto my back. What the hell was going on? I heard a loud hammering as people pounded on the doors leading to the balcony. They must have been either locked or jammed shut.

Flint climbed tentatively up onto the wooden wall surrounding the balcony and sat there staring off into space. His eyes were fixed on something that we could not see, something in his own field of view that was driving him to this final act of desperation. Tears were streaming down the man's cheeks. His hands were gripping the edge of the balcony, their knuckles corpse white. His lips were moving over and over in some sort of silent litany. Rapidly flickering over his teeth, they told of the hidden motive for this scene but I could not make out a word of it even with my new, improved hearing. Then, as if waking from, dare I say it, a dream, Flint's eyes were bright and full to the brim with terror.

"You cannot escape him!" He screamed, a tremulous falsetto grasping his tense vocal chords. "He will come for you in your dreams!"

"Oh no," I whispered. This was not good. Not good at all.

Flint tugged at the noose; it pulled taut against the railing. There were gasps from the crowd and the pounding on the doors increased. It sounded like someone was hitting them with something heavy like a fire extinguisher.

Satisfied that the noose was secure, Flint gripped the side of the balcony once more and opened his mouth shouting out, "*The Divergence is coming!*" before pushing off. There was a deep twanging noise as the rope stretched to its maximum and a resonant smacking as it hit the wall of the balcony. An almighty crash came from the doors as someone finally broke their way through and clambered through the seating to the railing. Arm over arm they heaved the dead weight of the caretaker up, but I, like everyone else in the Ashton Hall, knew Mister Flint was no more.

We were still there an hour later. The police had turned up alongside the paramedics. The ambulance guys had found little to do apart from shake their heads and respectfully cover Mister Flint's body with a cloth. The boys in blue, however, were definitely at the peak of their game. Everyone was questioned from shocked members of the public through to horrified production crew.

Then they reached me.

At this point they rang for backup.

Backup stormed into the hall wearing a perfectly pressed suit and a face like thunder. It grabbed me by the arm and dragged me away from prying ears and eyes as it growled under its breath, "I leave you alone for less than three hours and I have another body on my hands. Three hours, Sam! Are you trying to prove a point or do you just think I love my paperwork?"

I snatched my arm away from his grip. "Back off, Jitendra! It's not my fault!"

"Really?" His face was nose to nose with mine. I could smell peppermint on his breath and his pupils bored into mine. "Tell that to the bodies that seem to be following you around right now? One yesterday. One today. Not to mention five stiff actors."

I frowned. The actors. Two attempted and three completed suicides. My mind raced back to Philips, his terrified eyes and his gravelly voice. "The Divergence is coming," I whispered.

Jitendra backed off shaking his head. "Don't go all hoodoo on me, Sam. I need answers here."

"No, no. I'm not." Running my fingers through my hair I paced in a small circle. "Just before Philips dropped down dead, he said,'The Divergence is coming,' didn't he?"

The DCI nodded. "Go on."

"Well so did Flint."

"You're sure?"

"Positive. Ask your men. I'm sure all the other witnesses will have heard it. It was pretty hard to miss as he had centre stage somewhat."

Jitendra frowned. "So, you're saying that Flint was connected to your abductors?"

"No, not exactly."

"Well, what then?" Exasperation was touching the policeman's voice. "Come on, Sam. Give it to me straight."

"You're not gonna like it."

"I'm a big boy."

"Okay," I shrugged. "I first met Flint here during the week when I came to the Credete meeting. He had a bit of a run in with Wallace about the meeting overrunning. Then he seeks me out today and starts rambling on about how Wallace is a monster and how he somehow sets up people's illnesses by entering their dreams and how he controls the crowds and gets them whipped up into a frenzy.

"Flint was scared for his life. He was a man on the point of running away and hiding in a deep hole up a very tall hill, but then he just suddenly changed. It was as if someone had gotten inside his mind and told him what to do."

"You think Wallace made Flint kill himself?"

I nodded.

"You think Wallace killed those actors?"

I nodded again.

"Shit."

"I said you wouldn't like it."

Jitendra stood staring off into the middle distance, his mind working overtime. The longer he thought, the more I started to worry. I felt like I was in one of those situations where you find you have somehow backed yourself into an awkward corner. I had been unknowingly treading step after step, toe to heel into a very tight spot with zero space for manoeuvrability. There were long jagged spikes protruding from sheer walls and they would snag me whichever way I tried to turn.

"I need more info," he eventually said.

I groaned as the metaphorical spikes snagged me

and held on tight.

"I want you to meet up with Wallace again and get as much information out of him as is possible."

I desperately tried to twist and turn away from the barbs of my mind. "I don't have his number. I can't contact him."

"But I think you know someone who can."

"No."

"Is that *no* you won't or *no* you don't?"

"You know damn well which one it is." I pictured those sparking blue eyes framed by light blonde hair. Anger began to well up inside me. How could this arrogant copper ask this of me? "It's too dangerous."

"Sam, people are dying. You want that to continue?" He turned and left.

I stood panting heavily on my own. I had an awful feeling about this. My stomach was churning and I felt like a total cad, but he was right; people were dying.

More would die.

I fished out my mobile and flicked through the contacts.

"Hi, Abalone. How's it going?"

CHAPTER 13

It was a crisp autumnal afternoon as we drove out of the city. We drove east along Ashton Road out towards Glasson. Just past Conder Green, Abalone instructed me to turn down a freshly tarmacked drive. I let out a low whistle when I saw *chez Wallace*. It was immense; a wide stone construction that looked like it had been crafted by Hebrew slaves. There were wide, stained glass windows overlooking the rolling fields that surrounded the house. Stonework had been carved and fashioned into all manner of animals mythical and real along the roof top. Everywhere I looked the building screamed, "Money!" It had seen one hell of a financial investment over the years.

"I know," she whispered reverentially as if approaching the Holy of Holies, "it's an amazing place. A real testament to his message."

I forced a smile whilst feeling sick inside. How could such a bright, intelligent girl be completely suckered in by this guy? Then I remembered the dead fiancé. A car crash had claimed his life and Abalone had gone running into the avuncular arms of the reassuring Wallace.

A dark thought crossed my mind.

Had it really been an accident? What if..?

No, surely not. How could Wallace have orchestrated something like that? Yet, Flint had insisted that he could control peoples' dreams; that he had made the little Watts girl sick in her dream. Was it really beyond the realm of imagination that he could have contrived the death of Abalone's fiancé? Could he be responsible?

Possibly. But why?

"Therein lies the rub," I muttered.

"Pardon?" Abalone raised a blonde eyebrow as I pulled the car to a halt in front of the huge, rambling pile. "You quoting Shakespeare for some reason in particular?"

"Sorry. Just thinking out loud. It's a bad habit."

She leant across the hand brake and breathed into my ear. "I *love* bad habits."

I felt my cheeks glow hotter than a television bought down the local pub and she pulled back giggling lightly. Smiling, I let my eyes look at her there in the passenger seat. She was truly an amazing woman, full of life and vitality.

And I had lied to her.

I had rung her up and told her that Malcolm and I had argued the other day and that I wanted to go see him and apologise. I stressed that it was really playing on my mind (at least that bit was not a lie) and that I wanted to see him that afternoon. Could she arrange it.

She had said of course it was possible. She would ring Malcolm and arrange it while I drove over to meet her.

She had believed me implicitly like a child believes their parent will always be kind, careful and loving.

I had kicked this child in the face.

"What's the matter?"

"Nothing," I said dismissively, whilst building another falsehood. "Just worried about seeing Malcolm."

"I told you, it will be okay," she reassured me. "Now come on, let's go and see him."

Abalone, dear sweet Abalone, opened her door and climbed out of my VW Polo. I did likewise and as I followed her up across the drive we saw the front door swing open and there he stood: Malcolm Wallace, who some claimed to be the most evil man I had ever met. What did he do right then? Did he stare me down with those freakishly orange eyes of his? Did he shout tirades of abuse at me and slam the door in my face? Did he greet his darling disciple whilst giving the estranged acquaintance the cold shoulder?

He did none of these.

He walked across the drive, arms outstretched and enveloped his prodigal son in one all-forgiving hug.

The inside of the Wallace's house was just as impressive as the out. The creatures that had lined the rooftop were also to be found carved into oak panelling that lined the hallway and the study to which he led us. I made out lions, panthers, dogs, crocodiles...

And dragons.

Lots of dragons.

Dragons were starting to follow me everywhere now. It was creeping me out somewhat.

When dragons walk the Earth then all creation shall tremble.

What was the connection between them and the Divergence? There had been two dragons in my dream the previous week: one red, one black. Was Wallace one of them? Was he really going to be the cause of the Divergence? What was his connection to this mysterious Kanor? *Was* he Kanor?

All these loose ends and unanswered questions made my head hurt but I kept my discomfort well hidden and said nothing. I just smiled amicably as we sat on a plush upholstered sofa that looked like it cost more than my father used to earn in a year and Wallace poured us all a cup of what smelt like Earl Grey tea; its delicate lemony fragrance danced in my nostrils as I slowly sipped from the fine china cup.

Classical music played quietly from discreet speakers as Wallace told us how pleased he was that we had come out to see him. He had been terribly concerned about how he and I had parted company the other day. He had wanted to ring me but did not want to intrude. He had been so terribly afraid that I would just hang up on him. It would have broken his heart.

Damn, he was just as good a liar as I was.

"Tell me, Malcolm," I smiled, settling the china teacup down on its delicate saucer, "your collection must have increased quite a bit since you showed it to me at university."

"Collection?" Abalone asked, genuinely curious

and oblivious to the swathes of deception that swaddled her.

Wallace chuckled to himself. "Samuel is referring to my collection of esoterica. Something of a hobby and yes indeed it has grown immensely. Would you like to see it?"

"If it's no bother." I settled the cup and saucer down on a coaster.

"No bother at all." He rose and made his way over to a door at the back of the room. "This way."

Abalone and I followed him out of the comfortable study with its background orchestral accompaniment and delicately flavoured tea. To begin with the ambient light in the back room was low; there were no windows, just electric illumination. Wallace fiddled with a switch on the wall and the lighting rose.

Abalone gasped.

I had to admit that was also rather impressed. His collection had certainly expanded. What had once been confined to a box under his bed was now displayed in glass cases around a room that was roughly the same size as the ground floor of an average-sized house. Abalone was wandering around from cabinet to cabinet with her mouth open, obviously blown away by this side of Wallace that she had never seen before. There were scrolls, brooches, robes, pendants. All sorts of paraphernalia.

Wallace acted the benevolent guide, talking us through the most interesting pieces. "Most of my artefacts, as Sam knows, are pre-biblical. Here we have original texts from ancient Ur. Totally impossible to put a price on. Here is some Hittite cuneiform."

Abalone peered down at the small clay tablets he was pointing to. "What is it?"

"Cuneiform? It's an ancient alphabet, my dear. Very hard to translate. Fortunately, I have someone in the know," Wallace winked knowingly.

"Would that be your mysterious benefactor?" I asked, my eyes scanning the cases for anything familiar.

"Why indeed it would, Samuel. Indeed it would."

The thought of killer heels clicking on a kitchen floor flashed across my memory. "She must be getting on a bit these days?"

Wallace let out a bray of laughter. Abalone looked at me, perplexed. I shrugged. "Oh, Samuel. You still have no idea, do you?" He tapped his index finger against his lips in thought and his curious ring glinted in the light. "Come, let me show you both something familiar."

Abalone and I dutifully followed him to a wide cabinet at the back of the room. She gasped and I felt my mouth drop open in disbelief. "How on Earth..?"

There, tucked away reverentially in Wallace's private collection was a vast collection of small clay figurines. They all depicted a similar form: the bust of a woman presenting her breasts. Not only that, but in the middle of them stood a cast statue of about one metre in height. It was of a woman staring straight in front dressed in a long gown whilst holding two serpents apart, one in each outstretched arm.

"Is this Minoan?" I asked, peering closer at the statuette. "it looks like one I've seen before but..."

"Very good, Samuel," Wallace purred as if lavishing praise on a somewhat dim student. The patronising tone made me feel sick inside. "You're close, but not quite there. It is like the famous Minoan deities, but it is in fact Canaanite. Very old, very precious and totally unique."

"Why's it not in a museum?" Abalone frowned.

"Because it is mine, dear. And whatever I want I shall have because..."

"Anything is possible," I finished.

Wallace nodded silently.

I looked around the base of the statue. There were wooden sticks entwined with black and red ribbons. My mind darted back once more to Luneside University, this time examining Wallace's room. I had picked up something similar. Spliff had identified it. "It's Asherah," I whispered. "This is the goddess Asherah." In my mind's eye I saw Credete's banner of a capital T wrapped in two swirling lines. I glanced at the two snakes that made up Wallace's ring. "You worship her, don't you? That's what all this is; it's your personal shrine to your goddess."

Wallace bowed, his arms out to his side. "Guilty as charged. I became infatuated with Her Ladyship back when I was younger. I live to serve her."

"So you worship an ancient goddess?" Abalone's eyes were bright and wide in wonder. "That's rather cool."

"Thank you, my dear. Now why don't we go back to my study. I shall fetch us some refreshments."

We turned and headed back to the door through which we entered. As we did my eyes wandered up above the door frame and I caught sight of another statue. This one was displayed on a large shelf above the door. It was a creature with the heads of a lion and a goat and a tail in the form of a serpent.

The Chimera.

The same image that I had seen as a statue on a set at John O'Gaunt media, as a painting at the house of Howard Baines and as a necklace around the neck of Melanie Brande.

I snatched my eyes away from the beast of Greek mythology and couldn't help but look at our host.

He was smiling knowingly.

In my heart of hearts I now knew for sure that I was looking at a serial killer. Five actors, a waitress and a caretaker. How he had done it, I was not sure. All I could think of was his little mantra: *Anything Is Possible.* I shuddered and walked through the door into the study.

As I seated myself down, Abalone discreetly enquired of Wallace as to where she could powder her nose. Being the gentleman that he liked to appear, he offered to show her where the relevant room was on the way to the kitchen where he would brew some more tea.

As soon as they had left the room I was over to his desk in a flash. I needed information. What information, though, I was not sure. I was guessing that he would not have a list lying around on his desk entitled, "Innocent people I feel like killing on a whim". One by one I pulled out his desk drawers and rifled through them whilst classical music continued to be piped through his hidden speakers. The drawers

227

contained the usual things one would find: pens, staplers, scissors and a hole punch. No luck there. I rummaged through the books and papers he had neatly arranged on the desk's work-surface. Again, not much of any use. There were books regarding translations of ancient languages and archaeological finds and what seemed to be printouts of testimonials by members of Credete claiming how Wallace had changed their lives.

I shook my head and turned on the monitor to the computer. The screen flashed into life and I was presented with a login screen. I groaned.

Now, if this had been a film, I would have probably found the password on the third attempt. The first attempt would have been Credete as that was the name of Wallace's organisation and always the first attempt of film hackers. The next would have been Asherah as that which means something to the user is always the second choice. Then, if it had been a film, my trusted sidekick would come up with a comment that started something like, "Wait a minute. Don't you remember..." and we would input something blindingly obvious from three scenes previous. As it was, this was not a film and I had no perky little sidekick so I just turned the monitor off and gave up on that idea.

As I tapped my fingers against my teeth, my eyes were drawn back once more to the testimonials. I riffled through them again and paid them a bit more care and attention.

Here was a woman who had received a massive raise at work. She had been on the verge of suicide after her brother had gone missing the previous year.

Here was a man who had suddenly rediscovered the will to live after having been diagnosed with a mysterious illness a few months before joining Credete.

My heart started to pound as I read on. They all followed the same pattern: some sort of tragedy, join Credete, tragedy cured or relieved. They all also contained the names of the individuals. I whipped out my notebook and started to scribble down a list as I mentally made a note of their stories. I kept one ear cocked for the sound of footsteps approaching the study down the hallway. How long had Abalone and Wallace been gone? I had no idea. I had lost track of time. Was the same piece of music playing? If so, how long for? I ignored the sound of violins and wind instruments and carried on with the matter at hand.

As I started to write down the tenth name I heard a noise from outside the room. I quickly shoved the printouts back where I thought they should lay and sidestepped over to a bookcase where I pulled a random book off the shelf and pretended to peruse the volume of literature.

"You reading?" I turned to be greeted by a pair of sparkling blue eyes.

"It appears I am," I replied in as casual manner as I could manage.

Abalone looked over her spectacles at the book and frowned, "*Fly Fishing* by J.R.Hartley. I never knew that was really a book."

"Neither did I," I managed, closing the book and sliding it up on the shelf. What followed was one of those awkward little silences that seem to stalk me. It was

229

broken when I realised that Abalone had placed a hand on my arm.

"Sam..."

The moment was broken by a polite cough from the doorway. "If I'm interrupting..?"

Abalone quickly snatched her hand back and a slight red blushed on her cheeks. I turned to Wallace who was brandishing a silver tray containing a fresh pot of tea and some scones. "Actually, Malcolm, I've just had a text. I'm afraid I need to be heading off."

He actually looked disappointed at the matter. "What a shame. Ah well, can't be helped. I'd better let you two lovebirds fly out into the night."

"Lovebirds..." I floundered. "Oh no, we're not... I mean, we're just..."

He raised a hand to quell my babbling. "Say no more, Samuel. Well thank you for dropping by. It was good to put things straight, so to speak. I hope you found what you were looking for."

Ice shot down my spine. "Pardon?"

"I hope you found resolution to our unfortunate incident."

I nodded. "I got just what I needed."

As I parked up opposite Abalone's house on Dunkeld Street she unclipped her seat belt and smiled at me. "I really enjoyed that."

"Good." I managed. I had been scared somewhat shitless, personally, but then I had been there under rather false pretences.

"Listen," she cocked her head to one side and her

blonde hair fell down onto her shoulder. "How do you fancy meeting up tomorrow?"

The little man who lives inside my head with a trumpet for when nice things happen to me rushed to open his instrument's rather dusty case. "Sure. You want to go for coffee again?"

Abalone giggled softly and shook her head. "Been there, done that, Mister Investigator. How about a meal? You choose where. Pick me up about seven."

As I drove back down to Dalton Square, the gleeful music of trumpet fanfares was playing inside my head.

CHAPTER 14

I woke Sunday morning after sleeping like the dead, and that was the powerfully rested kind, not the zombified or vampiric kind. There had been no dreams, no dragons and, best of all, no librarians. Instead I had been lullabied to sleep on Saturday evening with the knowledge that Sunday was going to be a better day. The statue of the Chimera had linked Wallace to the John O'Gaunt actors which suggested that he was probably linked to Flint and the waitress. I had a list of members of Credete. I had a date planned with Abalone.

Yes. Things were definitely looking up.

Anything is possible.

I shuddered and kicked that corny little phrase into touch. This was all my own doing, *my* hard work. I had put the time in and now I was reaping the rewards, that was all.

I swung myself out of bed and headed for the bathroom.

After a shower and a shave I decided to hit the list. Ten names. No addresses. No telephone numbers.

What to do? First the obvious. I flicked my computer on and brewed some coffee while it booted up. Then, warm drink in hand, I lit up a Lucky before navigating to an online phone directory. Out of the ten names two struck out. At a guess they were ex-directory. Of the rest, seven had multiple entries but one, Matthew Slesinski, gave me a single hit. I checked the nearest clock. It was just past noon. I hazarded that Mister Slesinski could be at home unless he was church-goer, so I dialled the number and listened to the dial tone. On the fourth ring, someone picked up.

"Hello?"

"Oh, good afternoon," I said in my brightest, breeziest voice. "Is that Mister Matthew Slesinski?"

"It is. Who's that?" I detected that note of suspicion most people get when an unfamiliar voice rings them up and they start to think, *Call centre? Double glazing? Crazy guy?*

"Sorry to bother you, Sir," I continued as if all were sweetness and light and this was the most natural conversation in the world, "but I'm from the Lancaster Chronicle and we're running a feature about the group known as..." I pretended to read my notes, "Credete and I was wondering if you could give us an interview?"

There was a slight pause before he replied. "Oh, well, I don't know..."

Bingo! I had snared the right guy. Now I just had to lure him in. "I can assure you, sir, that it's all above board. We have heard all about the great things that Mister Wallace has been doing there and we would like to tell our readers all about his marvellous work."

There was another pause. "And it's all above board? Malcolm really is great guy. He saved my life. I wouldn't want to be part of anything seedy."

Slowly reeling. Slowly reeling. "Quite right, Mister Slesinski. I could meet up with you this afternoon if you were okay with that? It would only take a few minutes and a first-hand perspective could really paint Mister Wallace in a most favourable way."

There was a deep intake of breath on the other end of the line. "Ah, what the hell. I'm sure Malcolm would love the coverage. He'd love some new blood in the society and your article could do that. Okay. Let's meet up."

"Splendid, sir," I beamed. "How about two at the Borough? I believe that's just over the road from where your group meets?"

"Okay. Two it is."

"Could I just ask how I'll recognise you?"

There was a blast of laughter from the other end and when he told me what to look for I grinned from ear to ear. This would be a piece of cake.

Some people like to drink at a number of different watering holes. They like the variety of beverages and constantly changing sea of faces. Not me. I have to sit in the same chair, looking out of the usual window drinking the constantly appealing bourbon surrounded by familiar faces. It brings me comfort in an otherwise manic world. All creation can be going to hell in a handbag, but you sit me down in the Borough with a glass (or two) of Jack and I'm like a five-year-old on a bouncy castle. No matter what may come up and smack me in the face I will bounce back up, laughing.

Besides, where else in Lancaster would I have Grace as a barmaid? I don't even have to go to the bar; I just settle myself down in my chair and she brings over a good-sized measure of straight bourbon.

Hey there, Sam," the young girl smiled down at me as she placed my glass tumbler on the table, "not seen you since, you know, Tuesday. How's it going?"

I sipped at the whiskey and smiled as it warmed my insides. "Interesting, Grace. Very interesting. How about you?"

"Oh, you know," she shrugged, "the same old, same old. Lectures, essays, coursework. Spliff joining you?" she gestured to the empty chair opposite me.

I explained that he was not but I was expecting somebody else.

"Oh." A slight crease formed on her forehead. "Caroline?"

I almost choked on my bourbon. "Good God, no!" I spluttered. "I don't think I'll be seeing her for a *very* long time. Turns out she was using me all along."

"Oh, what a shame. Well if you need anything, you know where I am," she beamed and I am sure she was whistling as she made her way back to the bar.

It was just past two when the door to the Borough swung inwards and the pub descended into silence for that briefest of moments as drinkers turned to surreptitiously gawp at Matthew Slesinski or, as I had previously christened him, Matt the Tat. His spiked-blonde head swivelled from left to right, looking for the reporter that he had arranged to meet. I lifted my glass and he frowned. So it appeared that he recognised me. The facially-tattooed six-footer loped over to my table and peered down at me. "Abalone didn't say you were a reporter," he rumbled. I had to tread carefully here. He might not be a Sith Lord, but I still had the feeling that he could rip me in two if I pushed the wrong buttons.

"I'm not, Matt," I confessed, "but we need to talk. Please, take a seat. You want a drink?"

"I don't do that shit no more." His voice was quiet and threatening as he lowered himself down into the chair. "Just tell me what you want."

"A question first." I downed my drink and placed the heavy tumbler on a beer mat. "Tell me, Matt, why do you follow Malcolm? What's the attraction?"

His eyelids formed narrow slits as he tried to get the measure of me. "He saved me," he eventually revealed.

"From what?"

"From myself."

I nodded sagely. In fact my earlier suspicions about Matt had been correct. He went on to tell me that he had indeed been a biker and not one of those kind, hippy types that sell New Age jewellery at fantasy fairs. No, he had been a rather vicious leader of a gang that had hung out round Devil's Bridge over in Kirkby Lonsdale. For five years his gang had terrorised the local community, beating up those they saw as weak and extorting money out of local businesses. Then something had happened.

"How did you meet him?"

Matt leaned back in his chair and there he was, the biker of old. Cynicism adorned his face and anger glimmered in his eyes. "What's this about, man?"

"You had an accident, didn't you?"

"So?" he shrugged his colossal shoulders. "Abs tell you that?"

"No. But that wasn't the end of it, was it?"

Silence. Cold, glowering silence. I had hit a nerve.

"You were paralysed in a hospital bed after a fall from your bike, and I'm betting that you were dreaming some crazy dreams while you lay there."

The eyes flickered. Something was edging the anger out of its way: uncertainty. Matt shifted uncomfortably in his chair.

"What did you dream, Matt? What visited you while you slept?"

He ran his fingers through his spiked hair and let out a sharp breath. "How the hell do you know about that? No-one knows about that."

"Just a hunch. You're apparently not the only one at Credete who has been dreaming."

"Seriously?"

I nodded. I started to pull back on my fishing rod. Come to Sammie. "And I'm betting that the docs could find no physical reason why you were paralysed either."

Matt swore quietly under his breath. "Look, man, it was real freaky stuff. I can't remember half of it. At the time I thought it was just the morphine and stuff, you know? But remembering it..." His train of thought wandered off into somewhere unpleasant. "There were snakes."

237

"Snakes?'

"Yeah. Snakes. Big wriggly, slithery snakes." His hands undulated, illustrating the phantasmagoria that he was revisiting. "They came at me out of the grass and wrapped themselves around my legs and my arms. They felt so heavy. So heavy that I couldn't move. And all the time they were squirming against my skin. Damn it, I was *naked* under those things! It was awful. I felt violated. It was as if they just wanted to pin me down, keep me immobile. Every night it was like that. I'd dream of those wretched snakes, slithering and sliding all over me. I could feel the muscles of their long bodies undulating on me. I used to wake up soaked in sweat every morning. The nurses were constantly changing my sheets.

"Then one day it was different.

"I had the same dream. The snakes came up out of the grass and wrapped themselves around me, pinning me down. They even coiled themselves around my face. I was gagging for breath as they forced their way into my mouth! But suddenly I knew I wasn't alone. There was somebody else there. I could hear his breathing. I could feel a coolness as if a shadow had fallen across me.

"Then there was a word. One single word. 'Leave.'

"I woke up screaming and lurched upright in bed only to be caught in a pair of arms.

"He was there by my side."

"Wallace?"

Matt nodded. "He'd healed me."

Now it was my turn to sit back in contemplation. Slowly, I drummed my fingernails against my teeth.

"Matt, what was he doing there? In the hospital, I mean."

Matt frowned. "It never came up. I was just so grateful for him saving me. I guess he must have been visiting someone."

"Hmmm. Or perhaps, you were the one he had come to see."

"What d'you mean?"

Okay. Now was the time to tread really, really carefully. "Matt, Malcolm has incredible powers. You'd agree with me on that, yes?"

He nodded. "Sure. I've seen him do wonderful things. You saw him heal little Melanie on Wednesday. That was fantastic."

I placated him. "It sure was, Matt. It sure was. But here's the thing." I leant in close and beckoned for him to lean forwards too. This was going to be our own little secret. "Don't you think it's just possible that he may have been the cause of those illnesses?" I leant back and waited for the reaction.

Well, he didn't hit me, so that was a positive.

"That's not possible."

"Yes it is, Matt. Think about it. How many members do you know have all experienced a similar tale to you? Quite a few, I bet. All these mysterious illnesses which Wallace miraculously cures. It's far more than coincidence that he finds you. Perhaps he's in the right place in the right time, or perhaps someone gets handed a leaflet just when they're at their lowest. Hell, they might even have a dream about going along to one of your meetings. Let's face it, with Wallace, *anything is possible!*"

Matt's eyes turned to steel once more and lanced me to my chair.

Uh oh. A step too far, perhaps?

"I don't like what you're suggesting." His muscles rippled as he rose from his chair in one fluid movement. "I'm going now and I don't ever want to hear from you again, you here?" With that he stomped out of the pub.

I sat back into my chair and pondered the conversation. No physical violence, another mysterious illness and a miraculous healing. All in all I considered it a success.

As I rang the doorbell on Dunkeld Street I checked the time on my Tissot. It was bang on seven. I prayed that Abalone was not one of those types who took forever to get their gear together and leave the house. I had planned this almost to the minute. The door swung inwards and I was greeted by a tall, willowy woman with dark hair and brown eyes. "You must be Sam," she smiled, amused by my obvious confusion. "I'm Heather, Abalone's housemate. Come on in, she's almost ready."

I glanced again at my watch as I stepped over the threshold. *Almost* was good. I could do *almost*.

It was a neat little house which was currently occupied by a blonde tornado that was hastily whipping things up into its cyclonic grip: shoes, handbag, phone, keys. Then the storm subdued and there she was stood in front of me, grinning lopsidedly, the picture of demureness, all her hairs in the correct place and those bright blue eyes shining out from behind those cute glasses of hers.

"Well?" she asked.

"The lady doth impress."

She giggled then said to her housemate. "Right, not sure what time I'll be back."

"No probs," Heather winked mischievously. "I'm off to Tyler's for the night so you'll have plenty of *privacy*."

I'm not sure who blushed most as I ushered my date out of the front door.

"So, Mister Investigator, where are you taking me then?"

A cab pulled up outside right on cue and I opened the door for her. "*Alessandro's*."

That one word brought a visage of stunned shock followed by a look of total glee.

Nice one, Sam, I congratulated myself. *Nice one.*

There is one word and one word alone that describes *Alessandro's*: "Swanky."

I've eaten out a lot of times in my life and a number of the dining establishments have tried to achieve that certain finesse but have just missed out somehow: the lighting's too low, the music's too loud, the staff are too patronising. This place, however, had it *just right*. The maitre'd was pleasant, not fawning. The tables were smart and well-presented. The open log fire in the waiting area. I could just go on and on. I loved the place.

"I just hope there's something I can eat. I forgot to check when I booked it," I mumbled to myself, expecting it to be too good to be true. Abalone smiled up at me, her blue eyes twinkling in the glow of the fire.

"Don't you fuss," she soothed, stroking my arm in

241

a manner that I had to admit was rather pleasing. "We had a work's do here a while back. The menu is extensive and they cater for all sorts." She grinned, "Even nut munchers like you."

"Nut muncher?" I smiled. "Well I've been called a lot of things recently, but that is a first."

She tinkled a small giggle and handed me a posh-looking, leather-bound menu as we sat ourselves down on the very comfy couch. "Here, look at the pasta. They have a chilli version. I bet you like a bit of spice, don't you?"

My throat dried up. I was so out of practice at this game. "That would be nice," I managed eventually to yet another one of her mischievous giggles. "I think I need a drink first. Bourbon, if that's okay?"

"You don't need to ask, silly," she chided. "You're not one of my pupils, you know?" She called the drinks waiter over and placed our order. When they arrived, I noticed that she had ordered me a double. I drank it swiftly, all the more to her amusement. "You don't get out that much, do you, Sam?" she mused over her glass of white wine.

"That obvious is it?"

"It's sweet." She laid a hand on mine and lightly kissed my cheek. "Not to mention quite appealing."

As we mulled over the menu, the little men inside my brain who normally make sure that everything runs to order were having somewhat of a panic attack. Apparently someone had been tidying up and had decided that, as I had not been on a proper dinner date for a *very* long time, that the manual on *How to talk to a good-looking woman who wants to get into your pants* was just sitting around cluttering up the place so had stashed it somewhere. Consequently, at that moment in time, my head was full of the sound of running and shouting as the little men inside were trying to Google what I should do. They weren't having much success, but Abalone didn't seem to mind. She even held my hand as we were led over to our table.

The waiter took our coats and our order, then *it* happened.

The silence.

You know the one. The one where you know that you should be saying something, but nothing comes, so the silence gets broader and broader, an all-enveloping monster that is going to gobble you up whole. All the time you are aware of the silence and its all-pervading presence and the fact that the very sweet, pretty person you are sat with is patiently waiting for you to fill that silence.

Scenarios start to run through your head. Should you mention the weather? Too mundane. Should you comment on her dress? Too obvious. Should you say that you were traumatised as a child and are incapable of small-talk? Too freaky.

In the end, the silence gets bigger and bigger as sentences rise up to your tongue only to be swallowed up by the silence's voracious appetite. You may even go so far as to make a slight gesture before realising that there are no words to accompany it and this makes you look like a mild sufferer of social tourettes.

No. The silence is always victorious. You cannot

win. You just have to sit back, bite your lip and hope that your death by verbal insufficiency will be quick and painless.

"Not much of a talker are you?" Abalone finally ventured.

"More *out of practice*," I corrected her, relief washing over me as the silence was beaten back into its box with a very large stick.

"That's okay. I can't stand men who are always banging on about themselves. I prefer the quiet types."

I shrugged nervously. "My lucky day then, I guess."

Abalone's mischievous blue eyes twinkled as she lifted her glass of wine and took a sip. "So," she began, settling the drink back down on the restaurant table, "do you actually believe in all this stuff you deal in? You know, ghosties and goblins and the like? Isn't it all mumbo-jumbo?"

I thought first about a dark-haired vampire offering me as nutritious snack to her new-born and then about and insane, power-crazed lycanthrope being devoured by flesh-eating ants.

"There's some truth in it," I said.

She cocked her head to one side and her loose blonde hair hung over her shoulder. "Really? Tell me about it?"

I recalled firing a bullet into the chest of an unarmed woman.

"Not much to tell really. Early days. Besides, you saw what was going on at Saint Edmund's."

She gave an indignant snort and downed the rest

of her glass.

"What?"

"You really think the Ballcrusher let that live as some sort of ghostly phenomenon?" she reached for the bottle of Pinot grigio, then paused and started to wave her finger up and down. "We all saw what was going on. We know it was something spooky and whatever it was, you stopped it." Her finger continued to gesticulate. "But that sanctimonious cow has absolutely squashed it flat. 'Schoolchild high jinks,' she says." I watched her hand sway closer and closer to the wine bottle. "School-child high jinks my arse! We all know it was a ghost of some sort, but that bitch..." She let out a frustrated growl and swung her arms out.

My hand shot out to catch the toppling bottle, so did Abalone's. Mine got there first, hers a second later closing around my fingers. We stood the bottle upright. Neither of us removed our hands.

She smiled, not just with her mouth. Her eyes were studying my face, intently. I felt her thumb casually stroke the top of my fingers.

I shifted a bit in my chair.

It had been a while.

A long while.

Having said that, I had no desire to move my hand right away. That would have seemed rude, wouldn't it?

Eventually I nodded to her empty glass: "More wine?"

"Are you trying to get me drunk, Sam?"

"No. No! God no!"

"Pity," she grinned then removed her hand and

offered me her glass for a refill.

I obliged and quickly brought the conversation back round to safer topics. "So what's it like working at Saint Edmund's - Wetherington aside?"

So we chatted, laughed and relaxed into the arms of each other's company. As the courses came and went, we tucked into what was really splendid food and she told me all about how she loved her job but hated having management on her back all the time, pushing harder and harder for impossible results.

"I'd love to work for myself," she said as she finished off an incredibly indulgent chocolate fudge cake. "In fact, why don't I come and work for you?"

I chuckled. "I don't think I need a music teacher on my books."

"No, no," she shook her head as she scraped every last dribble of cream and chocolate sauce out of her dish. "I could be your secretary. You know the sort, the stay at home girl who secretly hopes that she'll be able to tame her boss so that they could drive off into the sunset. I'd spend half my time daydreaming about my fit boss and the other half answering the phone." She put her hand to her cheek and mimed a phone call. "Hello. Spallucci Investigations. I'm afraid the incredibly buff Mister Spallucci isn't here at the moment, but when he comes back I'll give him a message once I've extricated my tongue from his mouth." She looked at me intently with those blue eyes for a few seconds then dissolved into uncontrollable giggles.

I smiled. This was a welcome release from current events.

"Oh!" Abalone started, "that reminds me, *Mister Spallucci*, I've been meaning to ask, what part of Italy are your folks from?"

I laughed. "Oh God, that one."

She sipped her wine. "What one? A dark secret?" She showed mock conspiracy as she leaned forward into the candle light. "Are they *mafiosi*?"

"Anything but," I smiled. "You want the full story about my name?"

Abalone nodded as she refilled our glasses.

"Okay, my dad was born Eric Smith. As well as being a damn hot trumpeter..."

"Just like his son."

I shrugged off the compliment, "he also used to be a compulsive gambler. If there was anything you could place a bet on, my dad was there. From the gee-gees to the dogs to the toss of a coin. It was always double or nothing. Anything for a bet.

"Anyways, he met my mum, Marion Short and they started dating. Everything was going swimmingly until the stag night."

"I'm guessing we're not just talking a stripper here?"

"Did they have them back in the forties? I'm not sure they did. Anyways, I digress. It was a few weeks before the wedding and Dad was enjoying his drinks with some of his mates, all of whom were gamblers like himself. When one of them says, 'Hey Eric. Don't you think Smith is a boring name for your new lady?' My dad said that it had been good enough for his mum then it would be good enough for his wife. His mate then goes on to say, 'Yeah, well you always play it safe.' My dad denied this vehemently. An argument ensued, the outcome of which being that my dad's mates bet him he would not change his name to something bizarre before the wedding and furthermore, they dared him not to tell my mum to be until the moment of the vows."

Abalone was gobsmacked. She sat with her hand over her open mouth. "God, that's terrible! Wait a minute, what about the banns? Surely they would have been in his new name?"

I nodded. "They were indeed, but my dad was the canny one and persuaded my mum that she wasn't feeling well the first day that they were read out in church. As for the second and third reading, she must have missed them. They were never much in the way of church goers."

"So the first time she heard his surname..."

"Was when the clergyman said, 'Do you, Eric John Spallucci....'"

Abalone fell into fits of giggles. "Well I guess she still said, 'I do.' It must give them something to look back on a laugh at in their old age, I guess. Oh. What is it?"

I downed my glass of wine. It tasted bitter compared to my normal tipple. "My dad died about fifteen years ago."

"Sam," she reached out and took my hand, "I'm sorry."

"S'okay. You weren't to know."

"I guess you and your mum must be quite close then."

I let out a dry chuckle. "Not exactly. We haven't

spoken in about five years."

"You're kidding? How come?"

"We argued."

"What over?"

"Me refusing to eat her Christmas dinner."

"Sam!"

"Hey don't get all school ma'am with me. I'd been vegan for ages and every Christmas it was the same: 'Haven't you got over this silly phase yet?' I'd had enough."

"But she's your mother!"

I shrugged.

Abalone looked down at the table and whisked up my phone.

"What are you doing?"

"What do you think?"

"Don't you dare!"

"Try to stop me and I'll scream."

I sat and seethed.

"It's ringing," she smiled. "Oh, hello. Mrs. Spallucci? Yes, sorry to disturb you, but I'm a friend of your son's. He'd like a word with you." She thrust the mobile out to me and cocked a blonde eyebrow behind her spectacles.

I took the phone and started to speak. "Mum?"

"Sammy? Is that you?" After all the years, she still sounded the same and I could not help but smile. This was the woman who had raised and nurtured me.

She had been there when the noises in my head had brought night terrors.

She had been there as I had stumbled my way

through an awkward adolescence.

She had been there when my life had imploded after Caroline had trampled on my heart and Dad had died.

"Yes, Mum. It's me."

There was no, "Well, it's been a long time," or, "Are you still eating stupid food?" Instead, the first thing that my mother asked was, "Who's your friend? Are you dating?"

"Mum!" I sounded like an embarrassed teenager whose parents have told their teacher at parents' evening that they fancy them.

"Oh, I know. None of my business," she apologised. "I can't help but fuss. I am your mother after all."

I grinned. So did Abalone. "Yes, you are. It's good to hear you."

"Well all you have to do is pick up the phone. You know that, don't you?"

I nodded. "Yes, Mum. I do." I swallowed and fought back the tear that was rising behind my right eye. "Listen, Mum, I have to go. I'm sort of..." I drifted off. What was I *sort of* doing?

"That's okay, Sammy. You go have fun with your girlfriend. What's her name?"

"Abalone."

"Pretty name. It's a fish, isn't it?"

"A shell, Mum."

She paused before saying, "Don't be a stranger, okay. Ring me again soon."

I promised that I would. We said our goodbyes

and hung up.

"Well?" Abalone was sat back wearing a mischievous grin, her arms crossed.

"Well what?" I was also smiling. In fact I was probably grinning like a loon. Five years of avoidance, animosity and fear had been swept away in one fell stroke by this remarkable, young woman.

"A *thank you* would be nice."

"I think I can manage more than that." I rose from my chair a new man, confidence swimming in my blood stream. I took her face in my hands and pulled her mouth to mine. She resisted not a jot. As her lips worked slowly against me her floral scent filled my nostrils.

When we parted she groaned contentedly, "Well that's definitely worth top marks."

I chuckled.

"You see," she beamed as she affectionately stroked my hand, "anything is possible."

"Perhaps it is," I agreed. With my new-found mettle I was about to suggest we could go back to my place when her phone chirruped an interruption.

"Sorry. I'd better check this," she apologised, blushing and smiling. She tapped the phone and read the text message.

Her smile faded.

She stood up.

"I'm sorry, Sam. I have to go."

"What? Are you okay?"

She drew some money out of her purse and lay it on the table before turning and making for the cloakroom.

"Abalone? What's the matter."

"Please. Sam," she said, her voice dull, lifeless; her blue eyes downcast, avoiding me "I have to go now." With that she walked away, retrieved her coat and left.

I sat back in my chair, my gast truly flabbered. What the hell had happened? One minute there had been smiles, orchestras and cherubs; the next... I made to rise then thought again. No. I wouldn't pursue her. That would be the wrong thing to do. Something had obviously upset her. Something in the text. Something that she couldn't share with me. Something personal.

Yes that was it. Something personal had cropped up and she had to attend to it quickly. It would be wrong for me to intrude.

That didn't make it any less of a bummer, though.

I sighed, tossed my half of the bill on the table and rang for a taxi. Ten minutes later, I was half dozing in the back of a cab on the A6 back to Lancaster. The sweet scent of flowers kept enveloping my memory, causing my drooping eyes to turn up at the corners. The touch of her skin had been divine; her soft, beautiful skin. I longed to touch it once more. As I dozed off in the back of the cab images started to prod my memory. There was something odd. Something was nagging me. How could a personality change so quickly? My mind wandered as the headlights from other cars splashed over me. I saw Flint from the town hall, anxious and afraid as he told me about his concerns. Then just a short while later he was dead. Next I saw the young waitress who had been a bright, chatty thing until Wallace had apparently turned her into a self-sacrificing, murder machine.

Wallace.

Anything is possible.

Anything...

My eyes snapped open. Dear God!

I leant forward to the cab driver as we drove down Scotforth Road. "Quick, I need to get to Dunkeld Street right now!"

I rocketed out of the cab and charged across the pavement to Abalone's front door. As the car drove away, I hammered heavily on the dark blue wood. To hell with anyone watching.

The door swung inwards and my stomach lurched. I stepped over the threshold into darkness. "Abalone!" I called out into the unlit house. Unlit, that was, except for one light worming its way into the gloom from an upstairs room. I bounded up to the next floor two steps at a time until I reached the closed door with the light seeping out from underneath. "Abalone?" I knocked tentatively at the door.

There was no reply.

Cautiously, I grabbed the handle and turned. The door swung inwards and steam wafted over me, causing me to blink as I entered the small bathroom.

The thing that struck me more than anything else was how red the bathwater looked. There were no words, no expletives. I had no time for that, none whatsoever. I flew across the tiled floor and grabbed Abalone's slashed wrist. Blood was still seeping out into the warm water. I pushed my thumb down on the cut and raised it above her head to try and stem the flow. With my other hand I felt at her neck

No pulse.

"Abalone!" I yelled, my voice echoing round the small room. "Abalone!"

There was no movement. Not a flutter. I dropped the wrist and decided more action was needed. I drove one arm under her shoulders and the other under her knees – this was not a time for modesty – and hoicked her clumsily out of the tub onto the floor. I lowered my mouth to hers, pinched her nose shut, and gave two deep breaths then placed my hand together below her breasts and applied thirty quick compressions.

I swore violently as, with each compression, dark blood spurted out of her savaged wrist. I grabbed a towel and tied a tight tourniquet to her arm then went back to the CPR.

Two breaths. Thirty compressions.

Two breaths. Thirty compressions.

Two breaths. Thirty compressions.

Two breaths. Thirty compressions.

Two breaths. Thirty compressions.

Two breaths. Thirty compressions.

Two breaths. Thirty compressions.

Again.

Again.

Again.

Again.

Over and over. Each time I checked for breath. Each time I came back up and continued the same pattern.

Eventually, I realised that my hands were wet and it wasn't from her body which had begun to dry out. It was from my tears. They were flooding from my eyes as they realised the hopelessness of the task.

The compressions grew slower and slower as I gradually ground to a halt.

I had lost her.

This bright young spark that had only just entered my life had been so awfully removed. I sank back on my haunches and there, for the first time, I saw it; drawn on the tiled wall above the bath in her own blood:

An upper case T surrounded by two swirls. An Asherah.

My phone rang.

I tore it out of my pocket, slid the accept icon across and spat with venom into the mouthpiece, "You bastard! You utter bastard! Why are you doing this?"

"Now, now, Samuel," Wallace's patronising voice sauntered across the airwaves into my ear. "I did nothing apart from inform Miss Morris that the man she was sat opposite was in fact just using her to acquire knowledge about me and my machinations." He paused. Then with a wicked twinkle in his voice said, "I take it that she did not receive the news lightly."

"I'll kill you! I'll kill you!" I screamed down the phone. "I'll come looking for you then I'll rip that black heart out of your smug, puffed up chest."

"Yes, Samuel," he crooned, "such passion. Like when you dispatched that wolf and his wretched sister. Feel that anger. Use it. Come find me. It will be quite the family reunion." With that he hung up.

I slumped back against the wall and shut my eyes. I wanted none of this. I wanted a simple, quiet life.

And I would kill to get it. I would hunt him down, corner him, wrap my hands around his neck and...

My eyes shot open.

Family reunion.

Oh no!

CHAPTER 15

I thought my lungs were going to explode as my legs pounded left right, left right up onto Wyresdale Road and past Christ Church parish church. I've never been much of a runner, never had the need, but now I was calling on every last unit of energy I had to charge my way up to Caroline's.

He knew! The bastard knew, but *how*? I had not told him that John was my son. The old maxim came back to slap me round the face: *Anything is possible*. Sure, anything is possible, but how was he doing it? What was his secret? He had talked time and time about his benefactor about how she had changed his life. How could it possibly be the same one from university? If so, was she somehow pulling his strings? Was she this mysterious woman that Sophia had mentioned? "Devotion or death," that was what the curious librarian had said that Wallace's mistress demanded. Well she seemed to be getting plenty of both, but who was she?

After our little episode with Gerald the phantom caretaker, Spliff and I had discussed who Wallace's mysterious companion had been. Spliff had been insistent that it was some old, lavender-drenched spinster who was releasing some frustrated sexual tension with a young plaything. I disagreed. I had heard the killer heels and the seductive voice of Wallace's female companion that night and I was convinced that she was more of a leather and scent girl rather than wool and humbugs. Then, not to mention there was that voice at the Credete meeting in the Ashton Hall. The weird thing was, if it was the same person then it did not sound like it had changed at all. Wallace had said that she was old, but both times the voice had sounded young and, dare I say, sultry. A vampire perhaps? As I rounded the corner onto Coulston Road, past Williamson Park, I quickly discounted the idea. It didn't feel right. Not only was I known to the Children of Cain but it didn't seem their style. They were creatures of the shadows, watching waiting for whatever this Divergence thing was. They did not seem the type to be manipulators.

No, Wallace's benefactor was someone or some*thing* else. Of that I was fairly sure.

I pulled to a halt just down the road from Caroline's house. All this speculation was, right now, just that: speculation. I had to concentrate on the present, on the moment. Wallace had threatened Caroline and John, my family. He was either planning something or, more likely, had set something nefarious and spiteful into motion. The image of Abalone lying drained of blood in her red-stained bath flooded back into my memory. I pounded it back into the darkest recess with a big stick and cautiously crossed the road, looking up at Caroline's windows for any signs of life. There was none. No lights escaped from behind the curtains. No noise came from the house.

I walked up the small path to the door and pressed gently on the door. For the second time that night I found a door swinging into pitch black. This was most definitely not good. There was no shouting this time around. I walked as carefully and as stealthily as I could. Gently, I swung the door back into its frame, making sure not to close it in case the latch gave away my presence. I stood for a moment, allowing my eyes to adjust to the insidious gloom. The hallway led off in front of me, terminating at the foot of the staircase to the upper floor. To my right were two doors, first the living room and then the dining room which led onwards to the kitchen. I edged my way along the wall and found the door to the first room. The handle turned silently and I nudged the door open, my heart pounding. Inside was a sofa and an armchair facing a large flat screen television. I closed the door and made for the next room.

The next room was the dining room. The rear window's curtain had not been drawn and the moonlight aided me in noting that there was nothing amiss here. The dining table was clean and tidy; there was no trace of their evening meal. The Chas Jacobs still hung on the opposite wall. I progressed onwards to the kitchen. Pots and pans lay washed on the drainer, waiting to be put away. I ran a finger over a saucepan. It was dry. At a guess, they had eaten tea as usual, washed up and left them to dry on their own. From the lack of water on the pan, this must have been at least a few hours ago. If something had happened here, it had happened very recently. I scanned the rest of the kitchen. Everything was neat and tidy. There was none of the detritus on the counter that I would find in my kitchen: a packet of cereal, breadcrumbs and the ubiquitous stray teaspoon. What's more, there was no sign of any struggle.

I turned to my left and my eyes fell on the door down to the cellar. Rather than having a handle, there was an old-style latch which I lifted silently and tugged on to open the door. As I peered down the old, wooden stairs I could make out a dim light permeating from somewhere down below. I leaned my back against the wall and crept foot after foot down the stairs. Passing down below the dining room I could make out a room that seemed to run the length of the house. There was a slight musty smell that is found in most cellars due to the lack of air flow however there also the unmistakable scent of expensive aftershave.

"Do come down, Samuel," Wallace called out. "I think we need to chat."

With all attempts at stealth foiled, I walked with fake calm down the rest of the stairs. Most of the cellar was in darkness apart from one corner where Wallace was sat casually behind an old desk upon which were set a CD player of some sorts and a candle, which was the only source of illumination.

"Making yourself at home?" I was fighting back the overwhelming urge to lunge forward and choke the man to death but I knew it would be futile. I had yet to establish the whereabouts of Caroline and John. He was my only link to their safety.

And he knew it.

"So, Samuel," he purred, the glow of the lone candle giving his face a skeletal appearance, "how's life treating you?"

"It's been somewhat better." I descended from the bottom step and stood across the room from him. A quick lunge; that's all it would take. I could throw myself at him.

"Oh, I imagine that's probably the case, isn't it. I believe your little date didn't go so well this evening?" Those perverted eyes were dancing in the fire of the flame.

I clenched and unclenched my hands. My face stayed turned to him but my eyes flickered quickly around my surroundings. They saw nothing, just darkness.

"Nothing to say? What a pity." He wore a mask of mock sorrow. "Mind you, Miss Morris had very little to say either, when I told her about how you were just using her to get to me. I imagine it upset her... somewhat."

I could feel the muscles in my legs and my shoulders tensing. They were wanting to charge at him, right here, right now. I could end this. My hands around his throat, grasping, clawing, tearing; watching the life drain from those orange orbs.

But I had to wait. I had to wait.

The sorrow faded and was replaced with glee. "My, my, you really are playing the strong, silent type tonight. No little quips? None of your dull, little sci-fi anecdotes? Not in the mood are we?" Wallace shook his head. "Perhaps this will loosen your tongue." He raised his right hand in an upward motion and around the edge of the cellar candles burst into flame illuminating the far end of the wall. Caroline and John were there. She was bound to an old, wooden armchair chair the stuffing of which had seen better days and John was curled up in a tight ball in the far corner of the cellar with a circular chalk marking around his foetal form.

I had what I needed to know. Nothing held me back now. I surged forward, hands outstretched like talons. I made it halfway across the room until I felt my feet leave the floor and my momentum stopped to a shuddering halt. Frantically I tried to move my arms but they were locked by an invisible force, as was the rest of my body. I tried to twist and turn but to no effect. All I could do was scream in frustration at my captor who now walked up to me and inspected me as an artist inspects his canvas.

"So volatile, Samuel. So predictable." Wallace's voice was soft and low. He sounded like a cat preaching to a canary that is about to be served up as an hors d'oeuvres. "What did you really hope to achieve? I can see right through you. You wear but one face, whereas I, like the Chimera, wear many."

Chimera. I thought frantically back to my thespian abductors and the statue in Wallace's collection.

Wallace nodded. "Yes, you see it now. Well, part of it, anyway. Those bumbling fools were to serve my purpose. I drew them together, trained them and led them down a path that they thought would bring them riches and reward. Unfortunately they decided that they had to take care of you. Fools! You were a nobody, a hack. What harm could you have done. All they had to do was keep themselves hidden until I needed them and they couldn't manage that." He shook his head. "The five of them couldn't even kill themselves properly. Two botched attempts meant that I had to intervene.

"And then there was you." He stood before me, his arms crossed, pondering something. "I could have killed you straight away, be done with the matter. Your little girlfriend there would have taken the hint and scurried back to her news desk where she could have penned sweet little anecdotes about brave puppies saving drowning toddlers or whatever tripe it is she writes. However, my benefactor was quite insistent. You were to be kept alive. You were to be brought into our fold.

"She had *plans* for you. She alone knows why. Personally, I think you're a failure. Look at you: you chain smoke, you reek of bourbon, you have no life. I offered you a way out of your pitiful existence but you threw it back in my face." Wallace shook his head. "Very disappointing, Samuel. Very disappointing.

"What was it that my benefactor saw in you? I wondered. Then I realised that, for some reason hidden from me, she must have been afraid of you. Perhaps she feared that the two of us together could have risen up and wrested her power from her hands. I decided that like primordial dragons we could turn on our mother, breaking free of her constraining grip.

"But no, it wasn't to be. Your reaction to that young waitress proved that all too clearly. You are just like everybody else, Samuel, weak and pitiful. You do not have the strength to make the necessary sacrifices for the benefit of creation.

"I however suffer from no such compunction whatsoever."

As Wallace walked across the room towards Caroline and John I felt myself moving, gliding with him. He stopped and my body tilted backward to a horizontal position before being folded into a chair next to Caroline. I flashed my eyes to my left. I could just make out the rise and fall of her body breathing. At least she was alive.

"Now," my captor clapped his hands together as if about to explain the boundaries of the play area for children on a picnic, "I'm going to loosen your bonds. Not entirely. No, I have no doubt that if I did that then you would try something stupidly pointless again, but just enough for you to talk. All of you. What a gay conversation you could have." He blinked and I felt the muscles around my mouth loosen. I gasped a ragged breath and immediately tried to wrench myself from the chair. It was no use. Whatever power he was using, I was still held fast. There was a groaning from my left and I found that I could turn my head now towards her. "Caroline," my voice was dry and croaky, "can you hear me?"

"Sam?" Her voice was muffled and tired as if waking from a deep sleep. "Is that... What? Where?" She wrestled with the straps that held her bound. "Sam!" She screamed. Her dark eyes shot at me then across the room. "John! John!" she wailed as she tried desperately to free herself.

John started to come round. He rolled over onto

all fours and climbed heavily to his feet. "Mum? Sam?" He took a step forwards and was met with a blinding flash of light as his foot touched the chalked circle and he was pushed back into the centre of the ring. Panic rose in his eyes as it did in Caroline's. "What... what's happening?"

Caroline was now wriggling frantically against her bonds, her bobbed hair swaying back and forth against her cheeks. "Let me out! Let me out!" Her head snapped up in the direction of Wallace as he made a deprecating tutting noise. "You!" She was a trapped lioness whose cub was in danger. The problem was that her claws had been tied and she was in no position to attack.

"Just calm down," I said quietly. "You'll achieve nothing."

"Piss off!" she spat. "This is all your fault. It's always your fault." She turned back to John. "It's okay, sweetie. Mummy will get you out."

"Oh, really? And how do you propose to do that then?" I was tired. I was cranky. I couldn't help the sarcasm. I had left a lovely, young woman dead in her bathroom to come here and what was I getting? The same old, same old. "In case you hadn't noticed, we are both somewhat incapacitated."

We both looked up at Wallace as he chuckled quietly to himself. "Ah, the wonders of the modern family unit. And we wonder why humanity never progresses. Samuel is quite right Ms. Adamson; you cannot possibly escape. All you can do is sit.

"And watch."

My blood ran cold. "Watch what?"

"Samuel, Ms. Adamson, I have somewhat of a predicament facing me. For some time now, I have been planning the future, not just of humanity but of creation. As Samuel knows, I rather feel that our situation at the moment it corrupt, devoid of hope and totally irretrievable. As a result I have found it necessary to implement a plan that will ultimately rectify this.

"I am going to bring about the Divergence.

"My benefactor tells me that it is quite simple. All it requires is five willing sacrifices. Five individuals who are known to me that feel they have nothing left to live for. Five individuals who see this life for what it really is: totally devoid of prospect and hope.

"Now, I had those individuals prepared and ready to give themselves for the greater good in the form of the John O'Gaunt production team. However, something went terribly wrong. One went insane and did not receive my final call and then another seems to have hesitated and performed a less than satisfactory job."

"Philips and Brande," I growled, frustrated and annoyed at having to listen to my captor revel in his own story once more.

Wallace nodded at me. "Very good, Samuel. You've been paying attention. Anyway," he continued, obviously relishing every moment in the spotlight, "I had to dispatch the two failures and start again. I needed a clean canvas on which to create my masterpiece, so to speak."

Caroline: "Five new sacrifices."

"Indeed, Ms. Adamson. Five new lives to extinguish of hope and remove from this mortal coil. So far, I have clocked up three: a waitress in a dead end job, a scared caretaker and a betrayed lover. Of course, their predicaments alone were nowhere near enough to merit them taking their own lives, but I can be *very* persuasive.

"My benefactor has taught me well."

"You need two more." My blood had gone from chilled to frozen.

"Indeed I do. Indeed I do. I wonder what could make such loving parents lose all hope?" His orange eyes drifted over to our son, trapped in the magic circle.

All anger drained from Caroline's face. Her mouth hung open and her eyes widened. "No. Please, no. You can't he's all I have."

Wallace crouched before her, his eyes level with hers. "Oh dear. Does that make you sad? Does that make your little heart hurt? How does it feel to have something snatched away from you? Can't you play with it anymore?"

"Please... please..." Tears came with the words.

"Why should you really care, Ms. Adamson, ace reporter? You were the one who gave your son the wrist bands. You were the one who wanted him and his little friends to join my group."

Wallace turned his head towards me. "Such a caring mother, isn't she? Using her only son just as much as she used you. She willingly jeopardised both your lives for a news story. Such a doting lover and mother, don't you think?" He walked back to the table and started to fiddle with the controls on the CD player.

I looked at Caroline, tears flowing freely as she sat

slumped in the chair. She was a broken woman. John stood over in the circle, helpless, wanting to run to his mother. There was click from the CD and stringed instruments started to play a slow, doleful tune. Wallace closed his eyes and breathed deep. "Ah, *Beethoven's Seventh*. Magical. I had considered the *Moonlight* for this, but it had been used before in some film if I recall correctly, so I thought it would be a touch cliché."

"The captor wasn't murdered in cold blood in *Misery*. Just incapacitated."

Wallace raised an eyebrow at me. "Murdered? Oh! Ha ha! You think..." He clapped his hands together with glee. "Oh no, you have me quite wrong, Samuel." Woodwind joined the strings as he continued. "As well as changing reality for the better, I have a little side project that I want to try out. Have you ever heard of *Beyond*? It's a charming little place that was a sort of accident at the beginning of time. So I am told, three realms were created: Heaven with all its angels and love etcetera, etcetera; Earth and the physical realm with all its... well you know what *that's* like; then there was Beyond. Beyond was the place where the eye of God never looked. It was the place that even the angels feared to go. It was a place with no time or sustenance. If one was to go there, one would be separated from all creation.

"One would not exist.

"Well it appears that a travelling companion of my benefactor accidentally found a way to open Beyond. I've been dying to try it out for years and now I have a suitable subject."

My head played tennis between Wallace, smug and puffed up at his imminent victory, and John, forlorn and captive – not really sure what was happening. "Why? Why would you do that?"

Wallace frowned in confusion. "Why? Because I can." He turned side on from me and faced John as the music started to swell in volume. He closed his eyes and his mouth opened to speak.

"...

"...

"..."

There were words, there really were, but I could not possibly describe them. They were as if someone had taken the sounds and removed them. I could hear him speaking above the crescendo of music but my brain could not translate the uttering into anything that made sense. It left the space in my auditory processors blank.

What was not blank was the space in the circle behind John. It split open and a black maw widened behind the terrified teenager. Caroline rocked back and forth in her chair, moaning and crying. I tried to free myself but could not even stretch my fingers.

Wallace raised a hand and tendrils of blackness reached out from the split in reality, wrapping themselves around my only son. They snaked around his jeans and along his arms dragging him into a doomed embrace.

"Dad!" He cried out. "Dad!"

"John!" I screamed, my neck taught with grief, frustration and anger as the he slid backwards into the darkness. "John, I'll find you! I'll find you!"

And with that he was gone, sucked into God knows where. Wallace lowered his hand and the portal shut. The chalk markings rose from the floor and dissolved into the air. The music reached the end of the track and there was silence. Wallace walked to the table, unplugged the CD player, glanced casually over his shoulder and the next thing I knew, everything was black.

CHAPTER 16

When I came to, the first thing I realised was that I had the mother of all headaches. The second thing I realised was that I was completely alone. It wasn't just being in the cellar with nobody else, there was just that *feeling*. You know the one, don't you? It's the one when you wake up in the night after having that terrible nightmare: your pulse is racing and your skin is soaked with sweat. You wake up with a start into the grim reality of the night and realise that you are all alone to face your fears. There is no-one there to roll over towards and cuddle up against. There is no-one there to tell you that it was just a dream. There is no-one there to gently take your hand and stroke your fingers until you drift back off to a restful sleep.

You are totally alone and have to deal with the horror of previous night completely on your own.

I lit a Lucky and poked around a bit. There wasn't really much to discover. Wallace had meticulously cleaned up after himself: the CD player was gone as were the candles. I decided that the cellar was a bust and ventured back upstairs.

As I entered the kitchen I saw the light of morning creeping its way into the house. It was one of those grey, tiresome mornings where you would normally crawl back under the sheets and ignore the rain that drizzled down the window panes. I did not have that luxury. Even here, in the normally bustling heart of the home, there was that feeling of emptiness, that something had been untimely ripped from the womb of domesticity.

"Dad! Dad!"

John's last words rang out and I forced myself not to blink or shut my eyes as I would be forced to look upon the nightmare of him being dragged down into that creeping portal once more. Instead I proceeded to give the rest of the house a quick once over. It was, as I had suspected, totally empty apart from a useless investigator and a nearly burnt out cigarette.

My tour brought me back to the dining room. Where was Caroline? Where had she fled to? I wanted to track her down and make things right with her, check that she wasn't doing anything foolish. As I drummed my fingernails on my teeth, my eyes lit upon the picture that dominated the wall and I nodded to myself.

I headed for the front door.

She was stood by the viewing stations that overlook the city. I thought she was crying, but it was hard to tell as she was drenched from the continuous drizzle that had crept into town that morning. I walked over the mosaic pavement under the Ashton Memorial and approached her with extreme caution. "Caroline?" I ventured. There was no response. "Caroline?"

"I heard you the first time."

I winced at the simmering anger in the voice.

"Sorry."

"Sorry? Sorry? Is that all you have to say?" Her arms were wrapped tight around her middle and she turned her back to me. Her shoulders were shaking. There was no mistaking the tears now.

"I couldn't do anything."

Silence.

"I was held tight."

She turned on me, her hands clenching and unclenching by her sides, the increasing precipitation running down her brown hair and onto her face.

"You think that makes this any better? Do you?" Her face contorted in grief and anguish, her eyes half open as tears forced their way out to mingle with the rain. "He was all I had. My son. My boy. All I had."

I walked over towards her and made to put my arms around her.

"No!" she screamed, batting my arms away furiously. "No! Don't you dare. Don't you dare! Don't you touch me."

"Caroline, please. I want to make it right."

She shook her head frantically from side to side, the rain flicking off her fringe. "No. You can't. You know that. He's gone, Sam. Gone.

"And it's all my fault!" She crumpled down onto the floor, her head in her hands and cried in a manner I had never witnessed before. The sounds from her mouth were barely human and she tugged frantically at her hair as if trying to pull it out by its roots. "I set this up. I set this up. I condemned him!"

I bent to comfort her but she exploded up from the floor, her arms pushing me backwards causing me to stumble slightly. "I don't deserve your pity, Sam. I'm poisonous. I'm toxic."

I backed off, hands outstretched. "Okay, I get it, but tell me one thing."

"What?"

"Did you ever really love me?"

She stared at me through the rain, her brown eyes wide in disbelief. "You're asking me that? Now?"

"I need to know."

And we stood there, two people drenched by the rain and I looked deep into those brown eyes. What did I see? Did I see love? Did I see regret? Did I see any little glimmer to make me think that she had any care or compassion for me?

I saw nothing.

"Goodbye, Sam." With that she turned and ran out of my life her tears for her lost son blending with the rain that washed down her face.

I stood and watched her go. My heart ached to chase after her, to calm her down and bring her comfort but, for once in my life, my brain won through. It would be useless. She would just push me away, consumed with guilt for having sacrificed her child. My face would be a constant reminder of what she had lost. Every time she looked at me she would never see my love for her, but the pain of her ultimate loss. Besides she would never love me. She lost the one person that she had ever truly loved. Her greed for personal advancement had sent him into danger and the universe had punished her.

I shoved my hands into my pockets and sighed. What was I to do now? I was no challenge to Wallace. The man had powers that outstripped my mere mortal imaginings.

I needed something close to a miracle. I turned and made to walk away when I noticed something odd. Just off to the side was a dry patch of ground. All around it was drenched from the rain pouring down on top of it, but this little area looked as if there was something there – something *stood* there. I paused, lit up my second Lucky of the day, slowly inhaled whilst walking over to the curious patch of dry and puffed out a stream of smoke about head height. I was rewarded with a short, strangled cough.

"Peek-a-boo," I smiled. "I see you."

The air in front of me shimmered and there in front of me stood the mysterious Alec.

"Don't you think that's getting a bit tired now?"

"People never tire of a classic," he shrugged.

I tilted my head to one side. I'd let him have that one. Then, drawing slowly on the cigarette, I raised an inquisitorial eyebrow.

"There's been another suicide," he said.

CHAPTER 17

I watched the world through a fug of malaise whilst seated on an unforgiving metal bench at Lancaster train station. "1900," proclaimed an ornamented guttering on the opposite platform, a testament to the typically Victorian construction. Formal light brown blocks of neatly chiselled sandstone sat cemented one upon another, forming regular symmetrical patterns in the stout walls; just like so many of the older buildings in Lancaster – those which had not been turned into trendy wine bars. These old relics were memories of the Blakeian mills and the dark times of the slave trade (so conveniently forgotten: "How did we finance that fine building? Through linen and blood, my son. Linen and blood.") Also, like so much of Lancaster, this natural stone-work had been mutilated and scarred by more than a century of the vagaries of architectural fashion. Corrugated metal sheets and rust-reddened rivets made shabby canopies – a testament to the height of 1970's *good taste*.

The olden times were hidden behind the new;

disregarded, reviled, forgotten. Just like the thousands of black slaves whose lives and travail had brought their taskmasters the vast profits that paid for the construction of these once grand buildings. Not many know. Even less seem to care. Some things never change. The wonderment that is humanity. Beauty and cruelty walking had in hand: married, entwined, inseparable.

I sighed.

It was indeed a depressing line of thought, but then it was hardly surprising that my mind was wandering down that particularly grey and dismal avenue. Caroline hating and loathing me more than ever, had walked out of my life for good. John, my sweet, new-found son of only a few days, had been snatched away from me and taken God-alone knows where.

Beyond.

What sort of a place was that? How can something be truly *beyond*? Surely there is always something? There cannot be a complete absence of something if someone is there? Surely?

Then there was Wallace. Malcolm Bloody Wallace.

Still out there.

Still superior.

Still killing.

I looked down the train track to where police seemed to be wandering aimlessly, occasionally bending down and picking things up from between the dark sleepers. I did not want to know what they were putting in their little plastic bags. Christ. My stomach turned

277

somersaults and I prayed for Alec to get a move on and get back here.

I needed a smoke but even that was *Beyond*. All around me posters proclaimed that it was against the law to light up in this place. So is getting some poor bastard to jump in front of the nine o'clock express service from Glasgow. Perhaps Wallace hadn't read that particular poster.

I felt the pack of Luckies in my pocket and was about to say "Sod it!" and pull one out, but then I remembered that not only does a kick in the ass from some officious little prick hurt, but it would not pay to get people's backs up when we needed to get down and see the site of the suicide.

There went my stomach again.

Had I eaten yet today? I didn't think so. I had just gone home to change out of my blood-stained clothes before meeting up here with Alec. The mysterious Alec. He had snapped his fingers and I had come running, just like I seemed to be doing for everyone else that walked into my life at the moment. "Grow a spine, Spallucci," I grumbled to myself and kept my little lucky companions stowed away in discreet secrecy whilst sitting on my hands waiting for Mystery Boy.

I didn't have to wait that long, thank God.

"It's just down the track," he motioned to the milling of police I had been watching as he came out of the Supervisor's Office, "Let's go."

I lifted myself off the bench, its ridges still fresh on my behind and followed after the youth. Down the track was good. Down the track was away from the station, away from a public place of work.

There I could have a smoke.

I knew that when I saw what was waiting for us there I would need one.

They had hardly made any impact on the mess when we arrived.

It's very hard to describe what the scattered, drawn out remains of someone who threw themselves under a speeding locomotive look like. The feel of the macabre is immense. There is an overwhelming air of disgust at the pools of blood between the lines and the splayed edges of torn limbs lying casually by the wayside.

"Pesto sauce," said Alec. "When you get the mix wrong and it goes runny with lumps in it."

I ignored the flippant comment and, pulling my collar up close round my neck, made my way to the scene of the carnage. I felt ever so slightly unnerved as a uniformed officer marched over towards us. "I'd ask what your plan was," Alec whispered, "but you seem to make things up as you go along."

"What do you think you're doing here, Spallucci?" demanded the officer. I wasn't surprised that he had recognised me. The police seemed to have been my constant companions recently.

"I'm on a case."

"Well you can piss off back to your tarot cards. This is a suicide and nothing else, understand?"

I was about to plead my case when Alec stepped forward.

"It's very important that we see the remains."

There was a certain lilt to his young voice. "You *will* let us through."

For a moment the copper just stood and stared at us. Then he nodded and stepped back to let us past. "Thank you," said Alec.

As we made our way down to the train track I questioned the youth, "Where did you learn that trick, *Obi Wan*?"

He smiled. "At the Academy."

I let the matter drop. There would be a better time and a place for explanations later on, I hoped.

We encountered no more resistance. It was organised chaos down under the bridge. Police were scurrying about left and right. As of yet there was no sign of a forensics team and certainly no sign of an ambulance - the remains of the jumper were very visibly dead. You don't tend to survive losing both your legs and having your head ripped off while your internal organs are being pulverised along a train track.

"Quickly," urged Alec, "We don't have much time. We need to look closer at the body."

I decided to let him do the looking. I just kept watch. Sensitive stomach, you know.

"He jumped alright."

I dared a quick look over my shoulder to see what Alec was doing. He had removed his right glove and had actually placed his bare hand on a piece of fragmented tissue. "Jesus," I moaned as my stomach started to lurch. I fought down the urge to foul a crime scene with hot, steaming vomit and wrenched my gaze away from Alec's examination.

"There's something else though," he continued. "This man had lost all total hope." I grimaced as I heard a squelching noise from behind. What the devil was he doing? Treating it like Play-Doh? "He was afraid that his past was going to catch up with him. Terrified in fact."

I caught a sight of something amongst the strewn carnage and picked my way over carefully.

"This man," Alec continued, "must have had a real chequered history. He had gotten himself a real respectable life recently, but before..." He took a sharp intake of breath. "Well he was no saint for sure. There were girls, drugs, alcohol and lots of-"

"Bikes." I finished, peering down at the remains of a familiar tattooed cheek. "Lots of motorbikes." I heard raised voices and noticed that people were starting to look over in our direction. Apparently the little Jedi mind-trick had started to wear off. "Company's coming, Alec. Time to leave."

So we did. Quickly.

"You've gone quiet."

We were walking back down Market Street towards the city centre. Lancaster is quite small as cities go and most places can be reached on foot if people are willing to put the effort in. The train station is just a couple of minutes walk from the main shopping area, an area where the shoppers and workers would be busying themselves that autumn morning, unaware that an innocent man who had turned his life around from vice and violence to clean living had been ritually murdered by the man that he regarded as his saviour.

I took sweet relief from the tobaccoey heaven that was a Lucky Strike.

"Those things are really bad for you, you know?"

We stood outside Waterstone's book shop, waiting for the lights to change so that we could cross the one-way system. I blew out a long puff of smoke, looked at my new companion and gave a short chuckle. Companion. It made me sound like Doctor Who. Shaking my head, I decided I couldn't be bothered waiting for the lights and walked out into the flow of traffic. There was much screeching of brakes and presenting of fingers but I ignored them. A pair of trainers ran after me.

"Why do you do that?"

"Why are you here?" I had stopped next to the estate agents on the corner to stub the remains of my cigarette out on the nearby bin. "Tell me. Why this sudden interest in me? You were quite happy to lurk in the shadows before, all," I flapped my arms, "guardian angel style. Now, here you are, talking ten to the dozen, a mouth full of questions without so much as an explanation. I've had a really shit couple of weeks Alec and, quite frankly, right now I feel like finding the nearest pub and drinking myself to oblivion. So, just for once, give me a straight answer, will you? Why are you here?"

His dark eyebrows knotted together. "You need help."

I crossed my arms and let my eyes survey him from his feet upwards. His trainers had seen much better days; they were worn and muddy. His blue jeans were scuffed at the edges and covered in grass stains. His jacket was crumpled and had been roughly stitched back together in numerous places. His chin was slightly stubbled in the sort of growth that teenage boys would normally call in prideful delusion a beard. On his back was a grubby, well-loved back pack, that had the corner of a sleeping bag poking out of the top.

He shrugged. "That and I need a place to stay for a while."

For some weird reason, I couldn't help but grin and I don't think it was one of his mind tricks.

He talked almost incessantly on the way over to Dalton Square. About what, I'm not too sure. I think I zoned out once we turned onto Penny Street. I was still in a morose stupor from the events of that morning and the weekend. Suicides, deaths, one mystical disappearance and a shed-load of hatred from your ex can do that to you. Alec didn't seem to mind. He just seemed pleased to have someone to talk to. From what I recall, there were comments about the smell of coffee when we passed Starbucks, opinions on the decline in the economy when we passed the empty Next shop on Horseshoe Corner and other little snippets that washed over me as we headed south on Penny Street. To be honest, it was rather soothing to have someone who seemed more concerned with the day-to-day stuff for once rather than being bombarded with the paranormal horrors that had been dogging me recently.

It wasn't until we had entered my flat and he had dumped his pack on the floor that he said, "You did the best that you could, you know? Wallace is incredibly powerful."

I shrugged. It was little consolation. "I'll put the kettle on," was all that I could manage. I meandered off into the kitchen, leaving Alec to investigate his new surroundings like a puppy in a new house. At least he would not piss on the carpet.

"I love the clocks!" he called out cheerily as I spooned some instant coffee into two mismatched mugs. One was slightly chipped and I ran my thumb over the damaged glaze. So functional yet so fragile. The slightest thing could turn this simple utensil into a pile of shattered fragments. All you had to do was pick it up then drop it from a great height.

Just as Wallace had done with Matthew Slesinski.

Then once more I was stood over his tattered remains, chunks of flesh strewn along the train track and pools of blood thick in the gravel. My stomach churned and I ran for the bathroom. I made it just in time as my guts puked up into the toilet. This was just too much. How could I cope with all this? I felt like I had become an angel of death and everyone I touched was dropping down dead from an unseen plague. My stomach churned and more vomit spewed into the pan.

As I groaned to God on the great, white telephone I became aware of footsteps behind me. My cheeks flushed with embarrassment but I did not dare let go of the toilet as more bile began to rise.

Then suddenly it was gone.

The churning had quelled to a soft eddy and the burning bile tasted like clear fresh water which trickled softly back down my gullet. I knelt up, wiped my mouth with some toilet paper and looked up at the boy standing behind me.

"Better?" he asked.

I nodded. "Much. If you wouldn't mind?" I motioned to the wash basin.

"Sure." He filled the glass tumbler there with water and offered it to me. I drank it down slowly. Then peered in surprise at the clear liquid. It tasted of...

"Ginger is good for nausea," Alec explained.

I raised an eyebrow. "I didn't know I had it on tap."

"You don't," he shrugged, "but for now your brain thinks you do."

"Neat trick."

Another little shrug. "I found Israel far too hot so had to learn how to cope. That helped."

"Israel?"

"The kettle's boiled. I'll go finish those coffees for you." He turned and hurried out of the bathroom.

Curiouser and curiouser. I thought as I sipped at the clear liquid which, this time, was just water. I heaved myself up to my feet and followed him. As I walked through, Alec was bringing two steaming hot mugs of coffee through to the living room. He set them down on the table and settled himself on my sofa. I took the armchair. "So here we are," I said.

"Here we are, indeed," he replied.

We sipped our coffee and the rest of the conversation went unsaid. It was just not the right time. I had far too many questions and I had the feeling this young fellow was not going to surrender any answers too quickly.

So we sat and drank our coffee in silence.

Eventually I decided that it would be best to remain focussed on practicalities. "There's an attic upstairs. You could sleep up there if you wanted. It would give you some privacy and I'm guessing that you're not heavy-laden with possessions."

Alec smiled. "That would be great. Thank you."

"I'll get hold of a mattress or something you can use for a bed."

"Okay. The floor will be fine for now. At least I'll have a roof over my head."

I pointed towards the back pack. "You've been on the road for a while?"

"Yes," he nodded. "Talking of which, could I use your shower? It's been, as you say," he grinned, "*a while.*"

I chuckled to myself. "Sure. Help yourself."

So he wandered off into the bathroom and I drained my coffee before turning back to matters at hand. First things first: what day was it? I flicked on my phone. The screen announced that it was Monday and that the battery was incredibly low. As I sat the device in its charging cradle I shook my head. Where had last week gone? Also, was I any further to reining in Wallace?

The answer to both these questions was that I had no idea.

What was Wallace actually doing? Yes, he was running riot in his own little serial killer fantasy, and for what aim? He was convinced that it would bring about the Divergence. But how?

"Not too sure on that one."

"Jesus Christ!" I snapped jumping out of my skin in shock. "Alec, don't do that."

"Sorry, Sam. Old habit." He stood in the doorway bare to the waist and hair wet. I frowned as I noticed seven dark marks across his chest. They looked like the remnants of old wounds. Another question to file away for later. He wandered over to his pack and fished out a slightly less crumpled t-shirt. "I'm not used to being around people."

"Sure, I get that, but house rule number one: no head poking."

"No probs," he grinned. "But like I said, I really don't know how the suicides should bring the Divergence about. It doesn't really make sense."

I leaned back in my armchair. "So you've had a bit of experience in this already then?"

Water droplets dripped off his wet hair as Alec nodded. "I've seen similar."

"Really? When?"

Alec shook his head sending more water flying. "That's not important right now. What we need to be focussing on is numbers. Wallace needs five sacrifices, yes?"

"How do you..?"

He tapped the side of his head.

"Fair enough," I conceded. "Yes he needs five."

"And he has how many so far?"

I counted them off on my fingers. "The waitress and Flint were two. Abalone made three and Matt Slesinski was the fourth."

"Which means?"

I sat gobsmacked. "He only needs one more to bring about the Divergence."

At that moment there was a loud hammering at the door.

This time Jitendra had brought more than just one playmate. Three burly boys in blue muscled their way into my flat after him.

Oh, I was in deep trouble.

"Two more!" the DCI yelled into my face. "Two more victims, one of which I can place with you less than an hour before her death." He stood invading my personal space, breathing heavily as he ran his fingers through his jet black hair. "What the hell, Sam? I asked you to get close to Wallace, help me bring him down, not get him to up his kill rate."

"Jitendra..."

"No! Enough!" His nostrils flared as his normally well-guarded anger flooded over the brim. "Not this time. No, not this time."

I glanced over to the corner of the room where Alec was stood propped up against the door frame. The police officers were totally oblivious to his presence. Hope started to puff frantically at the small ember that it was desperate to nurse back to life.

"No," Jitendra continued, "this time... this time..." He wagged a finger vigorously in the space before my nose. "This... time..." He stopped and stared at the tip of the finger as if it was the first time he had ever seen such a strange looking object. "This..."

The uniformed muscle gave each other confused

looks. "Sir?" one of them asked. "What are..."

I saw a smile touch Alec's lips. He combed his fingers through his wet hair. "Go back to the station. Forget you were ever here. Go and save some puppies."

Jitendra's eyes snapped back into focus, alert, resolute. "Come on, men. We've got work to do. There are innocent canines out there that require our help!"

"Yes sir!" The bobbies snapped to attention before charging out of my flat in pursuit of their dog-saving boss.

I started to breathe again and closed the door behind them. Then, looking back to my young companion, I said, "Yes indeed, you are very useful to have around the place."

He grinned.

"But now, young Alec," I frowned as I slumped down into my armchair fishing out a cigarette, "I have questions and you *will* answer them." Flicking my zippo, I lit my Lucky. Breathing in deep, the tobaccoey goodness warmed a pair of lungs that were still chilled from the blind panic caused by Jitendra's sudden intrusion. I gazed out of the window across Dalton Square and observed that winter was starting to breathe down my city's neck. It always comes early in these parts: the leaves fall, the geese fly and little black and white pied wagtail birds can be seen bobbing their long plumage up and down around town.

What never seems to change, though, is the lack of clothing that people seem to wear when they go clubbing. Even on a night when the sky is clear and frost is starting to turn tarmac into ice-rinks young girls wear the shortest dresses and young lads sport silk shirts open halfway down their chests with no jacket. I shook my head as I thought about how they would stagger through Dalton Square later on, oblivious to any apocalyptic threat, then turned and faced my new lodger.

"So," I said, "here's the thing. I set myself up in what most would consider to be a less than conventional career and suddenly I find myself with a young shadow. This shadow appears from nowhere. Now, it is not a malign presence - far from it. Indeed on certain occasions it has indeed appeared to be quite useful. In fact one could call it a *life-saver*." There was a glimmer of a smile from the young boy's worried mask. "For that, I thank my newly-found guardian angel."

"You're welcome," he replied, graciously, his eyes trying to look everywhere but at my face.

I paused. "Indeed." A draw of nicotine suffused my bloodstream before I continued. "However, there seems to be a catch. Said shadow seems to have been dealt a better hand of cards in the game of poker that is my life at the moment. It knows things that I do not and seems to possess *attributes* that would not really be welcome by other players at a game of cards."

Alec's head raised and his eyebrows knotted. "Actually, I think it would be more correct to use the word *powers* rather than the word *attributes*. An attribute is a quality or feature regarded as a characteristic or inherent part of someone or something. The ability to manipulate minds or make someone perceive you to be invisible could not be defined as qualities or features. They are something that I *do,* they're not part of my character."

I raised an eyebrow as I drummed my fingernails on my teeth.

"Fair point." I stubbed the cigarette out and leaned back in the armchair, its soft embrace cushioning my tired joints. "Does being a walking dictionary also count as being a power too?"

The youth flicked his head to one side. "I have had a rather more extensive education for my years than most of those my age."

"And what would your age be then?"

"Seventeen or eighteen," he shrugged with an air that did not really care. "I've lost track a bit."

"Why would that be?"

"I've been travelling."

"Far?"

"Yes."

"I'm guessing not a standard gap year then."

A little head flick. "No."

I let out a sharp, exasperated breath. This was like trying to knock down a stone wall with a tooth pick. Alec was not for giving. It was not as if he was hiding anything, as such. He was just not telling me anything unless I asked him in a completely direct manner.

I stood up, poured myself a Jack, downed it in one, poured another and began to pace the room. "Why are you here, Alec?" I finally asked.

He paused, gathering his thoughts, before answering. "To help you and to stay safe."

That caught my attention alright. "To stay safe? What from?"

He shook his head.

I turned that over in my mind as the whiskey slid down again.

"Okay, not *what* from. *Who* from?"

"That is very difficult to answer, Sam."

"Why? Do you not want to tell me?"

For the first time in the conversation he looked straight up at me and those bright blue eyes were full of the deepest sadness I had ever seen. "Because there are just far too many people to list that would want me dead if they knew of my existence."

Wow! I hadn't seen that coming, but then... "Is that how you got those marks on your chest?"

He nodded, silently.

"How did it happen?"

"I was shot seven times." He unconsciously ran his fingers over his cotton t-shirt.

I sat down again, my knees suddenly weak. "Shot? When?"

"A month ago."

I had no voice. A month? Seven times? But the marks looked so old, not to mention the rather alarming fact that he should almost certainly be dead! My mind was racing now. There was so much that I wanted to know, that I *needed* to know, but I had to be so very, very careful here. I was going to have to tease the pearl-like information out of this tightly-closed oyster without managing to damage the shell.

"Who shot you, Alec?"

He crossed the room and sat down on the sofa. "That is complicated and it might upset you."

My stomach lurched, but I had to know. "Try me,

Alec. Please tell me. It's important."

His blue eyes shot to the front door. "The police."

"Oh, shit," I groaned. I had a wanted felon sat here in my living room. A wanted felon with supernatural powers who had just mind-warped the very authorities that had tried to kill him. The day was just getting better and better.

"I did say it might upset you."

"That's okay."

"Besides, it's not like most of them were real, anyway."

I frowned. "Not real police?"

"No," he corrected. "Not real *humans*."

Okay. Curiouser and curiouser. I filed that little snippet in the *come back to it later* box. "So how did you survive?"

"I heal quickly."

I snorted a quick laugh. No joking he healed quickly. "So, I'm guessing that you're not human."

His eyes drifted off again as his thoughts once more processed my question. "Again, that is complicated."

"Is it likely to upset me?"

He shook his head. "Oh, no. Not at all. Sam, do you believe in angels?"

Okay. So I had to admit, this was a new one. In the last few weeks I had encountered vampires, fairies and a werewolf. Wallace briefly mentioned them in passing when lecturing me about his beloved Beyond. So did this mean that I had some sort of cherub sat in front of me? Alec did not strike me as the type to spend all day sat around on cloud strumming a harp so I asked, "Are you saying...?"

"What?" He sat bolt upright, a mixture of surprise and amusement on his face. "Oh, God no! I'm not an angel."

I felt a sigh of relief escape my lungs and I tipped the glass of Jack back. Hooray for almost normal.

"It's my dad who's the angel."

I nearly choked as bourbon sprayed from my mouth.

"And possibly my mum, but we're not sure on that at the moment," he continued as I gasped for air, rasping staccato coughs through alcoholic vapour.

Dear Lord, why me? I thought to myself. I had never known that life could get this complicated. First a week from hell, then Caroline turning up, then Wallace, then John and now this. I sat and stared for a while. Alec contemplated his bare feet.

"When you say *possibly your mum*," I finally ventured once I'd calmed down. "Does that mean you're not sure who your mother is?"

He shook his head. "No. I know who my mum is. It's just we're not sure whether she was an angel at the time or not."

Okay. More weirdness.

"You say *we*. Would that be you and your father."

Alec nodded.

"So he's still on the scene, so to speak."

He gave a quiet chuckle that managed to unnerve the pants off me. "Oh yeah, Sam. He's very much around. It was him who said I had to come and find you.

He said that you could keep me safe."

My fingers did their little tooth tap dance. "He *knows* me?"

"Yes. In a manner of speaking."

My shoulders rose and fell as I gave an exasperated breath. This really was getting me nowhere apart from five steps closer to the cuckoo nest. "Look, Alec," I held my hand out to him, pleading, "you've got to give me more than this. These little riddles are doing my head in."

For a moment he looked up at me and, when those blue eyes locked on mine, I swear to God above that the pupils were burning with fire. Not only that, but they suddenly seemed far older than they should.

They were eyes that had lived.

They were eyes that had wandered.

They were eyes that had suffered.

Those eyes stayed fixed on mine for about thirty seconds before he checked his head to the side and looked away once more. "I'm sorry, Sam. I can't tell you anything else about me right now. Dad doesn't want me to. It's very, very complicated and there is a definite chance that you will not like what you hear."

He looked up once more and there were those attractive blue eyes of a young lad who was alone in the world and needed someone to watch over him, someone to protect him.

Someone like me.

I nodded. "Okay," I capitulated, fishing out another Lucky. "But do me this, if you can. Why don't you tell me about angels?"

Then suddenly, it was like a massive amount of pressure had been unburdened from his shoulders. He leaned forward, his eyes bright and his face animated. "Sure, I can tell you about angels, Sam. I can tell you everything that I know about them."

And he was off.

As he started to talk he rose from the sofa and paced the room, his arms gesturing in the air as he described things for me. His eyes wandered around the room although it was clear that they did not see a thing that was in front of him. Instead they were off with the very beings that he was describing.

I have read numerous books over the years which describe how theologians and mystics throughout the ages have stated that there is a hierarchy to angels. Alec told me that this was reality, though not as any old chap in a cave had described it.

At the bottom were the Angeloi. These were what most people thought of when it came to angels. They were white-robed, golden-skinned and possessed a single pair of feathery wings. They spent their time wandering the realm of Heaven contemplating God and His works.

Next were the Archangels. Of these there were only four: Michael, Gabriel, Raphael and Uriel. They spent their time in the Sanctuary actually in the presence of God. They were similar in appearance to the Angeloi, but they seemed to hold themselves somewhat different. You just knew that they were superior. I figured them to be sort of middle management types, but then I had an image of The Office's David Brent as cupid and quickly shoved the image out of my head.

One point of interest that all Archangels and Angeloi shared was a specific power. There were those who could create matter from nothing. Some could shift time. Others had more elemental powers such as control over fire and water.

I asked him if, perhaps these powers could be hereditary?

He grinned, catching onto my point. "My mum has the ability of psyche; she can get inside people's minds. She can see what they are thinking and distort what they perceive to be real."

"Neat trick," I observed.

He nodded.

I rolled my fingers à la Roland Deschain encouraging him to continue.

Next came the three mystical groups of angels: Thrones, Dominions and Powers. Thrones sort of spoke for themselves. They were the angels that made up the throne of God - small cherub-like creatures that made cute noises from time to time. Angelic Furbies, Alec called them. Dominions were somewhat elusive. All the other angels knew they existed, but none had ever seen them. It was believed that they dwelt here on Earth in the physical realm. Powers were the mad hermits of Heaven. They had no true form apart from what they felt like assuming for their own purposes and they spent all their time in a specific part of Heaven that was separate from the rest. Sometimes other angels went there to contemplate or seek their wisdom, but most of the time the rest of the Heavenly Host stayed well away. There was only one who ever went there on a regular basis, but he would not be going there anytime soon.

"Why's that?" I asked.

Alec stopped pacing. Suddenly the air was a touch too tense for my liking.

"He's the only member of the highest order of angels - the Seraphim."

Clocks ticked into my once ringing ears as I guessed the name that Alec was about to say

"Lucifer," I whispered.

He nodded. "Lucifer, the six-winged Seraph who spent most of his days, years, aeons dwelling in the heart of the Presence of God until one day he saw something that filled his heart with fear causing him to leave Heaven."

"*Filled his heart with fear?*" Now that was different. "What do you mean by that? Most texts say he fell from grace through pride and such stuff."

Alec shook his head. "Lucifer was a tragedy. He existed from before the beginning of time. He was the first of all angels, dwelling deep in the heart of God. As he slept he sang and God was so pleased with his song that he created Heaven and the angels. Then, aeons later, when Lucifer saw that God was to create a physical realm, he looked along Creation's timeline and saw something so horrific that it filled him with dread. He saw the timeline split in two.

"The Divergence."

There it was again. That phrase that seemed to be stalking me closer than a sad, greasy loner in Hollywood.

"Down one way there was Paradise. Heaven and Earth would unite. Love and Peace would rule for eternity. We would all be at one with God

"Down the other... Down the other was Kanor. Kanor and his Divergent Lands, the time of the Constructs. Heaven and Earth would not converge. There would be no peace. there would be a living hell on Earth until finally everything was put out of its misery.

"Total Oblivion."

"Shit," I whispered.

"That's not all."

"You've got to be kidding? there's more?"

"Sam, the Divergence is imminent. It will be caused by a man who is alive now. We will see it happening in our lifetime."

My blood chilled to sub-zero. "Wallace," I hissed.

CHAPTER 18

Four down, one to go.

Four down, one to go.

Four down, one to go.

I was smoking yet another Lucky as I paced back and forth in my flat. Smoke hung heavy around the room. Alec had made his excuses and gone to explore his attic room.

Alec.

I shook my head. So here I was, babysitting again. Last week a vampire, this week a... a... a goodness knows what child of one angel and one angel or human.

Oh, for the simple life!

Plus all the time Wallace was out there planning to take another innocent life in order to reform creation into some sort of post-apocalyptic paradise. Who would it be? Someone I knew or a complete stranger? Who was that monster going to reduce to such a wreck that they would end their own life?

Then there was the small matter of the Divergence.

What would happen when that final victim popped one too many pills or walked out into oncoming traffic? Would life as we know it cease? Would we enter into a new realm of horror and despair or was Wallace just a deluded sociopath?

The vampires had talked about the Divergence. Hell, they were even waiting for it, it had to be something tangible, but could it be brought about by just five suicides?

Anything is possible. Those three words, the little mantra of Wallace and his beloved disciples. Was it possible that five little acts of random cruelty could bring about the end of the world as we knew it?

My head was screaming. I was going round in circles. Literally. I paced round and round the room trying to grasp some slight straw of certainty in a field of confusion.

I needed to stop and rest.

I needed some music.

I flicked my stereo on and rummaged through the usual suspects of CDs that sat patiently next to it. I grumbled noisily as nothing grabbed my fancy. Too loud, too quiet. Too frantic, too chilled.

Then something struck my eye. A single CD lying there on its own with no cover. I picked it up and turned it over in my hand. It was the one that Boombox Betty had given me on Friday: *The Confessions Of Doctor Dream And Other Stories* by Kevin Ayers. I shrugged.

I might as well, I thought.

I popped it into the CD slot, lay out on the sofa and closed my eyes as the doleful voice of Kevin Ayers wafted over me.

The next thing I knew...

Rain hammered down like stair-rods but I remained remarkably dry.

"Another dream, then," I sighed to myself. "Ah well, let's go with the flow."

I surveyed my location. It was a dark, wet alley. Lancaster's full of them, a hangover one might say from the wonders of Georgian development that decided every last square inch ought to be put to good use as long as it didn't impact socially on those who actually funded the building of the storehouses and mills. To my left was the side of a building that I recognised as a furniture warehouse on Saint Leonard's Gate which meant that on my right was the Grand Theatre. Okay. Not so bad. Hardly an apocalypse. I let my feet lead me around the corner to the front of the large, Georgian building. The rain kept me company in its hammering manner, miraculously parting before me as I walked. Saint Leonard's Gate was bustling with theatre-goers hurrying out of the rain that seemed to prefer soaking them rather than me. They didn't seem bothered, however. There was not a scowl or a curse amongst them. They all seemed remarkably cheerful, which seemed unsettlingly unusual as, at the first drop of rain, Lancastrian folk will normally inform you, "It has never rained this hard as long as I can remember." Their other meteorological comments also include, "It doesn't snow anywhere near as bad as it used to," and, "The summers were definitely hotter thirty years ago, so don't you go telling me about this global warming rubbish." There were people of all ages piling into the theatre: parents dragging along chattering children, elderly couples reminiscing about the last play that they had been to see and young couples entwined arm in arm.

My heart ached at the sight of them.

"Losing someone makes you sad, makes you think that life is bad."

I turned at the sound of the voice next to me. There, crowned with his mop of unruly hair stood the late, great Kevin Ayers himself. I raised an eyebrow. "The last time I dreamt about a musician, they threw me off a flying horse. You're not planning something similar, are you?" I asked.

He just smiled and gestured for me to lead the way.

As I passed the billboards, I caught an unmistakable flash of lilac and saw emblazoned in large letters: "Tonight only, Doctor Dream!" I groaned inwardly. It had started out so promising, too.

Presently, Ayers and I were sat in the same box that Wallace and I had occupied the other night. I had no memory as to how we had arrived there, but there we were. The audience, as they had previously, were settling down and the lights were starting to dim. As a stuttering hush crept through the stalls, the curtain rose and the unmistakable sound of *The Confessions of Dr. Dream* struck up from the speakers. "Take your partners for the dance, quick before you miss the chance," Ayers spoke into my ear in an exaggerated stage whisper.

I had no partner right now. I was totally on my

own. Caroline had used me. Wallace had... I wasn't sure what. I shook my head slightly, oozing melancholy and watched as the show began.

A lone man stepped into the middle of the stage. He was clad head to toe in lilac: a lilac suit, a lilac shirt and lilac shoes. All this was topped off by a lilac top hat and an elaborate lilac cane that was entwined with two snakes: one red, one black.

"I take life!" he proclaimed to the audience at large who responded with whoops and shouts of joy.

"My knife cuts deep!"

I leaned forward to try and get a better view of the man but, from my angle, the brim of his gaudy top hat obscured any chance of glimpsing his face.

"Brings sleep..." He raised his arms out to his sides, his cane clasped in his right hand.

"Looks like a crazed Willy Wonka and an inebriated Robbie Williams mated and produced some weird love-child," I murmured.

Kevin Ayers touched my arm and whispered, "Watch out for Doctor Dream."

I could hear something else now. Behind the psychedelic tunes of Ayers' music, there was another voice; one that was sweet but insidious. It was a female voice humming low and quietly, just within audible range. Ice slipped down my spine as the members of the audience started to rise from their seats and gradually ascended into apoplexy. They were waving their hands in the air as they vied for the attention of Doctor Dream. Lovers pushed each other aside, parents fought to free themselves of their offspring, the elderly were trampled over as a body of grabbing hands and beatific smiles rushed towards the foot of the stage.

I caught a glimpse of Dream's mouth. It was smiling cruelly. "I'll fill your skies with promise that you'll fly," he hissed and the humming grew louder and louder in time with the incessant beat of the music. The audience were now totally hysterical, screaming and wailing for him to reach out to them. They wanted him to look at them, to touch them, to save them.

Dream raised his cane high in the air and it started to squirm. With languid fluidity, the two snakes detached themselves from the stick and started to elongate out into the air above him. Their eyes glittered with orange malevolence as they grew rapidly in size. In a few seconds they went from being extravagant ornaments on a walking stick to filling half the stage with their rippling bodies.

They slithered their way hungrily towards the edge of the stage, their huge muscles undulating along their bodies causing a harsh rasping sound as their bellies crawled along the wooden floor.

"I will return to feed on you!" he screamed out.

"Oh no," I whispered hoarsely. As the snakes opened their cavernous mouths, I made to rise from my chair but the hand of Kevin Ayers resolutely fastened me tight. "Watch out for Doctor Dream," he repeated once more.

Down below, there were no screams of terror as the audience were systematically devoured by the oversized serpents. Instead there were welcoming cries of, "Take me! Take me!" before the sickening sound of those voices being muffled out one by one. The snakes spared no-one; adult or child, male or female, they devoured everyone and not one person protested. Each meal gave itself willingly and joyfully to the vile creatures. All the time Doctor Dream stood on the stage, his arms outstretched, a look of satisfaction on his cruel lips, as if he were bathing in the glow of a beautiful summer's day.

I tore my eyes away from the horrific spectacle and looked in the one direction that I could to avoid the massacre, the opposite box.

A familiar pair of sunglasses were staring back at me.

The stranger from my dream about John O'Gaunt Media lowered the glasses and his eyes of fire fixed on me.

If ever there was a face that described anger, it was his. His hands gripped the sides of his box and smoke began to rise up in wisps from the painted woodwork. I was suddenly very aware that the temperature in the theatre had risen quite dramatically.

There was an enormous flash of flame and I awoke, drenched in sweat.

"I have got to stop listening to music before I go to sleep," I groaned.

CHAPTER 19

Monday lurched its way towards Tuesday. I spent most of the day brooding over my incapacity to achieve even the slightest action. Whenever I closed my eyes I saw the two monstrous serpents gobbling up willing sacrifices as Doctor Dream looked on with glee.

Then there was the other guy; the one from the other box, the same one from my dream of the John O'Gaunt studios. Who the hell was *he*? Like I needed any more to worry over.

I could not cope with this. It was all too much. In the end I got myself totally rat-arsed and collapsed in a heap on my bed.

The next day I sluggishly made my way through to the bathroom then the kitchen and back in circuit to my bed where I sat, drank coffee, ate toast, downed paracetamol and grumbled inwardly at how the world had been put in place just for the sole purpose of torturing me.

What had I ever done?

What was my crime in a previous life? I was too

old to have been Pol Pot. Surely I was too young to have been Hitler? Was there some other crazy serial-killing lunatic politician who had died the year I had been born? That must have been the case. It could not be surely down to just plain bad luck, could it?

A depressive cloud enveloped me as I finished off my toast. Eight-thirty, proclaimed my vintage Mickey Mouse alarm clock. No rest for the wicked. I had to get my backside into gear.

But to do what?

Good question. I considered hollering upstairs to my new lodger but something inside me resolutely shook its head. Right now I needed clarity of thought not brain-aching cryptology. I felt like I had been handed a pile of enigma codes and been told to decipher them without the slightest help from a code book.

In short, I was in an impossible situation. All I seemed able to do was constantly mull over and over images and actions that I had no hope in understanding or preventing. Wallace was always that bit too far ahead of me. He was a dark Pied Piper casually playing a haunting jig whilst everyone, myself included, merrily danced along to their doom.

Well, not today.

Today I was going to walk in a different direction. I had spent far too long chasing my tail and it had only brought me heartache and misery. Today, I was going to turn my back on the whole affair and clear my head before I came back to the task at hand refreshed and reinvigorated.

I glanced out of the window. It was a bright, crisp

autumnal day. Perfect for a walk. I needed a long, refreshing tramp either down the canal or up Clougha, the hill to the east of Lancaster on the edge of the Trough of Bowland. Either would do the trick. Just one foot in front of another; tread after tread, pace after pace. With each footfall dust would be dislodged from the nooks and crannies of my congested mind and the cogs would be allowed to turn once more, letting me see all around in a fresh light. Illumination would fall into the darkest recesses and that which was staring me straight in the face would be unmasked.

So what was it to be? The canal or Clougha? Only one way to decide, really. I fished a pound coin out of my pocket and tossed it high. Heads for the hill, tails for the flat.

The coin landed on the carpet with a dull thud. Heads it was. I scooped the coin up and pocketed it once more then rummaged under my bed for my walking boots.

I had to admit, I was kind of glad that the coin had landed heads up. Clougha is probably my favourite walk in the area. You drive out to Quernmore, look up and just go. I normally choose the route via an old, abandoned farm just to the east of the village. It provides a nice sloping ascent over rough grassland, then a slightly steeper incline over peat and heather before a final push over the short rocky outcrop.

I drove out of town and headed east along Wyresdale Road out past Williamson Park (not somewhere I wanted to visit right now) and off into the countryside. The Leisure Park and the Brewery skipped past my right, the motorway roared over my head and suddenly I was surrounded by a vast expanse of fields, fields and more fields. There, straight ahead of me stood my destination: Clougha Pike.

In a short while I had parked up in the village of Quernmore, pulled on my old, battered boots and was trekking away from civilisation. I had trod this path many times over the years, especially when I had been studying at Luneside University. Once I was out of my car, everything was left behind. There was the still air and the slightly acrid smell of rural industry.

I felt like I was home.

I walked out of the village and, turning off the road, headed up to the base of the hill. The footpath, as ever took me past the old, run down farm house that had stood vacant for at least ten years now. At least it had *used* to be empty. Right now it was a hive of activity with builders buzzing around its walls and up in its exposed rafters. Obviously someone had bought it and had decided that it needed renovating. I shrugged and passed by on to the access point to the land of Clougha.

I carefully closed the gate behind me and smiled as I looked up over the few miles of farmland that stretched upwards in front of me. First, there were the fields; mainly grassy with the occasional tractor ruts. Next, there was the heath land, riddled with becks and deep, boggy peat areas; the claimer of many a carelessly-fastened boot. Then finally there was the pike itself, a rocky outcrop rising up above the softer surrounding areas, fashioned by scraping and sliding glaciers of the last ice age. This was my Ultima Thule; my far destination. Once there, I would be free of all cares and separated from all that was dragging me down into the mire of everyday life.

For what felt like the first time since Caroline had walked into my office, tension truly slipped from my encumbered shoulders. The give of the ground under my well-worn boots felt friendly and reassuring. "Come on, old friend," it was saying to me, "let me take all your strains and burdens." Time was irrelevant as I continued to place one foot in front of another and ascended the slope. Cool, fresh air penetrated my lungs and the distant bleating of sheep danced delicately in my ears.

Before I realised it, I had reached the base of the pike and the rocky path climbed sharply in front of me. I loosened my walking jacket to allow my skin some room to breathe on the final push and progressed at a calm pace up the last stretch.

Then I was there. I have climbed higher peaks - Skiddaw, Snowdon, even the great Ben Nevis – but whenever I crest that last rise onto the summit of Clougha, I always feel that I am on top of the world. Sometimes, when I know there is no-one looking, I even do a god-awful impersonation of Jimmy Cagney.

But not today.

Today was a day for peace and quiet not daft black-and-white gangster movie antics.

I picked my way across the jutting rocks, made my way to the trig point and just stared out across the vast expanse of space. It was a glorious blue-sky day and I could see out across Morecambe Bay in one direction and over to Yorkshire in the other. I fished a fruit bar out of my jacket and nibbled at its juicy yumminess in a very satisfied manner.

This was how life was supposed to be: no creatures looming out of the dark, no ex-girlfriends, no big bad always around the corner. This was paradise. I could stay like this for ever.

I stretched and felt all the clawing pressure from my spine unkink. I wriggled my neck and the tension crackled out from between my loosening vertebrae. I yawned as I sat down on the ground with my back to the trig point looking out over the beautiful, verdant valley below. Yes, this was truly an unspoilt paradise.

I just had to rest my eyes for five seconds, didn't I?

There was a sound that would turn a man's heart inside out with terror. It was a cross between a shriek of an eagle and a roar of a lion but seemed to stretch across all possible boundaries of the human auditory range.

Then there was the smell. Charred ground and trees permeated with the unmistakable, sickening tang of blood.

I kept my eyes tight shut.

"This isn't real. It's just a dream. I am on Clougha. This is my special place. It will go away."

"I'm afraid it won't, Samuel."

"Sod off," I groaned. "Why don't you please just leave me alone?"

"I'm afraid that's not possible," stated the clipped,

educated female voice from right next to my ear. Even over the vicious sounds of carnage and devastation her quiet voice commanded total authority that demanded silence from boisterous readers of books.

I turned my head towards her then opened my eyes. Two pools of pure fire held me locked from behind a pair of dark-rimmed spectacles. "I hate you," I whined. "Don't you have returned books to file or happy children to terrorise?"

The librarian look-a-like cocked her head to one side. "You don't hate me at all and no, I don't." She stood up in one graceful movement that left her trim and immaculate whilst the world around her went to hell in a handbag. Casually she walked with supreme confidence to the edge of the pike and looked out at what could only be described as an apocalypse.

What was worse was the fact that I had already seen this montage before.

There they were, the two dragons – one red, one black – lashing out at each other with talons and claws, gouging chunks of flesh from each other that hurtled to the ground and spawned fires which consumed whole tracts of land. As their blood sprayed from their wounds it rained down on the devastated ground. From the rivulets, creatures arose. From the blood of the red dragon with seven heads angels were spawned; from the blood of the black, those faceless creatures of clay. Both sets of new-borns turned on each other and fought as ferociously as their parents; bloodied wings were torn apart and clods of clay were cast up into the sky.

"Is this for real? Will it actually happen?"

313

"When dragons walk the Earth, then all creation shall tremble."

There it was again. The same little psychotic soundbite I had heard from Philips shortly before he had shuffled off this mortal coil. I turned on my companion, my fists balled in anger. "Don't give me this prophetic crap!" I yelled across the noise of the war. "Will this happen?"

"One dragon already prepares for battle, Samuel." She squeezed my shoulder with her perfectly manicured fingers. It felt like I was gripped in a vice. "Do not let your inactivity cause the other dragon to join the fray!"

Then, as usual, I was left standing on my own.

"I'm really starting to hate my life," I groaned and my eyes flicked open to the once more calm scene of the Trough of Bowland. I let my heavy head sink into my hands and I rocked back and forth against the trig point. Dragons, dragons. What was it with dragons? First the late, not-so-great, Philips, then Wallace and now my ethereal, book-loving stalker.

And what the hell did she mean by, *Do not let your inactivity cause the other dragon to join the fray*? More cryptic codes even here at my fortress of solitude!

I delved into my pocket and fished out a packet of Luckies. Sod the healthy living fix; I needed the good old-fashioned crutch of roasted tar and nicotine. I flicked my Zippo and lit the cigarette. My hand paused as I was about to return the lighter to my pocket. I lifted it up and studied its pattern. Over sixteen years old and it still looked like new. It had certainly been made to last.

It had lasted a damn sight longer than our

relationship – mine and Caroline's.

It had lasted longer on this planet than our son. Tears welled in my eyes.

I turned the Zippo over as I rubbed away the stinging tears and read the fake Latin saying that my son's mother had had engraved for me. *Nil illegitimi carborundm.* "Don't let the bastards grind you down," I whispered to myself. Right now I was between a sod of a rock and an infeasibly hard place. I was being bashed about and smashed to a pulp.

I was not going to let them grind me down.

I didn't care about all their supernatural, mystical hoodoo.

I had no time for their dragons or their blessed Divergence.

Wallace had stolen my son. He had played his flute and my only child had been dragged screaming to the land beyond the mountains.

From the top of Clougha I could see that clouds had started to gather over Lancaster. They were dark and ominous, harbingers of an oncoming storm. As I made my way back down towards my car I let the storm swirl inside my guts, churning and gusting at the thought of Malcolm Wallace, self-proclaimed Messiah and destroyer of lives.

The bastard would pay.

CHAPTER 20

Arriving back at my flat I unscrewed a fresh bottle of Jack and poured myself a generous measure. I had boarded the train to righteous anger with a first class reservation and I was and was hurtling along the track at full speed. I knocked the bourbon back in one, swift glug and poured another.

Doctor Dream. Wallace was Doctor Dream, promising people that anything was possible, drawing them in like a fisherman with a tasty morsel hooked onto a cruel barb. Then, when they were close enough, all adoring and all worshipping, he devoured them. He drew on their devotion like a hungry, ancient god obsessed with immortality.

Caught up in this supernatural feast had been my son, John. He was an innocent bystander removed from our reality on a casual whim, a sideshow.

Thunder cracked outside rather dramatically. I rasped a rude noise and poured myself more whiskey. Right now I was impotent, unable to stop him. He was far too powerful. How could I bring down a guy who could send people to other dimensions with just three words.

I grimaced as I felt those three syllables slide around my brain. They writhed and wrestled with my synapses eager to be free. I felt my mouth twitch involuntarily. I slapped a hand across my mouth. They were not going to escape.

I needed a momentary distraction.

Slouching down into my armchair I flicked on the goggle box. It was the lunch time news. This was just as depressing as my life. In the Middle East people continued to blow each other up in the name of God. I sipped the whiskey as images of homeless children flashed across the screen followed by footage of young men with guns burning American flags.

Some things never changed.

Ironic really when Wallace was determined to change everything into a model that he would carefully shape with his own hands.

I drank my way down the glass as the national news gave way to the local. Murders, deaths, abductions. Even the local news was depressing. I didn't remember it being like this when I was a kid. Surely there were lighter topics that had been covered in my youth? Or perhaps that was just the rosy tint of approaching forty colouring my view of the long lost past? The long, lost past of playing with an Action Man on my parents' lawn.

"Don't forget the child you were, Samuel."

Then I nearly choked on my Jack.

The local news was showing live footage of an all-too-familiar location. There was Market Square in all its drizzly glory. I could make out the library, TK Maxx, Vodafone.

And a crowd of people.

My heart started to race as I downed the rest of the whiskey. I had a very bad feeling about this.

The reporter was prattling on about how in this time of despair people needed hope and how, here in Lancaster, one man was determined to bring people that hope. Indeed that man was determined to show everyone that *anything is possible*.

There he was, the new Messiah, standing tall in the drizzling rain, his white hair immaculately groomed and his orange eyes looking straight to the camera.

His hands placed firmly on the shoulders of the same little girl that he had healed the previous week.

"Do I look like a man who could kill a child?"

"You wear one face whereas I, like the Chimera, wear many."

I dashed out of my flat and down the stairs to my office. As I pulled open the bottom drawer to my filing cabinet and pulled out the heavy weight wrapped in an old tea towel, one thing alone was racing through my mind:

I had to stop Wallace by any means possible.

I would not let him take another innocent life.

Thunder rumbled in the distance as I hurled myself down Penny Street, knocking innocent bystanders out of my path. I had no time for social niceties as the fine mist of rain soaked my face and the storm brewed ominously above. I had one hand firmly planted on the revolver in my coat pocket. The last thing I wanted was for that little beauty to tumble out and cause me some interesting explaining.

My lungs started to burn as I reached Horse Shoe Corner and darted up Market Street. I chided myself once more with the fact that I really needed to get into better physical shape as I saw the mass of people milling outside the City Museum. I slowed down somewhat, approaching the rear of the crowd and took slow, steadying breaths. Two weeks ago, chasing across Williamson Park, I had endured the added inconvenience of raging tinnitus and poor balance. At least I did not have that to contend with this time as I hunted my new quarry. No, my prey had made sure that my affliction was a thing of the past. All he had wanted in return was my soul.

That was never going to happen. Just as he was not going to harm a hair on the head of the young girl he had healed the previous week.

I slowly elbowed my way through the thick mass of onlookers. None of them noticed the rumbling of the approaching storm or the wet drizzle that plastered their skin. They were all focussed on one voice, on one moment. There he stood, calm and majestic on the steps to the City Museum, his words cutting clearly across the growing crowd. I glanced around, suddenly aware of just how many people were here. There were far more than there had been at the Credete meeting the previous week. Were they all new disciples to his rallying call? I didn't think so. Some were dressed for work, others carried shopping bags. These were the good old general public; the average Joes who felt that they had to take a good look at what was going on. What was this new and interesting development in the heart of their city?

Each and every one of them hung on Wallace's every word.

I tightened my grip on the revolver in my pocket as I fell in behind the front row of the adoring populace. If only they knew.

He stood there, his kind, avuncular voice instructing all who would listen that they were destined for a better life. He explained that the world would change this very day, that in a few moments all the heartbreak and woe of their mundane lives would be washed away with one simple act.

My blood ran cold as I looked at the child who stood in front of him, his hands placed firmly on her shoulders. His reassuring words drifted in front me like a translucent veil that was attempting to hide a ravening beast. I had heard them all before and they just did not wash. The man was a murderer. Just look at how many had died at his hands in an attempt to change reality and bring about this *Divergence.* There had been the five actors to begin with then, when that had failed, he had started again. The caretaker from the museum, tattoo guy from Credete, the young waitress and of course Abalone. Poor Abalone. The thought of her smiling blue eyes almost caused me to squeeze the trigger and shoot myself in the groin by mistake.

Then there was John; not dead but sent somewhere else. Beyond, wherever that was.

This man was a destroyer not a healer, and now he wanted to destroy one more time to bring about his idea of paradise on Earth. He wanted to terminate the life of a young, innocent girl who, just the other day, he had healed.

Not while I still had breath in my lungs.

I stepped out of the crowd and pulled the revolver from my pocket. There were shouts and screams as people around me suddenly backed off in fear. I was the madman to them, not the calm, controlled harbinger of a new dawn who stood on the steps in front before them, his gentle smile framed by a halo of pure white hair.

"Well, good afternoon, Samuel." Wallace smiled. "So nice of you to join us for this momentous occasion."

"Screw you," I spat. "Step away from the girl." I motioned with the gun. Wallace just smiled at me with a curious look. It was as if I had asked him to walk around on his hands whilst playing a recorder from his butt hole.

"Really, Samuel? Now why would I do that?"

"Because if you don't, I'll blow your sodding head off!" My eyes flicked from side to side. I was aware of a surprising lack of movement from the crowd. In the back of my subconscious I seemed to be expecting someone, perhaps one of Wallace's devoted acolytes or an off-duty cop, prowling stealthily through the people, positioning themselves somewhere where they could pounce on me and save the day. In reality, there was nothing. All that had happened was that those around me had backed off, giving me a wide space and centre stage. Good old British bystanders.

Above, the thunder rolled deeper and the rain

started to increase in volume.

Wallace shook his head a faint smile touching his lips. "Ah, I think I see what this is now. You think that I want kill little Melanie here. How amusing. I've never killed a soul in my life." He bent forwards, lowering his mouth to her ear, his orange eyes never leaving me - mocking me.

"Don't you dare!" I pulled the hammer back on the revolver. "One word! I swear to God, one word..."

"Run along, dear," Wallace said, ignoring the gun, and the girl trotted off to her parents without a care in the world. There was no crazy guy waving a revolver around in front of her. There was no psychopath wanting to destroy humanity from the steps of the City Museum in a small, north west city in England. "So here I am, Samuel." Wallace spread his arms to sides, his cane held in his right hand. "What now?"

"Now you die."

"Ah yes, of course. I was forgetting. You are a killer, aren't you?"

"No." I swallowed. "You're the killer. All those people."

"Really?" He stroked his chin in dramatic thought. "I don't seem to recall laying a hand on anyone. Now *you*... Now there's a different story." A cruel smile formed on his lips. "Does it feel good, Samuel? Does the weight of the gun feel like the weight of someone else's life in your hands?"

My hands dipped slightly as the gun suddenly felt heavier. I raised them up level again, aiming the barrel straight at Wallace's chest.

"Tell me, Samuel," he continued as he walked down a step towards me, what did her eyes say when you pulled the trigger, that poor woman in the park? Were they shocked? Were they pleading? Or were they just dead - lifeless as her heart was ripped open and her soul expired?"

I took an involuntary step back and the gun wobbled once more.

There was a flash of lightning and Wallace's orange irises glowed like burning embers in the flashing unnatural afterglow. "Why do you want to kill me, Samuel? Tell me. Tell all these good, trusting people."

"Because... Because you have to be stopped." My throat was suddenly as dry as an abstainer's pint glass and the words were hard to form – tangled behind my rasping tongue.

"I have to be stopped? What from?"

"The Divergence." Rain streamed down my face and I blinked it out of my eyes. "I've seen it. It can never happen."

"And it's your task to decide what must happen? Your task to decide the future for these good people?"

The weight of the gun was unbearable. Sagging once more it took all my concentration to lift the barrel up. My head was light and my knees gave way as I sank down onto the paved square. Once more the gun sagged. I hefted it up with my right hand as my left propped me up on the pavement. This time, however, I felt like I had no control over my own hand. The gun seemed to rise up out of its own volition.

"Tell me, Samuel," Wallace was now just a couple

of metres away from me, triumph radiating from his smile, "what makes you so different from me? Surely we are just the same?"

"Never." It wasn't my voice. It wasn't my lips that moved. My body was displaced from my control of my basic motor functions. I felt like an observer, just another face in the swarming crowd. All I was fully aware of was my right hand lifting the gun up level with my head, the cold, wet muzzle pressed hard against my temple.

"Poor Samuel," Wallace crooned. "Poor, deluded Samuel. He came chasing demons only to realise that he was one himself – a monster in human flesh. An unbearable thought. Certainly not one that he could bear living with."

And he was right. I had killed a woman in cold blood – pulled a trigger and watched as she had bled to death.

What right did I have to judge this man? I was a far worse killer than he was. Wherever I walked, bodies followed.

Lightning forked across the sky and I heard an almighty crash.

It was not thunder.

CHAPTER 21

Anything is possible.

Anything is possible.

Anything is possible.

My head hurt.

My head hurt.

My head hurt!

I sat bolt upright. Could I do that when I was dead?

Damn, my head hurt! I placed my palm against my temple and rubbed, gingerly.

No gooey mess, that was a plus point.

Wiggled my toes back and forth. My shoes waggled at the end of my feet.

Okay, nerves and muscles seemed to be in order.

I looked around. It was dark. It was Williamson Square, the heart of Luneside University. It was also raining.

"This is Heaven? You've got to be kidding me!"

"It would appear that you misunderstand your situation."

I recognised that prim, crisp female voice. It was the voice that immediately made me want to check the dates in the front of my library books.

There was the light fluttering of wings and half a dozen or so of my little winged friends settled down on my legs and my shoulders. Sophia walked round into my field of view, her plain, sensible shoes making no noise whatsoever on the flagstones.

I noticed that, even with the night-time precipitation, she was bone dry.

But, then again, so was I.

"Well I'm guessing I'm not in Kansas anymore, Tonto."

She stood still and raised an eyebrow. "Curious, you have a wide-ranging knowledge of fantasy fiction yet you fail to remember that the dog from the Wizard of Oz was, in fact, named Toto. Tonto, on the other hand was the Native American companion of the Lone Ranger."

"Well, *kee-mo sah-bee*," I sighed, "perhaps that little slip was something to do with me blowing my brains out, just now."

Sophia cocked her head to one side in thought. "No," she replied, "I feel it is more in keeping with your trying to outsmart me in a witty manner. You failed. You cannot outsmart me."

I shrugged. "Yeah, yeah. Wisdom and all that." I gently removed the fairy-folk from my clothes and pulled myself to my feet. "So then, oh, fount of knowledge, perhaps you will tell me what it is that I'm doing here and, in fact, where *here* is exactly?"

"You are at Luneside University the night after you

326

found out that your father was dying and you have brought yourself to this place and time for the same reason that we want you here."

"What might that be?"

"We both want Malcolm Wallace erased from history."

I tapped my teeth with my fingers as I pondered this little matter. Erase Wallace from history. Right now, that did seem like a dream come true. Here I was, the very night that he went off with his mysterious benefactor and started down the path that ultimately led him to make me point a gun at myself and blow my brains out.

"What the hell," I said, smiling darkly, "I'm in."

Sophia cocked her head to one side and frowned. "Curious."

"What is?"

"You did not ask why we want him removed."

I shrugged. "I'm sure you have your reasons, but right now I'm sort of dwelling on the fact that I'm as dead as a third season of *Enterprise* which is something I would gladly correct." I paused. "The fact that *I'm* dead, not *Enterprise*, that is."

Sophia nodded, "Agreed then. You will dispose of Wallace and your life will return back to your timeline. Any act he committed after this night will never have happened."

"Sounds sweeter than my mother's apple pie." Not only had this man made me kill myself, but he had pushed my son into some sort of hell dimension. Oh yes, I wanted him gone from my life. "Where will I find him?"

"He will be here shortly. Approximately half an

hour or so. He is due to rendezvous with *her*." The word was fuelled with pure venom.

"Wow, am I detecting a history there?"

"No. We just feel that she has interfered in this realm's affairs too many times. She must be stopped on this occasion." The small fairies fluttered up from their resting places and hovered around Sophia. The air started to shimmer and as they started to disappear, Sophia said, "I believe there is a small matter you have to see to before Wallace?" and with that, she and the fairies were gone.

My brow knotted. A matter?

Then it struck me and I smiled my first genuinely happy smile that night.

Luneside University had not changed since I had graduated, but then of course it wouldn't have as I had not yet graduated yet. I shook my head as I climbed the stairs to Borrowdale Hall. I had to admit that I was rather enjoying this little trip down memory lane and as I walked through (yes, *through* – rather cool isn't it?) the door to my old kitchen I couldn't help but chuckle at the sight of Gerald the ghostly cleaner sitting forlornly at the head of a table upon which slumbered the forms of rather younger versions of myself and Spliff.

"Hello, Gerald," I smiled.

The moustache twitched as he took a rather comical double-take at me and my doppelgänger.

"Sam?" he enquired. "Is that you?"

"In the flesh." I spread my arms to my sides. "Well, sort of."

"You look older."

"I feel it too, mate. How you holding up?"

"Well, your buddy lasted about ten minutes before he 'just had to close his eyes a minute'. Then, well.... here we are."

I grinned. "He's good at that, trust me. He'll apologise in the morning." I rounded the table and crouched down beside myself (never, ever thought I'd get the chance to type that phrase) and gave myself a good looking over. "Less grey in the curls," I murmured to myself, "and less wrinkles, too." I was still smiling as I stood up. "So, Gerald, I believe you are in need of a psychopomp."

He nodded.

I waved my arms dramatically. "Ta da! Tonight's your lucky night."

My younger self snored and rolled in his sleep. I remembered what I saw back then and knew what I had to do. I stood in front of the cleaner and said, "So we need to get you home then?"

Gerald nodded. "Do you think you could do it?"

My hands suddenly felt pleasantly warm. I lifted them up between us and Gerald gave out a low whistle. I was aware of a slight moan from my left as the yellow glow from my hands started to spread out around me. "It would seem that I am adequately equipped. Must be some sort of after-life gift." Instinctively, I reached out and the glow spread towards Gerald. It snaked itself around him, shrouding him from head to toe. As he disappeared, his mouth didn't utter a word but his eyes quite clearly smiled a "Thank you."

There was a small noise and I kept smiling as I turned to the source. There I was, about sixteen years younger, looking up at me. My younger self made as if to speak and I shook my head. There was no need for words. Instead, he closed his bleary eyes and passed out again.

I chuckled to myself and looked out of the window.

I had to go.

I had a job to do.

I had things to put right.

When I saw him, whatever passed for blood in my dead form ran cold. There he was, the cold-hearted, murdering bastard. There in plain sight, waiting under the overhang of Williamson Square as if he hadn't a care in the world, as if he didn't have it in him to destroy the life of an innocent boy, my son, John.

Quietly, I walked up behind him and stood for a moment, collecting my thoughts. He was here, within my reach, ready for me to end it before it had begun. I reached out to grab him and he spun in an instant, the side of his arm batting mine out of the way. The recognition in his eyes was instantaneous. His mouth formed an "O" shape and he backed away, rapidly. I advanced and his legs twisted together causing him to fall flat on the floor.

I lunged forwards and grabbed him by the front of his jacket, not taking my eyes off his for a moment.

I had no weapon, but I knew exactly how I wanted to kill this slime. Oh yes, I knew exactly what I intended for him. I bent my knees and leapt up into the summer night. The warm air streaked passed my cheeks as we sailed up towards my destination, the top of the boiler chimney.

My ears were deaf to the screams of my victim as he flailed vainly in my granite grip. I had a purpose, a mission and I was going to follow it through to the vicious end.

My feet alighted on the red brick and I turned to survey the panoramic view. Off in the distance, I could see the lights of Barrow-in-Furness across the bay, beyond that the hills then the mountains of the Lake District.

And in my hand I held a worm. It squirmed, twisted and writhed between my fingers. It was a deformed worm as it had arms and hands – hands that gripped at my wrists in desperation. Deformed as it had a mouth that could speak and eyes that could weep.

"Sam! Jesus, Sam! What's going on?" the worm shrieked as I dangled it precariously over the edge of the chimney, its shoes scraping on the old, crumbling brick trying to seek out any form of life-saving purchase. "Sam! Sam!"

"Don't you DARE use my name, you filth!" I spat in the worm's face, at his creepy orange-tinted eyes. "You lost the right to address me like that a long, long time ago."

"What? Why?" Those freakish eyes were desperately scanning his situation, flitting from me to his feet to the long, fatal drop that awaited him. "What have I done? What in God's name have I done?"

"You killed my son!" I bellowed into the night sky.

"You took a sweet, young lad and sent him to a hell dimension where there's no time, no joy, no life."

"When? When?" His feet scrabbled loose and one leg swung back causing him to sway in my grip.

"In the future. Your future, my past." My knuckles were white, tight with gripping his jacket.

"No! No! I wouldn't. Couldn't!"

The first niggle of doubt started to squirm its way into my thought process. Would he? Would he really now? What if I had changed things? What if I had altered the future? How would I know?

Involuntarily I pulled him slightly closer towards me.

"Yes, Sam! Yes! Pull me in! Please pull me in. I won't do anything. Tell me about it and I'll make sure it won't happen. Honest to God I won't let it happen."

His eyes were wide open. Those orange irises glistened with tears, warm wet tears of a terrified man. I recalled a woman's look of shock as she died from a gunshot to the chest.

What the hell was I doing?

I pulled him in and wrapped an arm around his shoulders to steady him.

"Hold on," I said. "Hold on tight."

"Thank you, Sam. Thank you." His hands gripped me firmly as he looked down at his feet on the narrow rim of the chimney. "Thank you." He frowned. "Tell me. What did I do exactly?"

I was about to tell him when I saw his lips move around an empty word.

"..."

I pushed.

He fell.

There is an episode in Doctor Who called *Day of the Moon* where River Song (or Mrs Doctor as Spliff sardonically calls her) takes a backward swan dive from a ledge of a skyscraper in New York. Her arms fly out to the side and it all goes slow-mo as she gracefully plummets backwards until the TARDIS materialises behind her and scoops her away to a swift rescue.

The same was for Wallace.

There was shock in those orange eyes as his arms spread wide.

There was a rush of air that whipped at his hair.

There was, however, no TARDIS.

There was, instead, a sickening thump.

I think I may have smiled. Just a bit.

I stepped off the tall chimney and felt the warm summer night air brush against my flushed cheeks as I glided down to the floor below. As I descended, my eyes stayed fixed on the motionless bundle of flesh and bones that had been Malcolm Wallace – one time student, one time potential priest, one time wannabe bringer of Armageddon. The body was so still, so straight, so...

Not bleeding?

Surely there should have been blood. I mean, he had fallen from a terrible height. He should be oozing from jagged rips in his torn skin where fractured bones should be jutting out at grotesque angles. I knew this. I had read Stephen King novels as a teenager.

My feet lightly touched down and I walked

cautiously over to the body, prone on its back, arms out cruciform and eyes closed.

Drumming my fingers against my teeth as I held my breath, I crouched down and lay a tentative hand on Wallace's chest. There was no rise or fall. There was no heartbeat.

Nodding to myself, I was assured that he was dead.

It was then that his hand grabbed my wrist.

I let out a shout as his eyes flashed open, the cruel orange irises glaring in the glow of the illuminating lights around Williamson Square. He snarled like a wild animal as he flung himself upwards and lunged towards me. Instinctively I moved with him and he stumbled forwards, letting go of my hand. I had no time to think, only act. I rugby-tackled him roughly to the paved floor. We hit with a smack and I felt the side of my face tear harshly against an unforgiving man-made surface. We both scrabbled with our hands and our feet like beetles trying to avoid the burning rays of a magnifying glass in the hand of an immoral child. I was first to my feet and let loose a wide kick which he grabbed with his hands and twisted round causing me to fly over onto my side. I swore as I landed and yelled as Wallace's foot achieved what mine hadn't. My lower back hated me.

"You fool!" he hissed. "You damn fool. Do you think you can better me? Really?"

I twisted over and lurched up to my knees as my face and my back wailed louder than a cat on heat. I wanted to come back with a witty one-liner, something to put him in his place, but the words were just not there.

The pain had sent them packing to a land of no return. Instead, I just knelt there slumped, dejected.

Wallace was towering over me now, his hair wild and his eyes ablaze. "You have no concept of what I'm capable of, Sam, of what I'm destined to do."

I chuckled wearily. "Oh God, it's *that* speech again. Blah blah blah.... mankind is corrupt... blah blah blah... only I can right all that is wrong. Please change the record, already!"

For a second he was dumbstruck, amazed that I had mocked him, then he said, "I don't need words to silence you."

The little panic monkey in my head realised just what he intended and screamed for me to act. As Wallace opened his mouth to speak the first silent syllable, every desperate ounce of energy slammed into my legs causing me to pounce up onto him and slam him to the floor kneeling on both his chest and, more importantly, his mouth.

Angrily, he lashed at me with his arms which I pinned with my hands and my feet while his head tried to twist free from the pressure of my knee.

"Ah, ah," I chided him mockingly, not for once letting up on my body weight. "Two can play at that game."

I opened my mouth and this time the horrible non-sounds tripped from *my* tongue.

"..."

"..."

"..."

There was a flash and a hiss as the reality of

space time opened up in front of us. Wallace was now writhing even harder underneath me and was screaming muffled pleas into my trouser leg. Evidently he was no longer so sure of himself.

Then I heard slow, high-heeled footsteps echo across the square accompanied by a slow, appreciative clapping.

"Oh, well done. Well done indeed." I had to admit it was the goddamned sexiest voice I had ever heard and, apart from a few lilting hummed notes, I had only heard it twice before – once in the Ashton Hall and once on this same night many years ago.

I looked up and caught a proper sight of Wallace's benefactor for the first time, and what a sight she was. The ultimate femme fatale: there were the killer heels that I had heard before (scarlet of course); black, tight trousers that left no part of her legs to the imagination; a fashionably cut black leather jacket over a silky red top; reasonably long black hair cut perfectly to frame her beautifully cruel face.

Part of me actually thought, "You lucky, lucky bastard," until my more rational side reminded me that this was probably the last thing that went through the head of a male praying mantis, if you didn't count the teeth of the female praying mantis.

But *what* a female praying mantis!

She came to a stop and eyed some stone steps that rose up near to us. A small plume of dust rose away from their worn surface, leaving them spotless. Gracefully, she eased herself down into a casually seated position, stretching her long legs out in front of her. "Well go on then," she smiled.

"Pardon?" My voice cracked. I must have sounded like a hormonal teen. I certainly felt like one right then.

She pointed to the portal with a finely manicured finger. "Finish him off. I don't have all night and I've been so looking forward to this." She smiled callously, her upturned lips making her appear even more beautiful.

There was a grunt of protest from beneath me and I was rolled sideways as Wallace clambered to his feet. "What do you mean?" he whined. "You can't be serious!"

His benefactor give a tired sigh and admired her fingernails. They actually changed colour three times before she smiled with satisfaction and deigned to looked back up. "Oh, are you still here? Not taken over the world yet? You know that gets so *dull* in the end. 'Look, look, here's the universe I destroyed for you!' Bor-ring." She turned her attention to me. "I've had an eternity of that you know. It's okay the first few times, but its gets dull ever so quickly."

"You can't do this," Wallace groaned, running his fingers through his hair. "We had plans."

"*You* had plans," she snapped. "I was just having fun and now I'm not. You're boring, Malcolm. So damned boring." She stood in one fluid move. "I'm through with you. Finished."

Her one-time student fell on his knees in front of her and actually began to weep. "Please, please don't leave me. What will I do without you?"

She shook her head. "Actually, after what you are going to do to his son, I really don't think that's an issue. Goodbye, Malcolm." She turned and left, leaving the two of us alone in the square with a portal to some weird hell dimension, Wallace with growing confusion, me with growing rage.

He stood and asked over his shoulder, "Will I really do what you said? To your son?"

No words could form a decent reply. I just grabbed him by the shoulders and shoved him through the portal. Wallace screeched in frustration as the whirling material of the portal enveloped him and sucked him in.

I slumped down onto my knees, panting hard. I had done it. I had eliminated the source of my troubles. I had caused Wallace to cease to exist, cut him off from time.

The portal still hummed in front of me.

I stared at its spinning lights.

There was a dark spot at its centre. My stomach turned.

A hand slowly clawed its way through the undulating surface. It was followed by a shoulder then a head. Wallace glowered at me like a demented thing. He opened his mouth to say something when there was a loud bang and a black dot appeared briefly on his head before he was sucked back in once more and the portal hissed shut.

I spun around on all fours and saw a dark-clad figure in the shadows of Williamson Square. He stepped forward and the artificial lights showed the cruelty that inhabited his sallow face. A pistol was gripped in one hand and electricity appeared to spark from the other.

I made to speak but he just shook his head and my mouth closed shut.

He looked from me to where the portal had hung then turned and walked away before disappearing into the shadows.

Then everything changed.

CHAPTER 22

I was sat at my desk, my fingers resting on the keyboard of my laptop.

"There's somebody knocking at the door. Back in a mo'," were the last words that I had typed. I rose quickly, darted across the room and flung the door open.

There was nobody there.

Of course not. In this reality Caroline had not needed to come and see me about Wallace. She would not have been chasing that killer story. Yet I had still typed it out.

I opened the bottom drawer of my filing cabinet. The revolver was still there, wrapped in an old tea towel. I took it out, looked it over and set in down on top of the cabinet as I fished a bottle of bourbon from the top drawer and slugged down a good number of mouthfuls.

"And you don't even offer me one," sing-songed a feminine voice from the gloom. "Mind you, I would prefer a glass."

The bottle clunked to the floor as I whipped the pistol off the top of the cabinet.

There was a deprecating tutting followed by the sound of killer heels grinding into my carpet. "Now look what you've done. You've spilt it."

The intruder emerged out of the gloom and I recognised her at once. "You were there. In the past, egging me on."

She smiled. It wasn't a pleasant smile either. "Mmmm, yes I was, and I have to say I'm *very* impressed."

I kept the gun trained on her, although I had the growing feeling that this was a fairly pointless gesture. "Why would that be?"

"Power." She made the one word sound like a lingering orgasm. "It's rolling off you. Malcolm was powerful, true, but so, so gullible." She chuckled to herself, her laughter sounding like a stream eddying over the polished pebbles of a summer's brook. "*Divergence* indeed. As if he could bring that about."

"But the deaths. The storm brewing around him at the end..."

She slowly shook her head, her dark hair swaying hypnotically from side to side. "No. His little *Danse Macabre* was far from bringing about the end of your world. But it amused me to watch it." She held her hand out in front of her and casually examined her nails. "The Divergence *will* come and Kanor *will* rise."

Her eyes levelled with mine, fire burning in her pupils with glee.

"And then we will have a ball!"

"Poor Malcolm," she sighed dramatically. "He was so sincere in his quest. He so believed that he was going to be the focus, that he would be the ruler of the Divergent Lands. That made him so biddable.

"But you, I sense you are *different.*" With that she started to hum under her breath. It was a tune I had heard many years ago when I had been lying semi-comatose on the table in Borrowdale Hall and again, more recently, during the Credete meeting in the Ashton Hall. Once more the tune drifted into my head and danced seductively around my brain. However, unlike on the previous occasion, that was where it's effect on me stopped. There was no paradisiacal euphoria, no longing to follow this woman to the ends of the earth. I just stood there, the gun straight out in front of me.

The song stopped.

She smiled.

"Yes," she said, her voice brimming with curiosity, "*different.* Something has happened to you. Perhaps it was your little time walk. Perhaps it was blowing your brains out then coming back. I shall have to ponder the matter." She turned her back on me and made to leave.

"So that's it?" The anger and frustration of the last few days was overwhelming me now. "You're just going to walk out of here and leave me dangling like a marionette, ready to jig up and down at your pleasure? Well let me tell you, that's not going to happen. I'm sick of being played by women, using me for their latest whim and then discarding me. I've put things back to how they should be! I have! I'm going to drive over to Caroline's house and see my son. Then I'm gonna spend the rest of my life being his dad and no-one's gonna stop me. Not Caroline, not you!"

She turned and grinned wickedly. "Oh? It's going to be happy families is it? You and your little boy. Going to go and play football are you? Buy a puppy? Yes, you've changed things, alright, Sam, but consider this: how *much* have you changed?" and with that she walked out of the door.

She was playing with me.

She was toying with me.

I had killed her devotee and she was giving me payback.

I lay the gun down and fished out my mobile. I tapped the contacts icon and scrolled down to the "A" entries. There was no Adamson, Caroline.

My stomach turned.

I flicked on my internet browser and Googled the *Lancaster Chronicle*. I flicked to the *What's On* section. There grinning at me was some young chap with a neat goatee. Not Caroline.

No, no, no.

I drew up a telephone directory and entered her details. Nothing.

Then it started to sink in.

My last conversation with Wallace at university had been regarding my parish placement. He was going to give me the details the next day. As it had transpired he had run off with my visitor and left me a note.

Oh, God!

He had given me a note *after* I had killed him.

"But I still remember going," the words choked me.

"That's because you did. Just not in *this* timeline."

I turned and Alec was sat on the sofa. "How long

have you been here?"

He shrugged in a manner that only teenagers can. "I got here before Asherah."

Asherah. I remembered the statue in Wallace's collection and a little wooden stick in his room as a student. He had laughed when I had asked if she was older.

"Asherah." My voice was dry. My head was spinning. "*The* Asherah."

Alec nodded. "Strange to see her on her own, though. Asmodeus must be nearby, I guess. Either that or he's off looking for his..."

I cut across him. "*Asmodeus*? As in the book of Tobit? You're serious?"

He nodded again. "Last time I saw them was back in ancient Israel. He had this racket going with Solomon and the building of the temple. Then she waltzed in and things got kind of messy."

Two images melded together in my head. One was from the story Uncle had told me about a dark stranger in a Jewish ghetto, the other was of similar figure shooting Wallace through the portal to Beyond.

I grabbed the discarded whiskey bottle off the floor. Fortunately, there was still some left in the bottom. I downed the lot. A goddess and a demon? Here? In Lancaster?

"Bloody hell," I groaned. Then the whiskey took hold and the tears started to force their way out of my ducts. "John! What about John?"

"You never met Caroline. He was never born."

The bottle almost made a satisfying sound as it

smashed against the wall. I threw myself after it, screaming, pounding my fists time and time again against the hard surface. They must have started to bleed eventually as red smears streaked on the wallpaper. "Nothing," I sobbed. "All for nothing." I slouched down on the floor, put my head in my bleeding hands and wept openly. "What's the fucking point?"

I felt Alec crouch down next to me. He put his arm around my shoulders and guided me to the sofa. "It's a bit more complicated than that. There is still hope."

He looked blurred through my tears. "What do you mean?"

The youth took a handkerchief from his pocket, moistened it with his saliva and dabbed at my abraded hands. "Remember what I said Wallace had done with your son? Where he had sent him?"

"Beyond."

Alec nodded. "Well, Beyond is outside of our physical universe. The laws of time and space do not apply there. He'll still be there."

"Even though he never existed here?"

Again, a quiet nod. "There's a sort of paradox. If you look through your laptop all the things from your first week will still be there: Satanists, vampires, fairies and one big, ugly werewolf. This is because they *did* happen in your past."

"So I really met John at Saint Edmund's"

"In your timeline, yes. Just as the John O'Gaunt team were under Wallace's control. However, in *this* timeline things will be different. Perhaps those actors had different motives for kidnapping you and perhaps you had a different guide around Saint Edmund's. I don't know for sure, but we will just have to see what other people say or mention."

I looked at this young lad who seemed far more wise than I could ever be. "But you remember what happened in my timeline?"

"Yes, because I'm *special*."

"Angels?"

He smiled. "Angels."

I thought about my son trapped in some timeless hell and tears welled up inside me. "How do we get him back?"

"I don't know, Sam, but I know someone who might be able to help."

The next day must have been a week day. I didn't have a clue which one but people were bustling around outside earlier than I would have liked so it must have been somewhere between Monday and Friday. I glanced at my watch. It was just after noon. How long had I been asleep? At least there had been no dreams.

I crawled out of my pit, rummaged in the drawer for some paracetamol and downed them before lying back and listening to the silence.

No. Not silence.

Listening to the bells.

The fucking bells.

I think I screamed.

I hadn't realised that they were back the day before with all the comings and goings of supernatural folk, but I guessed it was inevitable.

No Wallace, no miracle cure.

Ah, sod it. I'd coped for almost forty years, I'd carry on coping.

I got out of bed, showered, shaved and dressed. As I entered the living room I saw my laptop on the table. Drumming my fingers against my teeth, I opened it up and pulled up Google Chrome. I typed in Caroline's name and waited.

"Well, well," I muttered as her face grinned up at me from the top hit. "Daddy's girl did good after all then." She was still a reporter, but not for some provincial little rag. She was working for a national TV network heading an investigative show that interviewed people with quirky lifestyles and obscure professions. Apparently it was quite popular.

I couldn't help but smile. Good for her, I thought. Perhaps the bitchy little cow that I had known and loved was just a result of a life that had never achieved its full potential.

I typed in another name. Again there was a result. I checked my watch. It was now just gone one. I had a couple of hours at least. I'd grab a bite to eat before I caught up with this one.

I arrived outside Saint Edmund Campion School just before three. God alone knew what I had in mind. First, would Abalone have actually met me? I remembered going to the school to investigate the so-called poltergeist, but did it really happen and, if so, did I meet her there or not?

Also, how could I be sure that I would see her

come out of school and at what time? I didn't want one of Jitendra's boys picking me up as a potential paedo.

Jitendra. There was another one. I had met him because of the little group of Satanists who had been devotees of Wallace. Damn. I was going to have to check over everything with Alec and see what had actually being going on in my life for the last week or so.

I was just about to Google the good policeman on my mobile when a flash of blonde hair caught my eye. There she was, over the other side of the road! Not only was Abalone still alive, but she was as cute as ever. There was a definite spring in her step and her locks shone in the dying light of the late autumn day.

But, I soon realised that she was not alone. There, jogging up to meet her was a man of a similar age who stood about six foot and sported a corduroy jacket with elbow patches. She rushed to hug and him and as they kissed I recalled the dead boyfriend. Had his accident been instigated by Wallace to draw her into Credete?

I turned and walked away.

She would be better off without me anyway.

I thrust my hands deep into my pockets and felt my fingers slide around my phone. I remembered with fond sadness the meal at *Alessandro's* which had now never happened. I remembered how Abalone had made me feel and I remembered the wonderful deed that she had done.

I pulled my phone out and hit speed dial. It was answered after three rings.

"Hello Mum."

I took my time walking home. It meant I was able to natter to my mum. She told me she was well, that the neighbours were well, that their pets were well and that someone who I had never met before but was a very nice man was also well.

I think this meant that she was happy to hear from me.

As I entered my stairwell she asked, "So when am I going to see you, Sammy? It's been a very long time."

I smiled. Indeed it had. "Tell you what, why don't I pop down later this week?"

She thought that was a fantastic idea and I said I'd check my diary then get back to her. We said our goodbyes and I unlocked my office door.

I groaned at the sight that met me.

"What the hell is a gargoyle doing in here?"

Coming soon
Sam Spallucci: Shadows Of Lancaster

AFTERWORD

So there you have it, my second foray into the beleaguered life of Samuel C. Spallucci, investigator of the paranormal. I hope you liked it. Please look out for the next instalment, *Sam Spallucci: Shadows Of Lancaster* which will be back to the previous format of a number of cases rather than a novel-length uber-case.

I ummed and aahed over the format of *Ghosts*. I had really enjoyed playing with the format of *Casebook*, using five individual stories that contained a background arc weaving through them and at one point it was my original intention to do the same with *Ghosts*. I had thought about using five or six cases with Malcolm Wallace lurking ominously in the background but it soon became clear as I developed his storyline that the topics of Credete and the Divergence were far too big to share the space in a book with other stories. So it was that *Ghosts* became a novel-length story and I'm rather pleased with the end product. This let me play about with older characters and bring in new ones hovering on the fringe, hopefully teasing you as to their purpose and identities.

One character I really enjoyed using more was Sam's mysterious guardian angel, Alec. We shall be seeing a lot more of him as the stories develop. Indeed, he has his own novel formulating in my head at the moment explaining his back history and all the little tidbits that he feeds Sam from time to time including the identity of his parents.

Another character that I have been very excited about unleashing is Asherah. She is one of my favourite creations, first seeing the light of day in the as yet unpublished fantasy novel *Fallen Angel*. The ultimate bitch, she is self-serving, self-worshipping and lacks any sort of compassion for any other life form including her various lovers and her long time on and off companion Asmodeus. She will return although not imminently as it is possible to have too much of a good thing.

So in the meantime, feel free to look me up on Twitter and Facebook. Don't be afraid to say, "Hi!" I don't bite. Well not all the time, anyway.

ASC. August 2014.

ABOUT THE AUTHOR

A.S.Chambers resides in Lancaster, England. He lives a fairly mundane life measuring the growing rates of radishes and occasionally puts pen to paper to stop himself from going out of his mind with boredom.

He is quite happy for, and in fact would encourage, you to follow him on Facebook and Twitter.

There is also nice, shiny website:
www.aschambers.co.uk

Made in the USA
Charleston, SC
30 March 2015